THE BOOKWORM

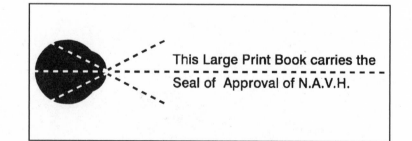

This Large Print Book carries the
Seal of Approval of N.A.V.H.

THE BOOKWORM

MITCH SILVER

THORNDIKE PRESS
A part of Gale, a Cengage Company

Farmington Hills, Mich • San Francisco • New York • Waterville, Maine
Meriden, Conn • Mason, Ohio • Chicago

LIBRARY OF CONGRESS CIP DATA ON FILE.
CATALOGUING IN PUBLICATION FOR THIS BOOK
IS AVAILABLE FROM THE LIBRARY OF CONGRESS

ISBN-13: 978-1-4328-5100-2 (hardcover)

Published in 2018 by arrangement with Pegasus Books, Ltd.

Printed in the United States of America
1 2 3 4 5 6 7 22 21 20 19 18

To Claiborne, for believing in me.

All that is necessary for the triumph of evil is that good men do nothing.

— Edmund Burke

PROLOGUE

Villers-devant-Orval, Occupied Belgium
August 1940

The monk walked out of the cool woods from the French side of the road. On the tall man's back, weighing him down, was the sort of rucksack the Dominicans use, fraying almost to the point of tearing where the canvas straps crossed his shoulders. He walked with a slight limp and carried a poplar walking stick that had seen years of hard use.

The grizzled man of the cloth looked back once and then set foot on the gravel road pilgrims had trod for centuries. The large wooden door of the abbey at Orval loomed ahead in the torpid summer twilight, and he made for it. A hundred and fifty years ago this was the cloister's side entrance, but that was before the French revolutionaries burned down most of the original abbey in 1793.

The traveler withdrew his letter of introduction from the Monsignor of Liège and, using the head of his walking stick, banged on the heavy oak door. An onlooker standing back in the forest with binoculars would have observed a member of the friary come to the door and, having been given the letter, usher the visitor within.

Once inside, he was greeted warmly by the brethren at their evening meal. Though not of their order, he was invited to break bread with them and, later, was given a place to say his devotions and spend the night before traveling on.

But their guest wouldn't be spending the night. Instead, a little after three in the morning, he slipped down to the abbey library where the medieval manuscripts were kept, dusty tomes that represented the labors of hundreds of the faithful over the eons. Placing his rucksack on the cold stone floor, he pulled on a pair of cotton gloves. Then he took out a flashlight and passed the beam over the bookshelves until he found what he was looking for.

Were any of the monks, unable to sleep, to wander down to the library now, what would they make of such a visitor? First, he used his hands to make a little more room on the shelf by sliding an illuminated thirteenth century Book of Job over from its centuries-long resting place. Then, from his sack, he carefully lifted the heavy cowhide-and-parchment volume he'd brought and slid it onto the shelf.

He took a little atomizer a woman might use to perfume herself. With it he carefully sprayed fine dust onto the book, the volume next to it, and all the nearby manuscripts — even the shelf itself. Returning the empty sprayer to his sack and dropping the gloves and the light in after it, he took up his walking stick and made his way, as quietly as he could, out of the abbey.

There was no moon to silhouette the tall man against the trees as he hurried back, without sign of a limp, up the road to the woods. Once there, he tapped on a tree trunk with his stick and was gratified to hear the same tapped-out signal played back to him. Five minutes later, standing in the clearing with the woman who had been his lookout, he took off the false beard.

So ended the first great Allied victory of World War II.

CHAPTER 1

Moscow, Russia
Monday

In a vast Stalin-era granite box several kilometers north of the capital's outer ring road, Larissa Mendelova Klimt checked her cell phone one last time — nothing — before packing up the box for the return leg of her "daily commute." Her routine never varied: pick up the *yashchik* in the morning, walk it along two rows of the *Osobyi Arkhiv* and then three rows over. Unlock the door to her carrel and set the box of old papers down on the desk. Turn on the light. Be seated. At night, pick up the box, lock up, and walk her burden back to its parking place with the other wartime files on the archive's shelf.

She was feeling pretty good about herself. Other people went away for the summer, enjoyed the weather, swam at the seaside or in a lake, maybe. But Lara the Good Girl worked right here while Russia's brief summer came and went. Unencumbered by her teaching load, she had waded through the captured Nazi documents in the box like an explorer. No, a cosmonaut — she was the Yuri Gagarin of academics, soaring through the unknown.

Take that day when she found two of the daily logs stuck together. Two not terribly significant days in May 1942, recorded down to the last, absurd detail by one of Hitler's secretaries at the time, probably Johanna Wolf. Even as she carefully unstuck May 15 from May 16, she realized no Russian eyes had ever seen the page underneath; no Russian fingers had ever touched it. Of 150 million people, only Lara knew that Hitler had visited Wewelsburg to promote a cadre of SS officers at Himmler's castle there before returning the same evening to Berlin by special train for a briefing on the Crimean offensive driving toward Baku. Okay, it was nothing special. Trivial, even. But it was all hers.

She knew what her friends called her: *knižnyj červ.* The "bookworm." All they could see was the huge iron door of the Russian State Military Archive that closed behind her in the morning, never the enlightenment to be found within the heavily

14

guarded Special, or *Osobyi,* section inside.

For the past eleven weeks, she had been doing exactly what she wanted to do. She spent nearly every waking minute plowing through the yellowed pages in this single box in the vast climate-controlled archive. Or else hunched over one of the preserved '40s-era Dictaphone machines in the Listening Room twenty meters down the hall, as the voices of Hitler, Himmler, and Bormann dictated letters and summarized staff meetings on the hundreds of recordings liberated from the *Führerbunker.*

Even so, Lara had her reasons for being euphoric. She could tick off at least five of them on her fingers, starting with her thumb: with this last page, she had the whole dusty job of reading and translating behind her for another year. Index finger: she had her big definitive book, her *Origins of the Great Patriotic War,* all but written on the desk in front of her. Middle finger: Viktor was finally served with the divorce papers and she could move on with her life. Ring finger: Over the summer she had been named to fill the vacant chair in her department and would teach her initial class tomorrow as the country's first full professor of geopolitical history. And pinkie: She had planned this summer's work with her usual care, and had been rewarded by arriving at the last page of the Chronologies on September 8, the final allotted day. She had calculated it perfectly, which just went to prove how weird the newly minted Lukoil Professor of Geohistory Larissa Mendelova Klimt — Lara to her friends — really was.

Still, as she gazed out the big, grimy window at the handful of people hurrying along the pedestrian walk of the *Leningradskoye shosse* on their way home and then down at the notes she'd tapped out on her iPad, she could feel the same old niggling doubt creeping back in. *Is it worth it?* Is this any way to spend a life, shutting yourself away in a musty archive?

Viktor certainly didn't think so. One time she'd read him something she'd written and he'd given that little deprecating snort of his. "Ashes to ashes, dust to dust. What difference does it make?"

Was she divorcing Viktor because he was a no-good unfaithful bastard, or because she couldn't bear to have him putting down her work? Did she surround herself with dead men talking because the actual live ones out there in the world were unknowable? From the time she'd been the tallest preteen in her *srednyaya shkola* in the closed city of Perm, Larissa had attracted the male gaze.

16

But what, really, had they seen in her? Her nose was clearly too long, her teeth — though perfectly white and even — had a space in the middle, and her inky-black hair would never stay where she brushed it. Worse, out of her mouth would come whatever she was thinking.

Lara returned her gaze to the single-spaced German record in front of her; she would read the last of the pages and deal with her life some other time. By now she knew Traudl Junge's machine, the typewriter with the chipped apostrophe. Guess they couldn't get new typewriters in the bunker by 1945.

And what was "A.H." doing on April 21, the day after his birthday party and the last day of the Chronologies? Was he in the map room, planning to move up his nonexistent Southern Army to block the Russians at the gates to Berlin? No, he did that yesterday. Was he in the radio room, directing waves of nonexistent V-2s to wipe out the Red Army's advance units (and most of the Berlin population)? He'd already tried that too.

Today he was playing with the Goebbels children. On other days he'd show them Speer's plans for the complete redesign of Linz, the Führer's birthplace, into the new seat of Germanic culture. Today, though, he was back to playing with Tibet.

Fraulein Junge recorded it on the same onionskin paper she once used for councils of war: "1100 hrs. to 1215: A.H. again had us roll out the scale model of Lhasa to instruct the children on the beginnings of their race. How the gods had lived on the continent of Atlantis and how, when it succumbed to the Great Flood, they had moved to the lands of Thule and Ultima Thule far to the north. Then, when some of them had had carnal knowledge of mortal women, an elite priesthood of Nordics had taken refuge in another icy stronghold, in the Himalayas, and established their kingdom far beneath the surface of the earth.

"With that he delighted the children by lifting up the model's mountains to reveal the magical city of the Aryans, the master race, as it had been recreated below. The little one, Heide, clapped her hands in joy as always."

Lara shivered and let the flimsy paper drop from her hands. She knew that ten days later, her mother would crush cyanide capsules into the mouths of little Heide and her five brothers and sisters so they might all perish with the Führer.

Did Germany's desire for lebensraum

make the war inevitable? Or was it simply about one twisted, murderous man with unlimited power? One thing she did know: it was time to put the box back on the shelf and leave pure, unadulterated evil behind her for another year.

Chapter 2

Aboard Air Force One, En Route to Moscow

"Okay, listen up, folks. The stewards will be serving dinner in a couple of minutes."

The press secretary took her work phone out of her purse and hefted it up to her eyes. All the encryption software made it heavy as hell. "Coupla things. I'm not naming names, but two of you filed stuff yesterday with the same mistake. This meeting in Moscow is with the G20; the World Trade Organization's a different, bigger group. Keep making these bonehead moves, and people might start to believe the campaign beat on the press for a reason."

She smiled her not-altogether-friendly smile. No one smiled back.

"Second: got an addition to the printed schedule. Mogul and the other bigs are invited to a celebration Friday night in Red Square. The bus for the airport leaves three hours later than it says . . . can't be helped."

She waited for the groans to subside and smiled again. "There's a new ETA for Andrews Saturday morning, so if someone's picking you up . . . we'll hand out revised schedules as soon as they're printed, okay?

"Now, the president needs to rest before we kick off the Q&A, so I'm going to ask you to hold it down out here during the meal." The secretary looked at her watch. "Let's reset to Moscow time." She twisted the stem of her Rolex for several seconds. "Right. Everybody, it's now 1748 hours. Thank you and bon app."

The two people on the far side of the bulkhead door and up a level from the press corps were in bed, true, but a nap was the last thing on their minds. It had been eight months since the inauguration and this was the administration's first full-scale trip abroad. Not many couples get to punch their membership in the mile-high club in America's most heavily armed aircraft . . . okay, *renew* their membership . . . and they'd vowed to make the most of it.

"Mogul" was a fairly big man, beefy in his nakedness but not bad for an older guy. She told him that his hair going from blond to gray reminded her of Kenneth Branagh in *Wallander,* which he'd decided to take as a compliment. Now he hoisted himself up on one elbow and looked over at her in her little lace "sleep teddy," the matching bottoms buried somewhere under the covers.

In the dim light, with all the cabin's shades down, there was still no missing that she was a former beauty queen and model, even now, on the far side of forty-five and after having had kids. She was looking back at him with that expectant grin he knew so well, her hair loose around her face and one long leg lying provocatively over the other.

She turned away from him briefly and shut off the little reading lamp built into the headboard. "This time, let's do it with the lights off. More romantic."

He could just make out the dimples in the small of her back, the ones right above her cheeks, that came and went as she rolled first away and then back toward him, dropping her reading glasses next to the tray of hurriedly eaten dinner on the carpeted floor. He knew he should be concentrating on their lovemaking, but he couldn't help himself.

"Not more romantic than our own plane, sweetie." He looked around at the bedroom cabin. "Where's the wood paneling, the gold fixtures, the silk pillows? And I wouldn't exactly call that dinky lamp mood lighting, not like our 757."

She ran one manicured finger over his chest, and then down, her grin becoming something a little more. "As I said . . ." She reached up and flicked the rest of the lights off. "More romantic."

After a few moments she murmured, "So, *that's* how they do it in the Air Force."

CHAPTER 3

Lara's mobile rang as she was packing up. Or rather, it vibrated, so as not to disturb the others in the *Arkhiv.* Not surprisingly, it was Pavel. Very surprisingly, he was calling to ask her to lunch tomorrow in the hotel restaurant beside the Moscow River's Crystal Bridge.

Lara remembered seeing the menu posted outside in a glass case. "Russian salad" (cucumbers and beets, no lettuce) all by itself cost more than Lara usually paid for her entire meal. Pavel said there would be three of them, and that the surprise guest ("Well, host, if I have to be honest") would be paying.

All right, then. Her summer's work behind her, a new job looming ahead, a fancy meal complete with mystery man — it was enough to make Lara put aside the way she felt about Pavel. "I'll be there," she answered. "But only if it's on the late side;

remember, I teach my class tomorrow at noon."

He said, "*Da,* Professor, I'll make it for thirteen-thirty," and rang off.

Lara looked at her watch. Cooped up every day in a world of the dead, a world without seasons, she needed to walk a little before going home.

You wouldn't call Moscow a pedestrian-friendly city. Not with its concentric ring roads breaking up the cityscape every other kilometer. At the end of the day, most of the office workers out here in the northwest of the city made for the nearest Metro, but Lara liked to decompress by cutting through the park of spruce trees that ran beside the water on the other side of the *shosse.* Not only was it quiet and fragrant in the woods, the path eventually found its way to Pokrovskoe-Streshnevo Manor, a forgotten three-hundred-year-old brick-and-stone curiosity that was once home to relatives of the Romanovs. From there it was a short stroll to the Shchukinskaya stop on the Number Seven line that led home.

Leaving the park, Lara was surprised to find the rush hour roads were emptier than usual. It was strange, too, not to be jostled on her way down the Metro steps. She was almost to the bottom when it hit her: this

25

was Monday of Conception Week, Russia's annual attempt to reverse its declining birthrate.

The thing had started in one of the Volga River districts as a local contest. Make a baby on September 12 and, if he or she is born nine months later on Russia Day — the holiday celebrating the end of the Soviet Union — you could win a refrigerator, or even a car.

More and more employers started giving their workers the day off to procreate. Soon, the festivities worked their way back to dominate the whole week leading up to the big Friday night celebration, the one that was supposed to put everyone in the mood to conceive babies.

Lara slowed her pace. There was no one at home to win a refrigerator with.

CHAPTER 4

Farther south, on the Kremlin side of the ring, the Broadcast Center's English-language tour guide planted herself in front of the ten-meter-high wall of TV monitors and began her last tour of the day. "Good afternoon, and welcome to the tallest man-made structure in Europe. The Ostankino Tower that rises above you the equivalent of 120 floors is now home to the most modern broadcast facility anywhere, the Television Technical Center, a state-of-the-art production and broadcast hub that transmits or retransmits more than five hundred domestic and international channels to every home in Russia and the four corners of the world.

"We employ nearly four thousand technicians, managers and on-camera personalities in this building. Look around; you may spot someone famous."

Dutifully, the tourists looked around before turning back to their guide.

"Behind me are 108 international networks, each playing on its own monitor. At the top are the American channels, as you can see. Beneath them, clearly labeled, are each of the European, Asian, and other foreign networks, a modern Tower of Babel, as you are about to discover."

With that, she produced an ordinary-looking TV remote and nonchalantly unmuted the 108 screens behind her. Instantly, twenty-seven languages began jabbering away, competing with each other for the visitors' attention.

The guide laughed before muting them again. "I could have turned them on one at a time, but it's more fun this way, no? Now if you'll follow me . . ."

The group moved toward the lifts that would take them to the observation deck for a view of Moscow at twilight. They left behind an elderly man gripping his walker tightly with both hands. The guide looked back to see if he needed assistance but the man waved her off. He was engrossed in something on the BBC's feed, and began to roll his walker toward the bank of monitors.

The British network's *News at Noon* had led with a one-line tease superimposed on the screen: "Worker clearing footings for new Family Court building unearths human remains." It was the image from the worksite that followed that had caught the viewer's attention: two figures were standing somewhat uneasily in front of a giant earthmover, the operator of the machine and a policeman beside him, stolidly holding a human forearm up to the camera.

The ulna, intact from the elbow to the hand, was yellowed and cracked in more than one place. But what made the picture so striking was the rusty metal handcuff still locked onto the wrist.

The old man extended an arthritic finger and pressed a button on the BBC's monitor, un-muting it again: "Good afternoon. In Parliament today, despite the austerity budget, the prime minister will ask thirty-two million pounds extra be allocated for emergency bridge and tunnel repairs in Scotland and Wales. But first . . . this morning, construction worker Davidson Gordon of Brixton made the grisly discovery of a handcuffed arm bone at a site near Gray's Inn that is destined to house the Principal Registry of the Family Division."

They cut to a one-shot of the worker, dark-skinned with a receding hairline, for his sound bite. "It was wartime work. Just pave over the bomb damage fast as you can and rebuild on top. You see it all around here and in the East End."

The newsreader returned to the screen. "Was this a long-forgotten gaol, uncharted on any map? Or something even more sinister? The BBC have learned City officials will suspend work until the Antiquities Division of the Home Office announce their findings. The police are also taking an interest in the case, and will sift through the site tomorrow for more human remains. Next, the PM's shock budget proposal in Westminster . . ."

The nonagenarian in the rotunda took out a mobile phone and laboriously dialed a local number, muttering in Russian before it went through: "Fools! You've no idea what you've got."

CHAPTER 5

Aboard Air Force One

The big man seated himself on the arm of a chair in front of the bulkhead and faced the reporters, who were crammed together in the aisle. He decided to break the ice.

"Kind of crowded in here. I'm thinking I should have shelled out the four billion dollars and sprung for a new Air Force One, whaddya say?"

Not a smile, not a titter. Maybe he should just open the bomb bay doors.

"Mr. President, Russia's leader has characterized this meeting of the G20 as Europe's bankrupt countries coming to 'beg the Kremlin to throw them a lifeline.' Your tweets and your off-the-cuff comments agreeing with him were described in the European press as 'incendiary'. How do you answer your critics?"

The President, looking particularly upbeat after his recent exertions, grinned. "The

Euro is in big trouble. If the shoe pinches, Howard, it pinches."

The *Times* reporter wanted to know if he was worried about security, given the ongoing protests in the Moscow streets against the government. The commander-in-chief went with his best, most dismissive smile. "We saw worse on the streets outside my rallies. No biggie."

"Mr. President!!" A forest of raised hands tried to get his attention.

He pointed to one of the pool reporters for the networks, a particularly short woman who was standing on a seat and holding her little digital recorder in front of her. "Barbara."

"Mr. President, the continuing question of hacking: Four months ago you rescinded the expulsions of thirty-five Russian nationals the Obama administration had banished in retaliation for the Kremlin's attempts to interfere with the election. *Your* election. Many people believe your willingness, your eagerness, to make this trip is proof of an unhealthy relationship with the president of the Russian Federation. And a way to get your own falling popularity in the polls off the front pages."

He sighed. "Unhealthy? Do I look unhealthy?"

The press corps gave up a few chuckles.

He continued, breezily: "Barbara, there's a word for the people who want to relitigate the election. They're called . . . losers."

Now to get all wonky on her. "And yes, Barbara, I'm the first to admit we have problems at home. It cost a Fortune 500 company six percent more last year to provide health insurance for an employee's family of four. Six percent in one year alone! Self-insured mom-and-pop places saw a seven percent hike. What's that tell you? It tells me it isn't the insurer gouging the public; it's the underlying medical costs themselves that are causing the inflation, medical costs inflated by the so-called Affordable Care Act.

"Am I surprised my numbers are temporarily down? Not a bit. We inherited a lot of problems from the last administration. Even worse, we inherited a lot of myths. Like the one that says the rising healthcare cost curve has been bent down. It hasn't. If we hadn't trimmed Medicare and Medicaid, the cupboard wouldn't just be bare. There wouldn't *be* a cupboard.

"As for this trip, eighteen other leaders are flying in right now for this business meeting of the G20. It's not a summit, but let's face it: thanks to the resurgence in the price of oil, the Russian economy is doing better than ours. Maybe we can learn a few tricks from them. Simple as that."

The questioning went on in that vein for another twenty-five minutes. The president looked out at the press corps, the doubting Thomases who, less than a year ago, were unanimous in their belief he could never be nominated, let alone elected. Now here he was, not just the first businessman to make it to the White House since Hoover, but the first ever with a billion bucks, and they were already writing off his *re*election. It was all he could do not to purse his lips and blow them all a raspberry.

In a few more days they'd get the news, a mackerel right across their collective kissers. It was going to be fun, watching them all change their tune, when the biggest oil strike in the history of the United States was announced right where the Democrats said they'd never drill — in the middle of the Arctic National Wildlife Refuge. And all he had to do to make it happen was look a Russian guy in the eye and shake his hand.

Piece of cake.

CHAPTER 6

Valdez, Alaska

Half a world behind the tail of Air Force One, Lara's twin brother Lev drove his Jeep onto the Valdez test station lot. In late summer this close to the Arctic Circle, day didn't break so much as bend — Lev could barely make out the difference between the two horizons, east and west.

His American colleague Craig always waited till the last second to begin his work week, so Lev would have the cinderblock facility to himself for a few minutes, which was how he liked it. He backed into the space reserved for "Len" Klimt, his adopted American moniker, and lit up a Winston. There was no smoking inside the enclosure, so this would be his last chance for a while.

Funny, the no-smoking thing, because standing outside the open-air test hut was no different from standing inside it, just on the other side of the fence. Overhead, the enormous pipeline blocked out the sky and most of the light as it traveled its final quarter-mile through the Custody Transfer Meters and into the field of holding tanks by the sea, the "tank farm."

He stubbed out his butt and headed over to the padlocked gate, key in hand. Once inside, Lev walked beneath the mammoth "proving loop" conduit and, using the wrench that hung from a chain, he tapped on the elbow pipe that ran down from it to break up any air pockets. Placing a clean Pyrex beaker on the flat cement pedestal in front of him, he used both hands to turn the wheel that opened the giant gate-valve, but left the stopcock closed.

The oil contracts stipulated that automated meters would measure the crude in bulk, but the transfer wouldn't be legal unless both the seller's representative — Craig for the consortium of producers — and the purchasing agent — Lev, acting on behalf of the refiners, both international and domestic — were present. Since the buyer and seller were always the same, it was always only Craig and Lev doing the 9:00 A.M. manual test.

All of this was a formality, of course. The North Slope Crude that made its way into the Valdez Marine Terminal always had the

36

same specific gravity on the American Petroleum Institute's scale, a fact they would ascertain once again this morning.

The Ford Bronco drove onto the lot a solid two minutes ahead of the church bell that would ring matins on the other side of Valdez. Craig was way early.

Lev held the gate open for him, and the American did what he always did, high-fiving him with his huge football player's paw. "Hey, thanks, 'Lenny.' Good week-end?"

The patter never changed. "You know it's 'Lev' to you. And yes, I had a good weekend. You?"

"Totally awesome." Craig, a bachelor with an apartment in the big, bad town of Anchorage, made the most of his weekends in 'Sin City.' At least he said he did.

Lev let the bear of a man do the honors, so Craig turned the small iron stopcock counterclockwise and they watched the crude begin to flow. After traveling the length of Alaska at less than four miles an hour, the oil that poured down into the glass beaker had lost much of the original 120°F heat it had a week and a half ago.

They stood there side by side, watching it slowly climb up the millimeter markings incised in the beaker. But then Craig went off script. "You smell something?"

Lev's nose wasn't his strong suit. "No. You?"

"Yeah." He walked toward the pipe that was disgorging the last of the oil and bent down, sniffing, before taking a hurried step back. "Damn, can't you smell it?"

Lev leaned over the liter of crude oil and inhaled mightily, overcompensating for his poor sense of smell. He nearly gagged at the odor.

Despite his concern, Craig was bent over, laughing. "What, you don't like rotten eggs?"

Ignoring the American, Lev stated the obvious. "It's sour."

"Tell me about it." Craig was carrying the beaker inside to the lab, so he was getting it full force. "*Way* sour. Wish I brought nose clips."

The seller's rep put the crude oil down on the test bench and fired up the spectrometer. He was thinking out loud. "Okay, a little sulfur I could understand, maybe they hit a pocket down there. But not enough so you could smell the stink a yard away at this end." He looked over at Lev and grinned. ". . . so *I* could smell it a yard away. You're getting off easy."

Lev was already dropping his dual

thermometer/hydrometer into the petroleum. He and Craig had had them made at the same time from the same supplier so no one could fudge the figures, not that either of them would. They were state-of-the-art instruments: beyond having the perfectly predictable 31.9 specific gravity of North Slope Crude incised in bold, the thing had Wi-Fi built in to send the results to any nearby computer.

Craig leaned in. "Temp looks good."

"Agreed. But . . . crap, API's falling short." Lev squinted. "I make it two points under."

"Me too. You got your laptop?"

"It's in the truck."

"Never mind." Craig kept his iPad locked to the shelf that was right behind them. Lev had given one to Lara for their mutual birthday, and it had gone over so well he had bought one for Craig for *his* birthday, but the guy was old school and always carried around just a phone. He never turned the iPad off either, but left it charging all week between their tests, some random bit of folk wisdom about extending battery life he'd gleaned online from *Popular Mechanics.*

The American unlocked it now and was already scrolling down the long list of world oilfield assays. No two fields in the world were exactly alike and, since it cost less to refine oil that was light and sweet, and more for crude that was heavy and sour, each field's "signature" was kept on file to assist buyers and sellers with current pricing on the New York spot market. If the instruments sitting in the suspect oil transmitted a match among the signatures in either density or sulfur content, it would be highlighted in red on the computer screen.

The domestic fields were listed on top. "There." Craig saw it first. "West Texas Sour is 31.7. Shit! This morning it's at $2.40 off Slope."

Lev shook his head. "See? The sulfur doesn't match."

They walked over to the twin pen-shaped instruments in the beaker of petroleum, just to be sure. Alaska North Slope usually flowed at 0.93% sulfur. This morning it was at 1.35%. Totally sour, beyond even West Texas Sour. Affecting his version of a cowboy's bowed legs, Lev walked a few steps and drawled, "Well, son, I reckon it ain't my Texas tea."

The two men knew the quality of the oil made little real difference to the buyer: what he saved on the purchase price of sour was lost on the added expense of refining it. If

40

the refinery's feedstock of crude was off in any way, the seller was the big loser.

Glumly, Craig scrolled down the table of foreign fields, looking for a highlighted one. He was almost down to Yemen, the last of the fifty-six producers on the list. "Bingo!" In his own faux–Texas twang, the big man said, "Levitsky my boy, it *is* your'n. Says right here Russian Urals is 31.7 and 1.35."

"Urals? Let me see that." They crowded in together, looking across at that morning's trades. Russian Urals Crude was going for a $2.61 discount off the North Slope price.

Lev dropped into one of the plastic chairs lining the cinderblock wall. "I don't get it, man. Since when does Alaskan crude start acting Russian? And how could it come as news to *you*? It must have been this sour days ago when your guys piped it in at the other end."

Craig slumped into the chair next to him. "Not a word. I can't figure it." If the American knew more than he was saying, there was no sign of it in his face.

The big man asked, "What you want to do?"

Lev sat there, thinking. Finally he said, "Let's come back tomorrow and test it again. Give you a chance in the meantime to make some calls to your people in Prudhoe, find out what's going on. If it's still running sour tomorrow at five, I'll file my report. Fair?" He held out his hand.

Craig shook it. "More than fair, you Russky creep. To seal the deal, I'll take you to Denny's . . . they got non-rotten eggs. Breakfast's on me, one-time offer."

Lev looked at his watch and got up. "No can do. Gotta go home and Skype my sister before she hits the hay."

"Funny, isn't it?" Craig was still sitting in the plastic chair, staring at his hydrometer. "They'll pump that oil out of the tank farm onto the ships, pump it again into some refinery somewhere, and pump it out one more time, light and sweet. The only two people who'll ever know how bad that stuff smelled will be you and me."

Lev pulled out of the lot first. He looked back and waved at Craig getting into his own truck, the last time he saw the American alive.

CHAPTER 7

Moscow

Back at her flat, Lara stood in front of her open closet, peeled off her blouse and dropped it in the wicker hamper. Then she reached into the closet for her terry wrapper. She'd make herself a cup of tea, sit in a cozy robe and wait for Lev's call.

The teacher found herself casting a critical eye at her closet. She owned only three kinds of outfits: stiff, slightly uncomfortable clothes to lecture in; loose-fitting pants and sweaters for working in the archives, shopping for groceries, and everything else; and a single cocktail dress, no longer in style, for those once-in-a-blue-moon occasions when Major Viktor Maltsev would come home with something left of his paycheck and insist he and the Mrs. "go out on the town." Oh, and her wedding dress, wrapped in yellowed tissue paper, in a box on the top shelf of the closet. The New Russian

Woman — the one who'd kept her own name to use professionally and now had the use of it full-time — whose closet held only Old Russian Clothes.

Meanwhile, she had a husband working his way through every shopgirl and waitress in the former Soviet Union; a few friends and colleagues, like Vera, busy with their own lives; and a brother on the other side of the world. Lara could feel one of her black moods coming on. She had some pills in the bathroom; should she take one?

And with the moods came the waterworks. Sure enough, an unbidden tear was starting to form in the duct of her left eye. That was another thing — who's born only able to cry with one eye?

She kept the bedroom door closed in case her roommate, Katrina, came home early from the bars with a guy and found her in her robe. Technically, this was Viktor's flat. Now that he'd moved out, Katrina was the tenant, helping with the rent by taking the smaller of the two bedrooms that shared the single bath. In reality, between the parade of men who came and went at all hours and the jumble of Katrina's makeup and cosmetics that wound up all over the bathroom, Lara was a virtual prisoner in her own room.

No, she wouldn't take the pill. She'd dry her eyes and freshen her lipstick a little. She had to look good when Lev called.

Lara was waiting in front of her computer, the clock on her Mac reading 2200 hours exactly. She had the bedroom dimmer turned all the way up so he could see her on his laptop half a world away to the east, beyond the Urals, Siberia, the Sea of Japan, and the northern Pacific. Ah, the power of Skype.

Looking down at her old-fashioned wristwatch, she studied the second hand as it took its time navigating the face. Luckily for them, Alaska was exactly twelve time zones from Moscow, so the twins simply needed to negotiate A.M. and P.M. to synchronize their calls. Should she be worried? The only time her brother, younger by eight minutes, had been late was when he was born.

The call came in at 22:02. "Hello, Larashka! Wonderful to see you, sis. You're looking fine, as usual."

"Am I?" She glanced down from his grinning image on her screen to the small picture-in-picture cameo of herself in the lower left corner and back again. It was scary how alike they looked: the same almost jet-black hair; the same big, dark eyes set deep in olive-skinned faces with

45

Asian-influenced features (their mother's doing). Lev still looked like Omar Sharif, the way he was in *Doctor Zhivago.*

"Tell me, Levishka, how's your week starting off?"

"Strange." A worried look crossed that strong face. "When Craig and I ran the test this morning, the crude was crazy . . . sulfur off the charts. I don't know what to make of it. Neither does he."

"Could your instruments be off kilter?"

"Two separate meters? No way."

She thought for a moment. "How many North Slope fields feed into the pipeline?"

"I thought of that too, *Professor.*" There were laugh lines around his mouth for a moment, the roughneck teasing the academic. "With over twenty fields and a thousand separate wellheads, any gas pocket they hit wouldn't make this kind of difference eight hundred miles downstream."

Five seconds of silence traveled back and forth along the 7,000-kilometer connection, much more if you added in the satellites they were bouncing off of. Lev switched the subject. "School start yet?"

"Tomorrow."

"Really? There's something I don't understand . . . why do they need a full professor to teach Rocks and Clocks to a bunch of *komya?*"

"They're not clods, they're future historians, I hope. And for the millionth time, it isn't geology *and* history, it's geohistory."

He had the exact same grin he'd had that time in Perm when he'd dropped the frog down her dress, the eternal brat of a younger brother. She was trying to think of a way to retake the offensive when a hurricane of noise suddenly slammed through the closed bedroom door.

Katrina was back, accompanied by most of the male population of Moscow, singing unintelligibly at the top of their voices and bumping into things.

The door flew open. Katrina's hair was mussed, and her lipstick looked smeared. Laughingly, she said, "Larashka, sweetie, a few stray dogs followed me home. Can I keep them?" The door was pushed open a little wider and Lara saw there were at least three of them, all soldiers, all drunk, all staring into the bedroom and swaying unsteadily. "Please, Mommy? They won't be any trouble!"

Gales of male laughter told Lara her quiet call with her brother was history. To the computer screen she said, "I'll call you back when I can."

"Okay. Sleep tight, Professor, and don't

let the geohistorical bedbugs bite."

Lara clicked off, and her grinning brother's face was gone from the screen.

CHAPTER 8

London, England
Tuesday

A little after two in the morning, anyone able to peer over the hoardings just down from the Chancery Lane tube station would have seen men with electric lamps and shovels digging quietly but furiously in the large hole. Within the hour they found what they came for: a small, mostly decomposed leather valise, no longer handcuffed to a human arm bone at the wrist.

Shining their lights on it together, they could see the damp had rotted away the leather at the bottom. There was nothing inside.

CHAPTER 9

In Brixton, a noise somewhere woke up Davidson Gordon in the middle of the night. The strange find at the site meant there'd be no work today; no work meant no money, curse the luck, and the Gordons needed the money. Still, it would give Davidson — "Davy" to friends and family — the rare chance to sleep in before going through the package he'd found in the hole next to the human bone, the one he'd kept hidden under his coat the whole time the cameras were on him.

His wife and daughter were still asleep when the noise came again, a discreet knock on the door. Bollocks.

Three men with muddy shoes stood on the step in the predawn, holding out identification cards that read, ANTIQUITIES DIVISION.

"Mr. Davidson?" asked the tallest of the three.

"Gordon. Davidson's me Christian name."

"Mr. Gordon, then. May we come in?"

"Family's sleeping."

"Oh, this won't take but a minute," said the heavily muscled one. "We want to hold up work at the dig as little as possible."

Reluctantly, Davy led them into the kitchen. The tall one's first question was, "Did you take anything from the excavation, sir? A package of any kind?" When he hesitated, the man added, "There's a finder's fee, of course."

With that, he led the men downstairs. Even though the overhead light was on, the massive one with a bull neck shone the flashlight he was holding on the workbench, where the package and its strange contents — the still-damp wrapping around the gunmetal-gray canisters — were lying open to view.

Davy wished now he'd done a better job of looking through his find. What if there was money in those sealed metal cans? Or jewels? He'd shaken them and hadn't heard anything. Still, he'd be in a better bargaining position if he knew.

The tall man continued, "I count six tins. Have you removed any?"

"No."

"Are you sure?"

"I'd know, woun't I?"

"Have you told anyone about finding this?"

"Just the wife and daughter."

"No one down the pub?"

"Didn't go down the pub."

"Your wife and daughter, did they tell anyone?"

"No, nobody. Must be pretty valuable, these things, the way you're asking all these questions."

The tall man was saying, "Questions? No, no more questions," even as he took the silenced gun out of his coat pocket and shot Davy in the heart and, just to be on the safe side, once more in the head where he fell.

The beefy man picked up the parcel and led the way back upstairs.

"Davy, that you?" a sleepy voice called from the bedroom.

She was sitting up in bed when the bullet went through flesh and bone, the pillow and the headboard.

The third killer, the young one with his red hair in a buzz cut and a little blue tattoo on his neck, grinned and went looking for the daughter. Beverly never made it to school.

Chapter 10

Moscow

It was 11:57, Lara knew, on the huge clock thirty-six floors above her head, having checked her watch against it on her way in. In exactly 180 seconds it would boom a dozen stunning notes across the Sparrow Hills in southwest Moscow and inform the newcomers who were hopelessly lost in the warren of hallways — there were 33 kilometers of corridors and more than 5,000 rooms in the Moscow State University building — that they were late.

Once the biggest structure in the world outside New York (if you counted the giant star on top), the building had maps of each floor, sealed in plastic, posted on bulletin boards under the heading IN CASE OF FIRE. The plastic had yellowed with age, so now the floor plans were totally indecipherable. It meant there were always stragglers who barged into the first class at the last moment, or even later.

For something to do while she waited, Lara walked over to the large map of the fifth floor above the elevator buttons. Pasted to the yellowed and cracking plastic was one of those oversized stars saying, *"Vy Nakhodites Zdes."* As if "You Are Here" would help anyone who didn't already know where "Here" was.

Around the map, the students had commandeered the remaining space on the corkboard. A thumbtack held in place the picture of a lost Siamese; good luck finding a cat in this place. A printed card glowingly advertised for a nonsmoking roommate, the same sort of card that had brought Katrina to Lara.

She was fingering a flimsy notice stapled to the board, the kind with a fringe of cut-apart phone numbers at the bottom you tore off if you were interested. In this case, a pretty Swedish student, smiling in the photocopied picture on the flier, wanted work as a nanny after school. Quite a few of the fringes had been taken. Could so many of the girl's fellow students need nannies?

She found herself reading an older flier under the fringed one: the Moscow City Chess Club was holding its monthly exhibition match and, this month, Garry Kasparov was taking on all comers. Refreshments would be served, "with a short talk beforehand by the Guest of Honor, former world champion and current Secretary of The Other Russia." His topic: " 'Why the Toothpaste Can't Go Back in the Tube,' an appeal for Russia to create closer ties with America and the West."

Make that a long talk, Lara thought — Kasparov's transmit button was permanently on. The event, she noticed, was this Thursday evening at 8:00.

The tolling of the bell overhead, always a surprise even when you were waiting for it, shook the windows in their frames. Lara let the echoing sound of the final note dissipate completely before briskly striding through the door to her lecture hall for the first time as a full Professor.

Greeting the seventy or so students who'd made their way to their seats with a curt "Good afternoon," she dropped the dogeared copy of her second published book, *An Introduction to Geohistory,* on her desk with a thud, the better to emphasize the gravity of the subject.

"What makes history . . . history? Do great men make history? Gandhi . . . Napoleon . . . Peter the Great . . . Julius Caesar? That's what all the textbooks used to say for hundreds of years.

"Or is it *the Big Idea*? 'All men are created equal.' 'From each according to his ability, to each according to his needs.' Even, 'the will of Allah is the law of the land,' as the Sharia would have it. Do ideas determine history?

"Maybe you are an economic determinist. Without onerous royal taxes, there would have been no Magna Carta, no Boston Tea Party, no summoning of the Estates General. Some say, absent a ruinous postwar inflation that had people trundling their currency around in wheelbarrows, there would have been no Hitler or Mussolini. That, without a generation of unemployed Third World youth, 'Islamic Fascism' would have no foot soldiers."

Lara withdrew a laser pointer from her bag and switched it on. "I suggest to you that all those beautiful theories are, well, theories." She turned and ran the red laser dot over the giant map of the world on the wall behind her from east to west.

"*This* is what causes history. All this . . . stuff . . . that's called the planet Earth. Question: why would an insignificant body of water, barely thirty kilometers long and three and a half wide, with no fishing to speak of, be fought over at least nineteen times in recorded history and another, ten times as large and teaming with aquatic life, be so unremarkable that two warring navies have never faced off in its waves?" After years of practice, she used her pointer expertly.

"Why is the Bosphorus the belle of the ball and" — she swung the laser way to the west — "why is Long Island Sound history's wallflower? Why are the nomadic tribes of one mostly uninhabitable desert in Arabia incomparably rich and another group living in the equally inhospitable Gobi unspeakably poor?

"Why were the political histories of the island empires of Great Britain and Japan, so similar in size, such polar opposites?

"By the end of the term — once we've had our field trip to the State Archives and you've learned the kind of material that exists to answer those questions and to prove or disprove all those beautiful theories — you will have mastered all this. As you will prove to me when you hand in your term papers."

It was a typical first lecture. Afterward, as she was packing up, Lara said, "For those of you who will be otherwise engaged this Friday, I leave you a question to ponder: if there had been no Great Wall, would the

Chinese be more — or less — dominant in world affairs than they are today?"

She closed the cap on her laser pen and stuck it in the outer pocket of her handbag. Turning to go, she noticed a hand was raised. "Yes, the young man in the back?"

A student with red hair cropped close to his head got to his feet; was that a smirk? "Does 'otherwise engaged' have anything to do with Conception Day, Dr. Klimt? Will *you* be otherwise engaged?"

The room broke out in laughter, and Lara went with the flow. "If it does and if I am, I'll *conceive* of a way to keep that fact to myself. Have a good day."

She watched them file out the door, the usual mix of eager beavers and slackers, trying to guess by their looks which ones were which. Turning back to the room, she was startled to see the young man who'd asked the question still sitting in the last row. Then he began to clap.

"*Bravo,* Dr. Klimt, excellent lecture."

"*Spasibo.* Are you a student of mine or are you auditing this class, Mr. . . . ?"

"Call me Alexei. And no, I'm not a student; more of a messenger. I have something to give you."

He got up, and Lara could see he carried a shopping bag under his arm as he worked his way down the aisle and over to where she was. She noted the dried mud on his shoes and the tattoos covering his neck. No, not a student.

"Something for me? An apple for the teacher?"

"A whole orchard."

He was standing in front of her now, holding the bag open so she could look inside. It held a standard shipping box, with a torn label addressed to someone with a name ending in "— simov." Nestled within some sort of old cellophane wrapping, brittle and disintegrating, were tins that looked a little like cans of tennis balls. The whole thing had a musty, dead smell.

A water-stained cardboard shipping tag, the writing on it lost in places, had worked free from the cellophane and lay loosely across the top. The remnants of a red wax seal still adhered to the tag.

He was smiling that I-know-something-you-don't-know smile all Russian men are endowed with at birth. "Before you teach another bunch of innocents your theory about the causes of war and peace and history," he said, "I thought you might actually want to know the truth."

Now *she* smiled. "The 'truth'? It's in there?"

"You bet your sweet ass. And it is sweet, by the way."

"I think you'd better go, Alexei."

"You're right, I was out of line. What can I say . . . I'm uncouth. But as a messenger, I'm first-rate. Here."

He put the paper handles of the bag firmly in her hand and closed her fingers around it. "You know what these tins are, don't you?"

She peered in once more. "They look like the Dictaphone cylinders I listen to in the archives."

"Once again, *bravo,* Dr. Klimt. Or is it *brava,* I can never remember. You're looking at six Dictaphone recordings that just came to light. They're full of testimony by one of the men who started the Great Patriotic War."

"How did you get them?"

He grinned. "The word 'commandeered' comes to mind."

"Have you listened to them?"

"No one has, not in almost seventy years."

"Then, how do you know what — ?"

"Trust me, Dr. Klimt, we have ways."

"This is madness." She turned and put the shopping bag down on the lectern behind her, reaching for her geohistory text to put it back in her shoulder bag.

The young man quickly shifted the shopping bag on top of her textbook, keeping it there. "Your whole beautiful theory . . . all that Romanian oil and Ukrainian wheat and lebensraum the Germans needed: bullshit, Larissa Mendelova. I dare you to go to your hideout in the Arkhiv, listen to the recordings, and see if your precious geohistory still holds any water."

Her professional pride at stake, Lara reached into the bag for one of the tins. He stopped her and rummaged in his pocket for a white cotton glove, which he put on before reaching into the bag. He saw the quizzical look on her face and said, simply, "Fingerprints," as he held out one of the cans to her.

Lara could see a label on top that read, "Coward interview, 04-10-44, Cylinder Three." In English. She looked back at him, questioningly. "1944? From the war? Who was the coward?"

The man smiled. "Not *the* coward. *Noël* Coward, actor and playwright. He was one of the conspirators."

She threw up her hands. "No, it's all too crazy. You're telling me an English writer started the war that killed twenty-five million of our people? I don't believe it."

"Painful, isn't it, to find out you've been

wrong all these years? Or would you rather go on believing in your own theory and unwilling to face the facts, like all those other historians you discredit?"

She took a breath and faced him. "All right, why are you *really* giving these . . . things . . . to me?"

"If you must know, I, we, think they're a road map to something, a treasure map if you will. And that you're the only person in all of Moscow with access to the Dictaphone machines who has the brains and the determination — and who knows the Arkhiv like the back of her hand — the only one who can listen to them and lead us to the treasure."

"Who's 'we'? And what kind of treasure?"

"Russians . . . patriots . . . people who don't buy the conventional fiction about the war. As for the treasure, it's a book; one that Adolf Hitler was given. Rumor has it he wrote something down in it, a confession, a message for posterity maybe, or a last will and testament. Whatever it is, it's valuable."

"I don't see how —"

He held up a finger. "You're going to say you don't see how a full professor can waste her valuable time on a 'wild-goose chase' looking for some musty old tome. We understand. That's why we're prepared to pay you a million rubles."

"A mil— I don't understand."

The tough who called himself a messenger pushed the bag of tins toward her one more time and said, "It's a valuable book, if it still exists. Listen to the recordings, my beautiful Dr. Klimt; follow the clues. Find what we're looking for, and there's a million-ruble . . . uh . . . finder's fee."

He was already on his way to the door. Lara picked up the shopping bag and hurried over to him, putting the handles firmly in his hand. "I'm sorry, I can't possibly."

"Is that your final word?"

"*Prostitye,* I'm sorry, it is."

The man turned to go. Lara went back to the lectern to gather up her things. She heard the door to the classroom close.

Lara turned out the lights and left the room. In the crowded corridor, with students hurrying in all directions to change classes, the scruffy young man was nowhere to be seen. Lara took a step toward her office down the hall and her foot bumped into something on the floor, a shopping bag filled with Dictaphone recordings.

CHAPTER 11

The Radisson Slavyanskaya, put up in the first wave of *glasnost*, loomed ahead of Lara against the threatening sky. There was more than a hint of autumn's coming chill in the breeze blowing off the Moskva, and Lara, hurrying because she was late, did up the next highest button of her light coat.

Other, newer hotels were located closer to Red Square, so the Slavyanskaya's proprietors were determined that dining should be their marketing angle. One could choose the Talavera Restaurant, featuring Mediterranean cuisine, or one of the two cafés catering to *mitteleuropeans.* To the left of the lobby, Sumosan boasted "the best Japanese sushi in Moscow."

A rack near the door of the bookshop/ newsstand held the German-language version of the afternoon paper, *Izvestia.* Its banner headline read, KREMLIN SET TO WELCOME WORLD LEADERS. Really? This week? Lara made a mental note to lift her nose out of her books every once in a while.

She quickly picked up the paper. A not particularly flattering picture of the Russian head of state was placed next to that of the American president. Lara noticed another headline, below the fold: WEST CONDEMNS USE OF FORCE AGAINST RED SQUARE PRO-TESTERS. She put the paper back in the rack.

In the vast Russky restaurant, "serving authentic Russian cuisine from the time of the tsars," Lara handed her coat and the unwanted shopping bag full of metal tins to the *garderob,* who must have been ninety if she was a day. Maybe, Lara thought, she'd leave the bag there on the shelf when she got her coat.

The woman on the phone taking a reservation was the *"Maitresse D,"* according to the plastic card on her blouse. Lara noticed the freestanding sign nearby announcing: THE RADISSON SLAVYANSKAYA CELE-BRATES INTERNATIONAL WEEK. Below it was the special "global menu" the chef had prepared in honor of the visiting dignitaries, which seemed to be mostly familiar Russian entrées paired with other countries' vegetables, starting with shashlik and Brussels sprouts. Hmm.

Next to it, a smaller sign announced: THE RADISSON SLAVYANSKAYA WELCOMES . . . TOR. A quick glance around failed to disclose at which tables sat the reforming firebrands of Garry Kasparov's opposition coalition, The Other Russia. Dismissed as a debating team years ago because they were unable to agree on a candidate to run against Putin, TOR was now, ironically, the official bogeyman, blamed for orchestrating the popular antigovernment protests that were popping up everywhere.

Political dissidents? The people having lunch here seemed accustomed to the nicer things, people who liked things just the way they were. Like the fact that the tablecloths were actually white, and they weren't shiny with too much washing, the way they were in the places the tourists never saw.

The officious Maitresse put down the phone. Lara gave her name, and the woman deigned to smile at this academic in sober clothes standing before her. Their host must have pull. "Dr. Klimt, your party is already here."

Pavel, in his one presentable jacket, stood up only because the other man did, a striking someone in an expensive suit. Lara took him at first to be Pierce Brosnan from the James Bond films. Pavel was saying, too

66

familiarly, "Grigoriy Aleksandrovich, this is the woman I was telling you about, my friend, Professor Klimt. Larissa Mendelova, may I introduce my boss's boss's boss, Director Gerasimov."

"*Prostitye . . .* I was delayed."

"Not at all." The head of the Russian State TV and Radio Company Ostankino — more familiarly known by its old name, Gosteleradio — held Lara's chair for her. This was altogether a different sort of Russian man than she was used to. When they were seated he announced, "I took the liberty of ordering a bottle of wine, Dr. Klimt. I hope you won't mind."

Hmm, she thought, wine with lunch . . . not your typical Tuesday.

He went on, in English. "Pavel has been singing your praises. He tells me you are one of our largest historians."

She turned to Pavel and, in Russian, reproached him with a smile. "Largest? Really?"

Immediately, Gerasimov understood his mistake. "*Prostitye,* forgive me, Larissa Mendelova." The tops of his ears were pink with embarrassment. "This is what happens when you teach yourself English by watching U.S. television. I know all the words but, still, my sentences . . . permit me to try my

67

compliment again: I am honored to meet one of Moscow's *greatest* historians."

Also in English, she replied, "Thank you, but that's only because all our truly great historians are still in the Urals, in the camps."

The man seemed about to laugh, but stopped himself. She figured he could *hear* English well enough. "Surely not anymore."

"No, I make the occasional joke." Lara watched the waiter open the wine bottle before adding, "Of course, actual history has only been allowed to occur in the last twenty years, so I suppose I got in on the ground floor."

Now the man did laugh. Pavel, on the other hand, looked stricken.

Gerasimov changed the subject. "I've spent the last couple of days with your writing, Dr. Klimt."

She quickly put in, "Please, it's Lara."

"All right, Lara. Your text on Soviet history . . . to have come at it from such a different angle, to have done so much, broken so much new ground while we were still under Gorbachev and his crowd . . ."

It wasn't phrased as a question, but he seemed to be waiting for a response. Lara said, "I was a junior instructor in America, earning a few dollars a month in hard currency from New York University for the Soviet Union, when my dissertation was published. I suppose I had the benefit of distance."

She thought about that for a moment. "If you've read me, then you know my specialty is *geo*history. How geography — rivers, mountains, climate, and especially the presence, or absence, of natural resources — determines a people's history far more than we like to think . . . and political dogma, of any kind, far less."

Gerasimov smiled. "Not something the children of Lenin wanted to have get around."

Lara smiled back. "No, I suppose not. As far as having *done* so much? Well, historians are thinkers, not doers. We need that distance I mentioned, whether it's measured in years or miles, so the things *other* people do can arrange themselves in patterns we're able to perceive. Still, thank you for the nice words, Director."

"My friends call me Grisha."

"Thank you . . . Grisha."

They ordered some impossibly expensive dishes. Then, back in the mother tongue, Gerasimov said, "I've been going to school on you. I know you've been a 'talking head' once or twice on a couple of our political

69

panel shows. One thing isn't clear. You were the girls' chess champion of Russia, weren't you?"

In the moment it took her to frame a response, Pavel jumped in. "Not just Russia, the whole Soviet Union. Once, she even beat Kasparov!"

She shot him what she hoped was a withering look. "No cheerleading at lunch, Pavel, please." She added, "He was playing ten boards at the time. I was just one of the ten."

Gerasimov, impressed, leaned in a little. "Okay . . . why? Why drop chess for History when you were so good at it?"

She thought for a moment. Why, indeed? "I guess . . . I guess I stopped believing everything was either black or white."

The man nodded in understanding. "I changed careers as well, but for a different reason: I wasn't good enough to be an actor, so I settled for being a weatherman. Now I give both the actors *and* the weathermen a living on television."

Over soup, Lara decided this would be her last lunch date with Pavel. She'd paid her dues. Her parents had been friends with his parents, that was all; taught them to speak Russian when they were booted out of England after the war. Then, when the

70

Colemans died, Paul — now Pavel — had attached himself to her family as an older "stepson." He had no conversational skills, no manners. A nothing-special job in the broadcast office's online division, maybe a little computer hacking on the side, like half the Russian guys she knew. When he wasn't running errands for the higher-ups, he was buying duty-free cigarettes for resale from his backdoor contacts at the embassies. A couple of times she'd seen his rusty Vespa, before it gave up the ghost, shoved against the wall of the British Embassy on Smolenskaya.

Look at him now, elbows on the table. He wasn't a brother or a boyfriend. Not even a colleague. Just an old *vlozhenii* . . . an attachment.

Grigoriy Aleksandrovich Gerasimov had been sitting back in his chair. Now he leaned forward again and said, "I have a proposition for you, Dr. Klimt . . . Lara . . . one that comes with a rather generous stipend. What are you doing Friday?"

Pavel seemed as puzzled as Lara. She guessed he'd only been told to set up the luncheon without being told why. Wait, the man wasn't talking about Conception Day, was he? About making babies?

Gerasimov reached beneath his chair and

71

picked up a thin calf-skin portfolio. From it he took a single sheet of paper, which he turned toward Lara. It looked like the TV listings from one of the daily papers. "There, near the bottom, the one that's highlighted."

It wasn't about sex. Relieved, Lara read aloud from the page. "Friday, 0930 hours . . . NTV, Channel One, RTR, ORT, Seaside Public Television . . . Moscow schoolchildren question the American president." She looked up. "Okay, but what's it got to do with me?"

"In America, I understand it's called an 'interactive Town Hall' . . . viewers call or text in questions during the live show. A moderator sits beside the person being interviewed, to take what the students send in and translate them in real time for the President.

"Well, at the networks we find ourselves in sort of a bind. Our in-house moderator, the person we would have used, rang up two days ago to say he has the flu. Even if he recovers in time, the doctors won't let him near the president. So we need a sort of 'substitute teacher.'

"And who better to fill in, to translate the students' questions, than someone who's not only fluent in English but actually lived for years in America? And in the president's own city, no less? Lara, you're perfect!"

Right through her olive skin, Lara blushed the deep, ripe-peach blush her family always made fun of. "Perfect? Hardly. Sir, I —"

"It's Grisha, remember?"

She blushed all over again. "Grisha . . . thank you for the kind words, but intrigued as I am, I have to decline. Perhaps Pavel told you, I have a new position at the University. The show trials — excuse me, classes — started this week. I lecture Tuesdays at noon and Fridays at ten. This thing . . . it's a direct conflict."

"I understand perfectly." The faint smile on Gerasimov's lips never changed. "He did tell me. So I was able to arrange a few things. As it happens, your Friday class has been given to a colleague. So you see, you're free to —"

"What? My class . . . ?"

"The Superintendant was very understanding. A twenty-four-hour sabbatical, she called it."

"But you, she, can't. Not without telling me. The material . . . it's a very precise lesson plan."

"But I *am* telling you. An honorarium to the History Department in your name seems to have necessitated a last minute reworking of faculty schedules. They're being posted in the Department right now. But never fear — your position, your students, your research, they'll all be there next week, once you've done your patriotic duty.

"Because that's what this is, a chance to expose young Russian minds to democratic ideas, face to face! It's the very thing hundreds of thousands of your fellow citizens are demanding, out there in the streets, and you'll be part of it. We'll be on five networks, with millions of viewers, piping it into classrooms from Kaliningrad to Vladivostok. Also, all the social media —YouTube and the rest. So I wouldn't turn it down if I were you."

Lara had a congenital dislike of the phrase "if I were you." And a deeper, more intense dislike of the Superintendent who had promoted her, reluctantly, finally, only after two male colleagues had died over the summer and she'd had no one else with testosterone to choose over Lara. Still, if it was just the one missed class . . .

The man was dialing a number on his mobile, right there in the restaurant. He held it out to her. "I wouldn't be coming to you if we weren't in a fix. Here, ask Superintendent Nazimova if I'm not telling the truth."

She waved her hand at the phone. "That

won't be necessary." She sighed. "Tell me where to meet you on Friday."

"No."

This time it was Pavel, the bystander, who blurted out, "No?"

"No, it's not quite that simple. Tell me Lara, have you ever worked with a prompter?"

"You mean a man holding cue cards?"

Gerasimov smiled indulgently. "We're a little more up-to-date. These days it's all electronic: the TelePrompTer operator types the questions as they're sent in from the schools around the country, and they show up on a clear glass monitor that sits right over the camera lens. You read the words a moment before you say them, trying not to look like you're reading, and translate them for the president. It's a little tricky, because you have to keep looking away when you speak with your guest, and then glance back to the camera for the next question."

Lara frowned. "Gee, I don't know . . ."

Gerasimov smiled. "All you need is an hour of practice in a studio and you'll do fine. I know where one's available; I could drive over and pick you up tomorrow."

Lara sighed. What choice did she have? "I'll call you when I'm free."

"Wonderful!" He looked over to the waiter

and snapped his fingers for the check. "And better bring a few changes of clothes. We'll have to see what works best on camera."

The waiter quickly put down the check on a small silver tray, and Gerasimov signed it with the gold Montblanc pen he took from his pocket. He scribbled his phone number on a piece of paper and gave it to Lara.

The three of them rose from the table. "I'm really looking forward to working with you, Dr. Klimt. Until tomorrow." Unexpectedly, he took her hand in his and kissed it. Then he looked up at her, and Lara saw that one of his eyes was blue-gray, the other blue-green.

Waiting behind another woman at the coat check, Lara was dismayed to see Pavel say goodbye to his boss and circle back.

"I was hoping you'd still be here. Larissa Mendelova, I have something important to tell you."

Uh-oh.

"I've been wanting to say this, Lara, ever since you returned from America, and, well, at first I was too shy. I mean, you were a big shot at the University and who was I? Just a guy from your hometown, you know, the boy next door, so to speak."

The other woman was putting on her coat now, slowly, so she could listen in. Without thinking, Lara stabbed both claim checks into the hand of the old *garderob* in the booth. This was going to be bad enough without a stranger eavesdropping.

Pavel, as usual, was oblivious. "And then you met Viktor, and all of a sudden you were married and, uh, the moment was gone."

She eyed him evenly. "And now it's back?"

He seemed to take her words for encouragement. "Yes, it's back! With you and Viktor, um, not together for much longer, I want you to know I have the deepest feelings for you. I always have, even before you left for America."

The stranger, her coat fully on, was still hovering. Lara turned to look directly at her. The woman, startled, smiled confidentially before walking away.

Lara decided to make this painless for both of them. "Pavel, I have only the strongest feelings for you." Which, technically, was true. "But not romantic ones. I consider you the brother I never had."

"But, Lara, you already have a brother."

The coat check lady was holding her wrap out to her, and she took it. "Exactly. Lev is the brother I *do* have; you're the brother I *don't* have."

"Huh?"

She pecked him on both cheeks, Russian

style, and was about to leave him there, befuddled, when the coat check woman produced her shopping bag and slid it across the wooden barrier to Lara. Not wanting to stand there for another moment with Pavel, Lara picked it up and walked out of the restaurant.

Afterward, crossing the Crystal Bridge on her way back to the Metro, Lara didn't notice the tins as they rattled around in the bag. She wasn't thinking of Pavel, either, or Gerasimov. Nor the changes she'd have to make in her meticulously crafted lesson plans. No, her brain was focused on something else entirely: In less than three days she'd be sitting beside the world's most powerful man on national television — not just the leader of the free world, but a world-class womanizer who'd been with beauty queens from all over the globe — and she was going to look like a complete mouse.

CHAPTER 12

A handful of dignitaries greeted the American president as he touched down at Sheremetyevo, people chosen because they spoke English, however haltingly. To prove it, they all had to say something longwinded out there on the tarmac. Then it was into the limos — late model, heavily tinted Lincolns and Mercedes — for the flying trip into town. The road they traveled was half a football field wide, lined with banners showing the American's picture alongside that of his Russian counterpart.

That was his up moment of the day. Downer Number One came when he took a call in the limo from Carl back in Alaska, one more proof that if you give a government bureaucrat a chance to mess up, he'll make the most of it. Apparently, some idiot up in Prudhoe blew it and started pumping oil into the pipeline from one of the tankers. *Before the deal was actually signed.*

They'd stopped him an hour after he'd begun, but the damage was done. To make matters worse, a second numbnut, covering for the first, hushed the whole thing up, pretending it never happened. So he was just hearing of it now, more than a week after the incident. And only because the inspector at the other end in Valdez was making a stink about something wrong with the oil.

There was only one thing to do. "The Valdez guy, buy him off. Make up a cover story and pay him whatever it takes. Just shut him up." Can't have any more screwups now, not when we're so close.

If ever a deal had to get done, it was this one. Executive Order Number One back in January made good on his campaign pledge to open the wildlife refuge and to drill, baby, drill — even if he hadn't coined the phrase — right where the geologists told them to. Seven disappointing seismic tests later, all he had to show for it were twenty thousand stupid caribou who couldn't come up with a new migration route, at least one angry Eskimo for every caribou, and a couple million fundraising letters filling the wallets of the guys he beat last time around.

This deal would buy him time; buy *Amer-*

ica time, that is. Had to be done, simple as that.

The follow-up call from Alaska found the President in a black mood. The afternoon papers were spread out on the bed in their suite overlooking Red Square, and one of them, the leftover Communist daily *Pravda,* had decided to pick up all the old tabloid lies about the women, pictures included. It was starting to rain and, as it turned out, you *could* have more screwups.

"Yes?" he shouted into the encrypted cell phone. The thing was great at scrambling your voice so no one else could listen in, but lousy at being an actual phone. There were thirty seconds in which the President listened to whoever it was explain Downer Number Two, and then his wife, freshening up in the bathroom, heard him explode. "Damn it Carl, if you had half a brain you'd be dangerous! When I said 'Do what it takes" . . . Christ Carl, I'm a little busy right now, getting our country's future straightened out. Do I have to fly back there and fire your sorry ass? Take a little initiative, that's what I'm paying you for. DO . . . WHAT . . . IT . . . TAKES!"

He slammed the cell phone down on the dresser. She hurried out of the bathroom to find him grinning that grin she knew wasn't a smile.

"When we get back, there'll be a new regime, honey. A whole new regime."

CHAPTER 13

From the restaurant Lara took the Metro, intending to cross over to the Number Seven line and home. But then she thought she would get off at Revolution Square and look for something to wear in the designer room upstairs at TsUM. Did she have enough to cover it? Lara thumbed through her checkbook. No, not for anything nice. All right, maybe she could borrow something from Vera. Her friend was the original clotheshorse, and on a teacher's salary too.

Lara was still plotting her fashion moves when her brain picked up on the fact that it wasn't the disembodied inbound male voice of the Metro system but the outbound female announcing the next station. She'd missed her stop and was instead, like some kind of mixed-up homing pigeon, heading out to the Arkhiv, where she'd spent the entire summer.

By the time the woman announced they

were approaching Vodny Stadion, or "Water Station" — named for the old pumping facility that once supplied drinking water from the Moskva River — Lara decided that fate or kismet or who-knows-what wished her to listen to the Dictaphone recordings in the shopping bag on the *Osobyi*'s ancient machines. She'd have to call Vera that evening. Lara got out and mounted the Metro steps, amazed to be back at the place she thought she'd left behind for the year.

There are truckloads — make that train-loads — of German World War II documents stored all over Moscow. Hundreds of trainloads. Through a bit of geographical luck it was the eastern half of Berlin, the half of the city Russian troops occupied in 1945, where most of the important Nazi government offices were located, like the *Reichskanzlei* and, of course, the under-ground Führerbunker. Government offices, naturally, meant government files. After the war, East Berlin eventually became part of the German Democratic Republic, and the city's Communist puppets were only too happy to ship anything of value or interest back to Big Brother in the Soviet Union.

For decades, the most secret Nazi papers, the so-called *"Osobyi"* files, were kept under lock and key in the middle of town near the

Kremlin. Then, in the last days of Gorbachev, when everything was breaking down, they were opened up to Russian scholars like Lara. Under Yeltsin, even more of the boxes, the monthly *yashchiks,* were brought out into the light. Lara could walk over from the flat, flash her plastic ID card on its chain, and immerse herself in the Third Reich.

Putin put an end to all that. The ex-KGB man ordered the *Osobyi* section moved to the Russian State Military Archives out past the airport. A twenty-minute drive along the outer ring road when Lara had the car, it was nearly an hour on the Metro from the University, requiring a change in the middle of town.

The clock over the entrance said it was after 3:00 when Lara swiped her ID through the updated card reader. Two hours was all she had before the place shut up tight. She nodded, as usual, to Leonid, the guard, and opened the shopping bag to show him the tins. Without a word he affixed six white stickers on the six cans to indicate she'd brought them in with her.

Lara hurried toward the double glass doors of the Listening Room. Finding it unoccupied, she parked her things against the far wall before seating herself at one of the three 1940s-era Dictaphone machines.

Okay, in for a penny, in for a pound: If the long-dead Englishman Noël Coward knew something that could blow a hole through her life's work, she wanted to hear about it before someone else trumpeted the fact.

On top of the tins inside the shopping bag was the cardboard shipping tag she'd seen before. Lara could make out the words, preprinted in English: OFFICIAL MAIL OF THE MILITARY COURT OF THE UNITED KINGDOM. DO NOT OPEN. Underneath, in smaller type, it said, "The contents of this bag are vouchsafed proof from inspection by order of His Majesty, Directive 31.2."

"His" Majesty. Interesting. She took the tin marked "Number One" from the shopping bag and, breaking the seal, allowed the wax cylinder inside, as pristine as the day it was recorded, to slide out. Lining up the machine's lever with a guide on the side, she dropped the recording in and pushed the lever back. Because the original hand-held listening tubes were tiring to use over long periods, they had been modified to accept modern over-the-ear headphones. So, with her iPad powered up and ready to take notes, she lifted one of the Bose QC15s from the shelf above the machines, plugged it into the old contraption and settled down to listen. It was a man's voice that began:

Now that I've figured out how to work this infernal device, I suppose I should start by saying this is Dictaphone cylinder number one. Fair warning, Robert, old friend — oh, sorry, it's *Sir* Robert now, isn't it? Well then, Sir Robert, your man has given me a half-dozen of these thingies, and I intend to fill them up over the next six evenings.

Lara typed "Sir Robert?" on her computer pad. Over the next two hours, she would make dozens of entries.

For the record, my name is Noël Peirce Coward and I was born in Teddington, Middlesex, as a Christmas present to my parents in 1899. The date today is the second of October 1944, which makes me not quite forty-five, still in the full flower of manhood. I don't know how you swung it, Robert, tracking me down in the city of palms and swimming pools from five thousand miles away for something as inconsequential as a war. But here I am in a little soundproofed room off La Cienega Boulevard — which, I'll have you know, in Spanish means *The* Cienega Boulevard — "thoroughly documenting" an incident from the early days.

"Tattling" is more like it, and during the cocktail hour, too, after slaving all day over a hot movie studio, trying to pry a few dollars for my next production out of some tight American fists. Still, if it will help poor Anthony . . .

So, I have consented to do as you ask and prattle into this microphone whilst your earnest assistant on the other side of the glass takes notes, disgorging everything I know about the matter for you and your colleagues to use in his defense before the Court of Inquiry.

It's quite a lot, actually. And I'm going to tell every scrap of it, because Anthony may be a lot of things, but of one thing I'm certain: he's no enemy of his country. The government perhaps, but never the country . . . of that I'm sure.

Then too, given the Military Secrets Act, this will be the one and only time the story will be told, so I intend to do it justice. No editing myself, no euphemisms for the naughty bits — I'm trusting you to see to all that when you come to have this typed up. For now it's the truth, the whole truth, and nothing left out.

It all began with Celia Johnson's toothache. Well, to be honest, even earlier than that, four years before Celia's tooth ever thought of becoming inflamed. In 1935, one morning out of the clear blue, Marlene Dietrich rang me up to say how much she'd liked my performance the night before in *The Scoundrel*. We've been best pals ever since, in keeping with my firm practice of fawning on every admirer.

The party for Marlene in '39

is where Celia's tooth comes in. Or rather, out. I had prevailed upon her and her husband, Peter Fleming, the travel writer, to motor down from Oxfordshire right before the war to take a villa in Cap Ferrat, next to where I was staying with Willie Maugham. I was thinking of her for *Private Lives,* and I wanted to twist her arm a bit. Sadly, she decided to take *Pride & Prejudice* instead. We wouldn't actually work together for three more years, until she played my wife . . . imagine . . . in the picture, *In Which We Serve.*

Anyway, Peter had his younger brother Ian join us all for the fortnight, ostensibly to get in some golf but really as a sort of unpaid nursemaid for their newborn baby, Nichol. Which freed Celia and Peter to pop over to our place next door to celebrate Marlene's U.S. citizenship, which had just come through. Are you getting all this?

Then that blessed molar made

its presence known and they had to call in a dentist from Ville-franche. Peter was gallant enough to stay with his wife and Ian was sent over to us in their stead. Ah well, the best-laid plans . . .

Because Dietrich's new citizenship was the pretext for the party, Willie and I commandeered the Americans who had taken the villa on the other side for the month: Joe Kennedy and his two grown sons attended while the Ambassador's wife was back with their younger children in America.

Lara lifted the lever that was playing the cylinder. This couldn't be right, could it? Dietrich? Maugham? The Kennedys? What did any of it have to do with a long-lost book?

Lara looked around. Through the glass of the Listening Room door she could see one or two scholarly types, nearly buried behind the piles of books they were using for their research. She let out a huge sigh. What the hell — she was all the way out here already. So she lifted the lever and put it back on the cylinder.

The evening was a strange one, even for me — one woman and seven men, Marlene having in tow the writer Erich Maria Remarque, an inconvenience as they were both married to other people back in Germany.

Over dinner, I found the eldest Kennedy son, Joe Jr., to be as smart as he was strapping and obviously his father's favorite. Sorry to say, he was killed when his plane went down on a training run over Suffolk last month. The younger boy, John, slightly built and somewhat unwell-looking with his suit hanging off him, was "doing Europe" before beginning his last year at university. John, who insisted everyone call him Jack, was as taken with our guest of honor as his father, who never took his eyes off her as she regaled the table with stories of the well-known and the well-off.

The topper came over coffee,

when Marlene produced from her evening bag a telegram she'd received that afternoon, forwarded from Berlin by the German consul in Nice, or was it Monte? She passed it around for our viewing and Maugham prevailed upon Ian as the "new boy" to translate it aloud for the Kennedys and me, lest Marlene have to do all the work.

"My Dear Blue Angel, Your fleeting presence in Europe compels me to request the pleasure of your company at the Berghof at a time of convenience to you. I again implore you to return to the country of your roots, for your artistry is all that is lacking for the new Reich to be gloriously complete. I await your reply. Your most ardent admirer, A.H." This last bit he did looking straight into Dietrich's eyes, as if the words were coming from Ian Fleming and not Adolf Hitler, a nice bit of stagecraft if I say so myself.

Marlene smiled. But all she said was, "This is the third

cable from Hitler this year. What he refuses to understand is that *he* is the reason I'm not coming back.

"You see, he considers me his good luck charm. Years ago he went to a movie theatre in Munich and saw *Die Blaue Engel.* The following day the National Socialists won ninety-five new seats in the Reichstag. Then, when *Dishonoured* was playing in Berlin two years later, they won another one hundred twenty-three.

"As luck would have it, nothing of mine was available next time around and he watched a Bette Davis picture instead, with subtitles. For the first time, they lost votes." She laughed and lit a cigarette. "So now I'm his 'Blue Angel.' "

She took a pull on her cigarette and exhaled. "At least Roosevelt doesn't think I'm a human rabbit's foot." Marlene was putting the telegram back in her evening bag when she said, "He had an astrologer, did you know that?" Sitting next to me, Maugham rose to the bait. "I thought that sort of thing went out with Louis Quinze."

She said, "Apparently not. This one called himself a clairvoyant."

Joe Jr.'s laugh must have sounded like disbelief, for her companion, Remarque, leapt to her defense. "No, it's true. His name was Hanussen. When they lost those 'Bette Davis' seats in '32, the Bavarian corporal was worried and he called the man in for a private reading."

Marlene interrupted. "Let me tell it, Ricky." She got up so she could pantomime the action. "So this Hanussen comes to Hitler's place and seats him in the exact middle of the room. The man examines his hands, counts the bumps on his head or some such rot and sinks into a mystical trance. Then he declares, 'I see victory for you. It cannot be stopped.' Can you imagine?"

Remarque added, "And here's the

95

best part. The faker was a Jew! Erik Jan Hanussen began life in Vienna as Hermann Steinschneider. Everybody knew he was Jewish except the Führer."

I thought what Jack Kennedy said next was just to prove he was listening. "So what became of this astrologer?"

Dietrich told him. "After the *Nacht der langen Messer,* they found his body in a field on the outskirts of Berlin. You see, he was the one man who had seen the Führer worried. They couldn't have that."

As Maugham and I were getting ready for bed we talked over the evening, and I don't recall either of us mentioning the bit about the clairvoyant. It was only when I again saw the younger Kennedy boy that the episode took on a different aspect.

CHAPTER 14

The wax cylinder had come to the end and was making a little hiccup every time it revolved past the machine's lever. Lara stopped it, grateful for the chance to get up and walk around. She found it tiring to take notes, especially when you don't know what you're listening for. Besides, was any of it real, or merely a long-dead playwright's imaginings?

She performed a few knee bends and back twists, and flapped her hands in the air to get the kinks out and the blood circulating. Then she reached down for the second recording, wondering not just what Coward would say next, but what any of it had to do with the origins of the Great Patriotic War.

```
This is Dictaphone cylinder
number two. I saw Jack Kennedy
again by chance (or so I thought)
the next June at a club in
```

Harlem, New York, the kind of place where they keep bringing out extra tables and chairs for the crowd until everyone is sitting in the laps of everyone else.

I had just taken French leave from running our propaganda office on the Continent, having concluded that, if his Majesty's Government aimed to bore the Germans to death, we didn't have the time. I was working directly for Winston now, attempting to charm the Americans with song and dance into supporting our cause despite a little thing called Dunkirk.

My last night in the States, I went to see Marlene perform after hours with Cab Calloway's band, and visit backstage after the show before returning home to sing for the troops. Earlier in the day she had made a personal appearance at Radio City, where *Destry Rides Again* was doing wonderful business. Now, fourteen hours later, she was still fresh as a daisy, warbling her tunes through the blue haze of a thousand chain-smoked cigarettes, when I looked around and saw the manager, Patrice, carrying a chair over his head and leading someone in evening clothes through the throng.

Patrice shoved the chair down in the two inches next to mine and a tuxedoed Jack Kennedy was saying, "May I?" even as he was peeling off bills for the tip.

Capping an evening that must have included some formal affair, he appeared to be over the jaundice or whatever it was the previous summer. We sat together, entranced by La Dietrich. I didn't know then that Jack and Marlene were already lovers . . . she hadn't breathed a word.

In her dressing room afterward, she introduced me to Calloway, the man with the largest set of incisors I have ever seen. Eventually I tried to take my leave, explaining I was sailing in the morning, but Jack insisted I join them for a nightcap in his hotel room. "I have a car outside." Don't they always.

Riding down Fifth Avenue I was in a rotten mood watching this boy, not yet graduated from Harvard, nibble the ear of one of the world's most desirable women. I mean, he hadn't *earned* it, as far as I could see. Worse, this stripling's room proved to be, in fact, the Carlyle's best suite, with a panorama of Central Park beyond the balcony.

It was just going 2:00 A.M. when Marlene excused herself to "take off my face." On her way she said, "Noël, Jack has a wonderful idea I think you should hear."

"For a show?"

As Kennedy walked over to a little steel bar on wheels he said, "For a 'production.' " He fixed us both brandies, which he brought over on a tray. "Mr. Coward . . ."

"It's 'Noël'. 'Mr. Coward' is, was, my father."

"All right . . . Noël. It's my

father who's the problem. As far as he's concerned, Britain's already lost the war, so he won't lift a finger to help me. Even if he did, he wouldn't be of any help, since the Prime Minister knows Dad's a defeat-ist and refuses to see him. That makes me persona non grata as well."

"I shouldn't worry. A lot of people are non grata with Win-ston."

"Well, my brother and I don't share Father's views. But the way things stand, this idea of ours will be dismissed out of hand."

I was thinking the brandy was very good and did it come with the suite when I sensed he was waiting for me to ask, "What idea?" So I did.

"What idea?"

Kennedy stopped to swirl a single ice cube in his liquor before going on. "We've come up with a way, my brother Joe and I, possibly to prevent the inva-sion of the United Kingdom."

He let that sink in before adding, "To be honest, most of the Irish over here think the fall of Britain is the best thing that could happen."

"And you don't?"

Right in the middle of his narration, Noël Coward sneezed. Not a little one either, but a great big honker. The recording clearly picked up the sound of a handkerchief being unfolded, used, and refolded again before the man continued speaking.

I apologize, Dear Listener. I must be allergic to telling stories for which I'm not being paid. Now, where was I? Oh yes, Kennedy was about to tell me why he and his brother Joe weren't pulling for a German victory like the other Irish.

"Not if it means us here in America facing Hitler with all Europe behind him. So I thought . . . that is . . . well, I've heard you have the Prime Minister's ear."

I shifted a little in my chair. "A gruesome thought, young man.

And even if I did, and even if your government will stop being so dashed neutral, any ships or guns wouldn't get there in time."

"I wasn't thinking of arms. My idea is more of . . . a trick."

I didn't take his point. "Meaning . . . what, precisely?"

Kennedy looked into his glass and began. "Remember that story Marlene . . . Miss Dietrich . . . told, of being Hitler's good luck charm? Of his getting a clairvoyant to predict the future? Well, what if someone prophesied that Hitler is going to conquer *the Soviet Union* within the year? And what if Hitler believed him? What would he do?"

I went along. "I don't know. What?"

"We're guessing he'd swing the Wehrmacht around and attack to the east."

My internal cogitator seemed to be running slowly that evening. "And just who would predict such a thing? Don't you remember . . . they killed the fortune-teller back in '34."

Jack leaned in a little, his eyes brighter than I had seen them before. "What if the greatest fortuneteller of all time said it would happen?"

"And who, exactly, is —"

"Michel de Nostradamus, a French prophet of the sixteenth century."

Kennedy got up and moved over to the bookcase on the far side of the bar. It occurred to me, did the books, too, come with the room? The young man kept talking. "Before FDR took him on, Father was something of a movie producer. In the '20s, he sank some money into a picture with Gloria Swanson that was shelved when talkies came in. *The Swami.* He bought these books on Nostradamus for background material. Here, look for yourself."

He opened a small volume entitled *The Prophecies of the Seer* to a page with four-line stanzas running the length of it. Not poetry, exactly, and the English was rather stilted. I fancy myself something of an antiquarian, and I was more taken with the binding than the text. I do remember one bit: "The towers will be set ablaze and the river run red."

Not knowing what to make of it I said, "His English is rather Biblical, no?"

The American flipped the pages back to the front. "See, it's a translation. The original French is even more Biblical."

Alcohol doesn't usually muddle my brains, but I couldn't see where the conversation was going. I bought some time by getting up to stretch my legs and look out the window at the park and the city beyond it, a sleeping city at peace. "And people believe such rot?"

"Some people do. The Greeks had their Oracle of Delphi. A seer warned Caesar to beware the Ides of March. Charlemagne and Napoleon . . . still, one person's belief is all we need."

I turned to face him. "But did this Nostradamus *really* write that Hitler would defeat the Sovs four centuries before there were any Sovs? Or a Hitler, for that matter?"

Kennedy looked down at his brandy. "Not in so many words. Not in any words, as a matter of fact."

"Then how —"

"We'll make it up. Create a false prophecy, make it look musty and old, like a prop in one of father's movies. Don't you see? That's why I'm telling you. *You* make up things for a living, don't you?"

By now it was after three in the morning and my tolerance for the harebrained had expired, so I decided to let the boy down gently. "I write comedies. Drawing room stuff. And patter set to music. This isn't my cup of tea at all."

Jack put down his glass on the metal tray with a rather loud noise for the middle of the night. "Noël, Marlene tells me

you know everybody who is anybody over there and, most of
all, you have access to Churchill. Couldn't you at least
produce this thing? I'm twenty-
one; I have money in my own name
now. Hire a writer, a scholar.
Hire ten if you want and send me
the bill. But it has to be done
right away. Look at this."

He thrust that day's *Herald-
Tribune* in my face. "There. PÉ-
TAIN NAMED NEW FRENCH PREMIER. Father
has been talking to him right
along, says he's about to make a
separate peace with Hitler. That
means, in days, Britain will be
all alone."

He took my silence for permission to continue. "Seriously,
why couldn't we? Right now,
tonight, your country is just
sitting there, with the Nazis
twenty miles away, licking their
chops. You think of yourself as
a patriot, don't you? I know if
America was up against it and I
could do what *you* can, I'd . . ."

I tried to set him straight.
"Even if we could convince them

107

it was genuine, why would the bloody Nazis give a fig what some medieval crackpot dreamed up?"

Instead of answering me, he lifted his eyes. For a moment I thought he was reconsidering the whole thing. Then, solemn as a mortician, he uttered the following words: *"The young lion will overcome the older one/On the field of combat in a single battle/He will pierce his eyes through a golden cage/Two wounds made one, then he dies a cruel death."*

I didn't know what to say. So I said nothing.

Kennedy looked back at me. "In 1559, a vision came to Nostradamus in the bath. He wrote it down afterward and sent it off to the king in Paris. Eight months later, Henri II died an agonizing death in a jousting accident when a lance ran through his helmet, the 'golden cage', and broke off, piercing his eye in two places. Catherine de Medici, the king's widow, brought the man who'd foreseen it to Paris and made him the court prophet."

"And Hitler knows all this?"

"I doubt he knows *any* of this. But when they tell him, and they will, he'll *believe* it. Everything is destiny with him — you saw the way he begged Marlene, his good-luck charm, to come back to Germany."

Kennedy freshened my drink from the bottle on the rolling bar. "Look Noël, I have to go up to Cambridge and graduate from college next week. You're the one who's going over to raise morale. Not being invaded would raise their morale, wouldn't it?"

In my journal entry the next day I wrote, "Maybe it was the lateness of the hour, but I let myself get caught up in the idiocy of the moment. This boy could sell ice cubes to the Eskimos. I found myself saying, 'Ummm, how would this work, exactly?' "

After ten more minutes, I promised to see what I could do.

109

We hauled Marlene out without her face and I gave her a farewell hug and a kiss. But I still had my doubts. Turning back to the lovers at the door, I asked Jack how he knew so much about French kings and mystics: "What did you study up there at Harvard? History?"

He wrapped his arm around the shoulder of the woman beside him, pulling her close to him, and grinned. "International Relations."

I sailed for Southampton in the morning.

CHAPTER 15

London

The newsreader was beside herself, blond curls aflutter, positively quivering with the excitement: "The mysterious find at the Inns of Court has deadly consequences: family of three found shot to death in Brixton." The *News at Noon* film editor had had a field day, cutting from the Gordon house in Brixton as the bodies were brought out to the file footage of Mr. Gordon at the work site the day before and back again.

There was speculation as to the connection between the two events and the usual interviews with the shocked neighbors. Then it was back to the studio. "DNA testing has ascertained the wrist bone unearthed yesterday is approximately one hundred years old; Metropolitan Police have further determined the handcuff affixed to it is one couriers used in the war to secure attaché cases to their persons. In addition, the BBC have learned the building housing barristers that was originally on the site took a direct hit from a V-2 rocket in 1944."

Then it was back to Brixton for the stand-up with the police spokesman: "All right-thinking Londoners are shocked at today's developments. We ask anyone who has information to come forward and assist the police with their inquiries."

The bear of a man trying to close an overstuffed suitcase grinned and told the screen, "*Prostitye,* chaps. We'd love to help, but the tin cans are long gone."

CHAPTER 16

Moscow

Lara was agitated. Excited and dismayed, both. John F. Kennedy and Noël Coward working together to keep Britain from invasion? And, instead, enticing Hitler to go to war with Stalin's Russia? Her Russia? This was History with a capital H . . . *if* there was anything to the man's story.

If a few well-placed individuals could get together and rearrange world events . . . then her classroom interloper was right — the tins at her feet would sink Lara's own book on the origins of the war, the one she'd just labored to finish in manuscript form in this very building. And it would go a long way to torpedo her "precious geohistory."

This story of Coward's . . . "story" was the key word. He made them up for a living, didn't he? Why couldn't this all be an elaborate script for some film or play, complete with a fictional Sir Robert he was telling it to?

Her mind raced ahead, like the chess player she once was, seeking the ways she could prove if it was real or not. Not, she hoped. But first, leaving her things where they were, Lara pushed through the double glass doors. She'd walk around the Arkhiv, making as many circuits of the floor as it took to get herself thinking clearly again.

CHAPTER 17

The half-hour bell rang throughout the Arkhiv just as Lara returned to the Listening Room after three full circuits of the place. Time for one more recording before she had to pack up and go.

This is cylinder number three. Nigel, your faithful assistant stationed across from me on the other side of the glass, who is now frowning at the mention of his name, has given me the photocopies you obtained from the steamship people — does one have no privacy anymore, even in the middle of an ocean? — so, yes, I attest that these are the very cables I sent my secretary en route to the mother country after meeting with Kennedy in 1940. And yes, I will read them now into the record, to further attest to my state of mind at the time. As you bade me do, Robert.

Twenty-three June/first day out. "Aquitania First Class service no better than prewar steerage . . . don't think Cunards have got their hearts in it. We're to be dumped in Liverpool instead of Southampton, thanks to U-boats; Lawrence my lamb, please arrange alt. shore transport. Also, get what you can on 16th C. French prophet Nostradamus. Ask around clubs for art historian, fluency in antique French and Latin required."

Twenty-four June/second day out. "Lawrence: Any luck with Nostradamus? Broadsheet slipped under cabin door this morning shows Hitler at Eiffel Tower whilst Nazi leather boys stand around, goggle-eyed to see actual culture. Must act before same toadies start taking snaps of Nelson's column."

Twenty-seven June/fifth day

out. "Cable received. Well done, my boy. Sure this chap from Courtauld has requisites? Hope so . . . thought of hitting Austrian paperhanger with 'Blunt' instrument too good to pass up."

So that's how I came up with Anthony Blunt. It was his name, don't you see? I'm sure I never laid eyes on him till that day at the restaurant. All right, you asked me to "re-create" my conversations with Anthony. Here goes, best as I can recollect.

I arranged to meet him for lunch at Simpson's-in-the-Strand. Now, I've found you get two things when you ask for a "menu" in Simpson's: a baleful look from the server and an oversized card headed BILL OF FARE. No Frenchy words and no Frenchy foods. Now that Pétain had capitulated to Hitler, I felt it only right, if we were to discuss *ancien français,* that we put on an Olde English nose-bag.

Blunt, when he arrived ten

minutes late, was lanky, well turned out and unapologetic. "Mr. Coward? Anthony Blunt. Waiting long?"

"Not overly. Join me." I shook the hand he proffered, noting it was dead-fish limp. Right then and there I decided that, manners or no, we were going to get on. We had to.

Blunt settled himself across from me in one of the high-backed booths that line the room. But not before extracting a handkerchief from his breast pocket and ostentatiously whisking the cushioned seat where his posterior would go.

I plunged in. "I'm informed by impeccable sources, Mr. Blunt, that you are —"

"Dr. Blunt."

"Beg your pardon?"

"It's Doctor Blunt. I have my doctorate."

It was all I could do to keep myself from saying, "And I'm the Archbishop of Canterbury, so you can kiss my bloody foot." But I was determined, as I've said, that we get on. So, all meek and mild, I replied, "Then welcome to my humble abode, *Dr.* Blunt. Would you care for a drink?"

The word "drink" had the same effect on Blunt that "Open, Sesame" had on Ali Baba's cave door. It prised the thing open. Alcohol softened Anthony Blunt just enough so that fifteen minutes later, when a husky young waiter of pleasing mien — one of the tableside carvers who was presumably too young for the Army — moved past us pushing a silver dinner wagon loaded down with mutton for the party in the booth next to ours, something telling occurred. Rationing had been on since the middle of March, and I was amazed to see so much meat in one place. Blunt's eyes, though, lingered on the youth's athletic form. So we had that in common.

"Anthony, let me get down to cases. As part of the war effort, I wish to engage a person such as yourself to create a seemingly ancient document, a

119

ruse that must have impeccable bona fides."

"Are you with one of the services?"

I had practiced my response. "Yes, a rather secret one, I'm afraid."

Blunt smiled for the first time and finished his drink. "Oh, don't be afraid. I love secrets." He held out his empty glass to the waiter, an old gaffer who had been hovering nearby. "Another of the same," he said.

I waited until Blunt's eyes were back on me. "We require a man of your resources to help devise a medieval forgery."

"A simulacrum."

"Beg pardon?" I wasn't sure what Blunt had said.

"You want me to create a simulacrum, I hope, and not a forgery. Something that appears genuine in all respects but isn't, as opposed to a faked version of something that actually exists. I don't do fakes."

I don't mind admitting that it

seemed a distinction without a difference. "A simulacrum then, if I'm pronouncing it right."

"You are. And I will. If the compensation is appropriate."

"How much do you require?"

"Oh, there will be expenses, to be sure. But I don't expect coin of the realm."

"Then what —"

"I wish to be taken into your service. To enlist . . . in the war effort."

I suppose now is the time to declare, for the record, that I had absolutely no knowledge Anthony was already working for the Soviets. That, in fact, he had been doing so ever since his Cambridge days.

Your young Nigel here has put me "in the picture" as regards Anthony's frequent rendezvous with Ivan Stoichkov, their sinister London Head of Station. Robert, you have specifically asked me who first broached the subject of his joining the Service. I now state, unequivocally, he did.

As I wasn't a talent spotter, I made no reply at the time. Or rather, I tucked into my leg of lamb, which another of the farm-boys-turned-carvers — this one with ginger hair — had just put on my plate. Anthony's gaze was riveted just above another leg, on the boy. The conversation was, for the moment, over.

Afterward, I redeemed from the cloakroom the Hamley's shopping bag I'd got when I bought some electric trains for my nephews. In it was the material my man Lawrence had assembled on Nostradamus, as well as Kennedy's little book of prophecies. I handed it to Blunt, who gave it a jaundiced eye and promised to "look at it over the weekend."

Oh, hold on, Nigel is tapping on the glass. I . . . I'm wanted on the telephone. I see there's more room on the cylinder, so we'll pick this up again in a few moments.

CHAPTER 18

Time for a little fact checking, Lara told herself. First step: learn if there was any truth at all to Noël Coward's story — Coward, the playwright and songsmith, but definitely not the historian.

Taking off the headphones, Lara scrolled back through her iPad notes of the man's testimony and started with "Sir Robert." No last name, so there was no help there. Moving on to *In Which We Serve,* she dragged the phrase over to the Google search box. What came back was, "The 1942 film boasts an impressive cast, which includes Noël Coward, John Mills and Celia Johnson."

She then typed in "Celia Johnson." Google showed her the woman's obituary: "Celia Elizabeth Johnson. A fine actress and beloved mother; wife of Peter Fleming. Born December 18 . . ." All right, Ian Fleming *did* have a sister-in-law named Celia who *was* an actress alongside Coward.

Next, Lara determined the old RMS *Aquitania* had indeed crossed and recrossed the Atlantic during the war, first as a passenger liner and later as a troop ship, before finally being sent to the scrapyard in 1950. So, that part of his tale, about cabling his assistant from the ship, was plausible.

While she was considering what to do next, her phone vibrated soundlessly. Outgoing calls were discouraged in the Arkhiv. Incoming ones were absolutely prohibited unless one's mobile had the ringer off. It was her tenant, Katrina.

"Trina?"

Lara could hear the buzz of the busy TsUM department store in the background. "Larissa Mendelova, I'm sorry, I know it's Tuesday and I'm supposed to pick up dinner, but something's come up. Maxim is taking me to the Lokomotiv football match."

"Who's Maxim?"

"You met him last night. He was the tall one, the soldier. We're going straight from work, so I'm afraid you'll have to do your own shopping. I'd do it myself on my lunch hour, but I have an errand to run and —"

"Don't worry about it. I'll be getting home late myself."

"A date?"

124

"Not exactly. I —"

"Good for you, Lara. Oh, I almost forgot. Viktor called again."

"What did he want?"

"I'm not sure, something about the divorce papers. He said you know the number."

Lara sighed. More stalling tactics. "I know the number."

"Look, I've got a customer."

"Okay, see you . . . whenever."

"Umm, don't wait up, you know?"

Lara sighed again. "I know."

Noël Coward began clearing his throat and she turned back to her work.

I apologise for that telephone call just now. It was another call, from Blunt a few days after we'd met, that brought me to the Courtauld Institute of Art at 20 Portman Square, a Georgian home I believe was once the official residence of the French Ambassador to the Court of St. James. A century and a half later, he would be chagrined to know it's populated by art students.

Fearing that German artillery

and the Luftwaffe's dive bombers would begin their "rain of terror" any day now, the faculty — many of them German-Jewish refugees from Hamburg's Warburg Library — and the entire student body were engaged in taking down the artworks from the walls and packing them for removal to the safety of the countryside.

In his "Technological Department," the art restoration workshop one storey down from his own top-floor digs, Blunt insisted on giving me "the shilling tour." There must have been a hundred different varieties of the canvas, board, paper, and parchment used by artists through the millennia. And untold numbers of paints, inks, varnishes, and shellacs, side by side with the pens and brushes of every size, shape and material needed to apply them. Blunt called it "my playroom, which doubles as the best-equipped art supply shop in the world."

As my own Technology Department consists of a pen-and-pencil set, I was suitably impressed, and I told him so. "When I said at lunch we needed a man of your resources, I had no idea how . . . resourceful your resources were."

"Thank you, Noël —" Blunt was interrupted by two students, a young man and a woman, carrying a Van Gogh self-portrait, the one with the bandaged ear, down from his rooms for safekeeping. He said, wistfully, "I'm going to miss the crazy old boy." It would be the only vaguely sentimental moment I would ever see the man have.

We followed the students carrying the picture down the wide central staircase. As best I can remember, I tried to ease into the topic of his "payment." "Yesterday I telephoned someone I know in the Government and, if we can pull this thing off, there might be a place."

He said, "This 'thing' of yours, this simulacrum — who knows about it?"

"In this country? No one."

"You mean no Grand Poobah has vetted your idea?"

I laid it on the line. "That's precisely what I mean. With your help, I intend to present Churchill with something very like a fait accompli as far as the book itself is concerned. Otherwise, the thing would be too fantastical for the PM to grasp. It's almost too fantastical for me to grasp."

"Then, come with me." Abruptly turning on his heel and with a brusque "beg pardon" to the small knot of people standing in front of a door directly under the staircase, he led me down an interior flight of steps, saying, "When the nobs lived here, these were the kitchens and pantries. It's easier to control the temperature and humidity down here than it is upstairs."

I was a little slow keeping up. Blunt stopped and looked back. "I said I was giving you the shilling tour. Don't you want your money's worth?"

We made our way through a

warren of storage rooms, some still with washing-up sinks in the corners, that were lit by a few bare bulbs. Paintings in their frames were stored on their sides in the first of these rooms, dozens of them chock-a-block. Unframed canvases were rolled up in cardboard tubes and stacked in pyramids, like so many wine bottles in the caves of a French chateau. In another room were altarpieces, disassembled and leaning against the walls three deep. Blunt waved his hand. "Italian on this side, German over there."

The next set of rooms held leather-bound books from floor to ceiling. "All of this is available for study." He began ticking off the centuries as we walked: *"Ottocento, settecento, sei, cinque . . ."* We walked through a door into another, similar room. "Still cinquecento. Notice anything?"

I looked around. All I could see were more leather-covered volumes. Maybe these were a little thicker than the previous ones. "I don't know what I'm looking for," I admitted.

Blunt beamed, the teacher indulging the dull student — something I'm sure you're familiar with, Robert, having been my maths tutor that lamentable winter term. "We've left paper and now we're in vellum. That door we just walked through was the year 1450."

When I didn't know enough to go "ooh" or "aah," Blunt grew peevish. "The printing press, man. Movable type. Everything from here on is pre-Gutenberg. Handwritten and illuminated." Whilst the twentieth century was going about its business upstairs, we had traveled back five hundred years in the time it took to walk from the front of the old kitchens to the back.

"Think of it," Blunt was saying. "It's always the year 1375 where you're standing. Westminster Abbey is still unfinished. Martin Luther won't be born for another century. Constantinople is still — well, you get the idea."

I got the idea. It was a boring idea, but I got it. I followed Blunt, who was walking toward five or six large canvas carts of the sort commercial laundries employ. Inside each were more volumes piled one on top of another, willy-nilly. In all, there must have been three hundred old books in the carts.

My guide waved his hand over them. "Depressions aren't bad for everyone. They're quite good for art historians. We picked these up for a song. And it's not just private collectors; the Catholic Church are hurting quite badly just now. Those three hold the contents of a monastery that closed in '38. Of course, with a war on, I have no one to do the cataloguing. So here they sit."

Blunt crossed his arms. "Our tour ends here. Noël, I thought you ought to know what we're up against. If you want me to fabricate something, it had better look right and feel right and smell right if it's going to fool the Germans. Their art historians are the best in the world."

I knew I musn't say what I was thinking, but you know enough about me to know I said it anyway. "Smell right?"

Blunt grabbed a heavy book at my elbow. He opened it and immediately slammed it shut again. The dust and whatever else was in there nearly choked your humble correspondent. I coughed and then sneezed for nearly half a minute. When I finally could get the words out, I managed to say, "It smells something horrid."

"Mold." Blunt was triumphant. "Fourteenth-century mold. If you don't have mold, the boys in Berlin will know it straight off." He put the volume back where it had been. "I've read the things you left with me in the bag from the toy store. You were quite right to do so — I find this sort of thing to be child's play." The man was simply insufferable.

He turned on his heel and walked back through the door by which we'd come, the one he'd said was the year 1450. I found him fingering the volumes along the left-hand wall. He extracted a book from the shelf, opened it, and closed it again almost immediately, gently this time. He said, "Do what I'm doing on the next shelf down. Look for one with a hole in the flyleaf."

I did as I was told.

Blunt pronounced, "I have a stratagem."

It was at least thirty seconds before Lara was aware the cylinder had run out. And, lost in thought, another minute before she realized the Arkhiv was closing. She packed her things and walked the six tins containing Noël Coward's words back to her cubicle before locking them up, wishing the Englishman a pleasant evening.

CHAPTER 19

Five hours later, Lara found herself trapped in a nondescript dance club way out on Ulitsa Shchepkina, all glammed up in one of Vera Lebedova's slinky Diane von Furstenberg wrap dresses and pasting her last smile of the evening on her face before sitting down.

Her so-called friend had gotten her into this evening of "mixing and mingling" as the price of going through her closet and borrowing clothes for Friday morning's telecast. Vera had said, "I just happen to be signed up for this thing tonight. You should come."

"Thing?"

"A flirt party. They're fun, a way to meet guys. You remember guys, don't you?"

"I've still got a guy. At least until he signs on the dotted line."

"You think that's keeping your no-good Viktor home nights? Larashka, you've been a hermit long enough."

Her final "flirt partner," waiting at Table 14, was a handsome enough guy, blond like a lot of Russian men but with unusual dark gray eyes. He'd clearly polished off most of the bottle of vodka that was on the table, and was leering at her through eyes at half-mast. It occurred to her as she sat down that the only difference between Moscow flirt parties and American speed dating was that, over here, the women did the moving while the men sat. The leers were identical.

His nametag read "Yuri." Lara fingered the sticker on her blouse that read "Larissa." No last names or even patronymics allowed. The Master of Ceremonies rang his bell and the guy jumped right in. "I like men without hats."

Wait . . . was this a test? Lara smiled a little and said, "So do I. I notice you're not wearing one."

"No, I mean I like Men Without Hats, the '80s band. They're in Moscow this week and I've got two tickets."

"Aren't we supposed to get to know each other first?"

"What's to know? I dig Eurasian chicks."

"So do I."

That threw him. Lara followed with, "The Eurasian Chicks, that country band from

Kazakhstan. Know them?"

He didn't laugh, he didn't chuckle, he didn't do anything for about ten seconds. Then all he managed was a surly "I don't think so." Men. Can't live with them, can't use them for firewood, as an American friend used to say.

So much for lively banter at Table 14. She couldn't wait to share a laugh about it with Vera, who was just at that moment being chatted up by the hottest guy in the room. Easy for her. Vera Lebedova was pretty in a Maria Sharapova sort of way, blond and willowy. *"Lebed"* was Russian for "swan," and her long, elegant neck lived up to the name. Guys fell all over themselves for her.

Lara knew she was too picky, looking for a Russian guy who could take as well as he could give. One who was not just interested, but interesting. Ilya Kolkov, he'd been interesting. There was a moment back then . . . before Viktor had shown up with his medals and his war stories and seemed the more interesting one . . . before she understood how many other women found Viktor interesting, too . . . when it might have been Ilya.

The emcee announced, "Okay, *smeshivat-sya!*"

His call of "Mingle!" set off the final cattle

call, when people who'd been sizing each other up all night exchanged mobile numbers. Or simply decided to go off together. Over near the bar, Vera was mobbed. Guys competed to get her a drink, to light her cigarette. Was it all about how you looked; were Russian guys that shallow? Or was it something Vera instinctively knew to say, some magical combination of syllables in those quick moments sitting across from each other, when the guy was cute and the moment was right . . . something Lara would never master.

Three nondescript men came up and pressed slips of paper with their table numbers into her hand, one of them Mr. Men Without Hats. Then someone tapped her from behind and said, "I think I can help you. Forget Table 9; guy's a washout."

Lara saw it was one of her fellow competitors. The tall, well-dressed woman wore a nametag that said, "Tati." Her face was vaguely familiar.

"Do I know you?"

"Possibly. I used to be the weekend weather person on Channel One . . . Tatiana Ivanova." She held out her hand.

Lara shook it. "Yes, I remember now. You were good with the maps."

"*Spasibo,* Dr. Klimt."

137

Dr. Klimt? How did this woman know her —

"Larashka!"

It was Vera, waving, leaving with the hot guy. Lara waved back, but in the meantime Vera's date whispered something funny in her ear and Vera was turning to him, laughing, the swan forgetting all about the duckling she'd taken under her wing.

In a low voice, the stranger at her elbow said, "I . . . we . . . know about the book."

Lara turned back. "We? Which book? One of mine?"

Tatiana Ivanova snorted. "Don't be coy, Dr. Klimt, it doesn't suit you. We'll double what anyone else will pay."

The place was quickly emptying out. The emcee switched the lights on and off, his signal that they were closing up.

"Pay for what? Who *are* you?"

"I told you . . . I'm a helper, a friend."

"A friend?"

"All right then, call me a secret admirer. You have many such admirers in The Other Russia."

"You're working for the opposition?"

"The democrats, the people who want a more open government, a free press. Garry asked me to —"

"Garry Kasparov? You know him?"

The two women were standing by a table where some guy had left behind his cheat sheet, a crumpled list of crossed-out girls' names. Lara's was one of them. Tatiana Ivanova picked it up. "Look, the people you're dealing with . . . they aren't very nice. Afterward, they'll cross you off like a name on a list."

"What — what are you talking about? You must have the wrong girl."

"No, Professor, you're the right girl. We'll double any offer . . . think it over."

Before Lara could respond, the emcee doused the lights, longer this time. In the dark he said, "Show's over, ladies. Nighty night."

When the lights came on again, Tatiana Ivanova was gone.

CHAPTER 20

The nighttime laser lights beaming from the top of St. Basil's cathedral were trying to find a way through the closed blinds of the suite when the call came in on the cell phone with the American eagle on it. The President, still up reading policy papers, pushed the blue "privacy" button and was wide-awake in a hurry.

"You did what?"

The voice on the other end back in Alaska repeated what he'd said. For a moment the commander-in-chief took the receiver from his ear and looked at it in disbelief before replying. "When I said 'do what it takes,' I meant pay him anything he wants. Not . . . *eliminate* him."

"We tried that. We couldn't buy him off. Said he wouldn't . . ."

"Wouldn't what?"

"Wouldn't be 'a party to what we're doing.' Exact words."

"Christ, Carl."

"I know, sir. The good news is, the buyer's rep and him, they never filed a report. And now that things are running smooth again, there's no proof anything happened. No proof, no paper trail. Plus, we made the thing look like a suicide."

"That's your idea of good news?"

"Well . . . I mean . . . you're in the clear."

"Except there's you, isn't there, Carl?"

Without waiting for an answer, he carefully placed the portable phone back in its leather carrying case with the embossed Presidential seal. Then he threw the case against the hotel room wall.

His wife, used to it all by now, didn't even look up from the book she was reading. "Problem, Hon?"

Friday and the plane home could not come soon enough.

CHAPTER 21

Valdez

The weak Alaskan sun was dropping in the west when Lev drew up to the testing station. Craig wasn't there yet. Five o'clock came and went, but the American didn't show. Lev left three voicemails while he waited. Nothing.

By a quarter to six, the Russian decided to run the test on the petroleum, unofficially, by himself. He opened the large gate-valve, unlatched the galvanized "thief hatch," and then the stopcock. When a liter of the goo had filled the Pyrex beaker, he stepped forward and, bravely, took a deep breath. No rotten eggs, no sulfur, just unrefined petroleum.

He dropped his hydrometer in. After a moment he squinted at the result: 31.9 API. North Slope Crude was acting like North Slope Crude again.

"Len" Klimt cleaned everything up,

locked the station and, more than a little confused, drove away. A pair of eyes followed him down the road.

CHAPTER 22

Moscow
Wednesday

In the morning, Lara arrived at the Arkhiv with her rolling suitcase packed full of Vera's "on-camera" wardrobe options to go over with Gerasimov later in the day. She had come to terms with not being able to lecture on Friday; instead, she'd settle for interviewing the president of the United States.

Leonid the guard opened the bag and went through her clothes, handling, *feeling* her lingerie. Afterward, he put a sticker on the suitcase. No hello, no nod, nothing to acknowledge he'd been touching her intimate things; all in the name of state security.

Leaving the suitcase in her study carrel — she'd call Gerasimov later and tell him when to pick her up from the Arkhiv — Lara carried the bag of recordings that supposedly led to a million-ruble jackpot (or more, if Tatiana Ivanova was to be believed)

144

and headed back down the corridor to the Listening Room and Mr. Coward.

We now begin cylinder number four. I've given instructions I'm not to be interrupted for anything but a true emergency. Now, where were we? Ah yes, the Courtauld.

In the end we brought two books upstairs with us. One was a Bible, in Latin, with a thick cowhide leather binding and pages of vellum, probably printed in Germany, though not by Gutenberg. The other, thinner, also on vellum, had a cracked spine. "Our sacrificial lamb," Anthony called it.

Back in the Technology Department, he closed the door to the room and turned the lock, saying, "Have you got the quatrains?"

I patted them in my breast pocket. "I *wrote* them and, even so, I don't understand them. Heaven knows what the Hun will make of our ditties in your Old French mumbo-jumbo."

"The Hun, as you say, is smarter than you think." Blunt fingered a couple of the small bottles of different liquids that lined a nearby shelf before taking one. "And it's Middle French. *Moyen français.* There's a difference."

Then he spread a large white sheet of paper on the table and took out a doctor's scalpel from a drawer. "Here, take this." He brought over the thinner of the two books and set it down. "While I gather a few things, why don't you do something useful, Noël, and make us some ink?"

With that, he opened the book at random and, taking the scalpel, began to scrape the page. A few bits of the black ink fell off in flakes onto the sheet of paper. "Now you do it. Not so hard that you scrape the parchment. All we want is the ink."

For the next fifteen minutes I destroyed several pages of what I had originally assumed was a priceless volume, creating in the process a small hillock of the former lettering and causing my wrist and forearm no end of pain with the repetitive motion of the knife.

Blunt was assembling things from around the room over on his end of the table. Then he came closer and saw me rubbing my arm. "Be thankful I didn't send you back downstairs to harvest dust. Beastly job, and you have to wear one of these." He slid open a drawer full of surgeon's masks, and shut it again. "Okay, that's enough ink for a start."

The art historian used the scalpel to scrape some of the shavings off the paper and into a Petri dish. Then he took an eyedropper and dipped it into the bottle of nearly clear liquid he'd chosen earlier. It said "Linseed oil" on the label. As soon as he poured two or three drops into the dish, the black scrapings dissolved in the medium, turning it dark.

"You see? Ink made from iron gall will reconstitute itself." He swirled the mess in the dish with a glass pipette. "We let it sit for a couple of days *et voilà*, new 16th Century ink."

"A couple of days?" I was stunned.

Blunt was unmoved. "Can't be helped. You don't fool meticulous people like the Germans with slapdash work. Besides, the bookworm will still have her job to do."

Now I was totally unstrung. "Who . . . who's this 'bookworm'?"

Blunt picked up a matchbox from among the jumble of things on the table. He held it out. Mystified, I stared at it.

"Go on, open it."

I did as I was told and found what looked like a common beetle.

"You asked who the bookworm was." Blunt touched the beetle. "This is dear Mater. Oh, you've laid your eggs. That's my good girl." Blunt put the box back down on the table.

I could feel my entire plan crumbling away. I'd chosen a

madman for the job just because his name was Blunt. "I don't know what you're playing at, Anthony, but I assumed . . . that is, the urgency . . ."

"Sit down, Noël, and I'll explain."

"I don't want to sit down," I said.

"All right then, go on pacing, I'll explain anyway." Blunt picked up the other book, the Bible, from the table and opened it to the flyleaf. He held it up to me. "This page where our faux prediction will go . . . do you see this hole here?"

"I thought it was just an imperfection in the paper." Wrong thing to say.

"Not paper. Vellum. Big difference. In the Middle Ages, vellum, or parchment, was made from calfskin that was wetted down, dipped in a bath of lime and left there for more than a week to get all the hair off, stretched, dried, scraped, and possibly dipped in the lime again until it was nearly trans-

149

lucent. Okay, now what's the biggest difference between vellum and paper?"

Without even waiting for me to attempt an answer, he went on. "It's made from the skin of an animal. Animals get all manner of insects gnawing away at them. Some of them deposit larvae that do *their* gnawing from the inside, making a hole in the animal's hide so they can get out."

"I see," I said, though obviously I didn't.

"Sit down, Noël. It's easy, really. Let's say we're Germans. Art historians, very good ones; we get an old book and want to make sure everything is on the up and up. What do we do? If we were French or Italian, we'd flip through the pages and see if it looked all right. But no, we're German. We do scientific tests. On the ink. On the paper, the vellum in this case. On the hole in it. Did someone in England make the hole last month, or did some hungry insect chew his way

150

through it four centuries ago?

"All right, let's recall our plan: we want it to seem as if Michel de Nostradamus, this apothecary who has visions, was traveling around the countryside in the 16th Century, dispensing his little prophecies about this and that, when he had one of his brainstorms about the future.

"We have a wonderful library here, and I dug a up a few little pearls. From a letter he wrote in 1562, we know Nostradamus visited an abbey at Villers-devant-Orval. So, what if he were overcome in the night by another of his terrible visions — this one four centuries in the future — and wrote down what he had seen on the only 'paper' he could find at the abbey: the flyleaf of a Bible?"

"And if the crazy old sod wrote his vision down in someone else's Bible, he couldn't very well carry it off with him; books were rather valuable back then. We know he spoke of some final prophecies he never published before he died. Perhaps this was one of them."

I was still confused. "But that doesn't explain the beetle in the matchbox."

"Oh, you mean my *Anobium punctatum.* She's a furniture beetle. And she's just become a mother many times over."

With a cloth, he cleaned the glass pipette he'd used to stir the ink and now poked the beetle with it so we could better see the eggs she'd laid. There were dozens. "When these eggs hatch, the larvae, the bookworms that emerge, are ravenous. And they do what baby furniture beetles do: eat through anything in their way, boring long cylindrical holes in the leaves of books, the bindings, even the bookshelf.

"So, while the ink is steeping, I intend to take your poetry" — at this he held out his hand, leaving it there until I withdrew the lines I'd laboured over and placed them in his palm — "and translate it

152

into something Nostradamus might recognise as his own. Then I will write it upon the vellum flyleaf with the quill pen over there, taking care to go directly over the hole you see in it now.

"That hole is our starting point. When the ink is thoroughly dry I will encourage these brand-new and very hungry beetles to create a hole at the exact same spot in the binding and in the overleaf. When we are done, it will appear that bookworms, over the ages, created one continuous hole in the pages on either side of the prophecy, partly obliterating Nostradamus's writing. Effectively we will have 'married' our simulacrum to the original text of the Bible."

I had been waiting for Blunt to take a breath so I could ask, "And how does one 'encourage' a bookworm?"

Blunt drew out a pot of school paste. "With this. The little buggers think it's caviar. I'll just dab a bit where I want them to go and let Nature take her course."

I felt my restlessness coming back, so I got to my feet. I tried a smile. "And how much time does Nature require?"

"Not more than six weeks."

"Six weeks! Why that's . . . that's almost September! The whole country might be forced to learn German by then!"

Blunt carefully shut the matchbox with the beetle in it and put the gluepot away. "Well, that's where I have you at a disadvantage, old man. I already know German."

CHAPTER 23

Bells were going off in Lara's brain; unconscious connections were being made. Hadn't she read something, somewhere in the Chronologies, about a book; last year or the year before? Could it have been a Bible? She knew the way her mind worked; if whatever was lodged in her cerebrum was important enough, her subconscious would bring it to the surface — sooner, she hoped, rather than later.

Lara was making a note to herself about it when she noticed her iPad telling her she had email. She touched the Mail.ru icon on the screen and typed in her user ID and password. Russians were the world's greatest generators of electronic spam, offering cheap watches and pharmaceuticals, sex aids (or just plain sex), and phony "phishing" messages from financial institutions, requesting personal information to "update our files." Often, spam was all Lara received in a day. But today she had — *tseluyu!* — thirty-four new messages in her Inbox. One, from her department chairman, had nine Reply All responses from her fellow teachers. She started with the original.

"Dear Colleague, Superintendent Nazimova tells me a member of our professional staff has agreed to appear on various TV networks and be compensated for said appearance. As you know, University rules forbid such compensation during the academic year, and only the entire Faculty Senate can grant a waiver from the rule. Therefore, I solicit the Faculty's opinion: should we hold a meeting on the matter, with a vote to follow, of the History Department tomorrow in the Faculty Dining Room at 10:00? Please reply soonest."

Lara quickly scrolled through her follow-up emails. They amounted to her colleagues trying to guess which teacher it was and what to do about the "waiver," Nazimova's way of trying to turn Lara's friends against her. Some of those friends solicited Lara's own opinion of the matter. When she hadn't answered, several more implored her to make her whereabouts known.

The woman took money to make Lara appear on Gerasimov's program, and then she reported the deal as some kind of honor violation on Lara's part.

She knew only too well how a Department meeting would go. The Modernists, her friends, would be all up in arms over Nazimova trying to keep her off an obviously educational program. The Tsarists, sitting by the coffeemaker to get the freshest brew, would submit to the administration's intrusion, as if by divine right. The acolytes of the "Greats," Peter and Catherine, would talk and smirk among themselves at the three tables at the far end of the room. And all fifty-eight of them would have to have something to say, whether or not they actually had an opinion. All over a done deal. As the hypocritical Superintendant had said, in the new Russia, money talks. And talks. And talks.

"*Suka! Samka!* Bitch!" The bilingual anger came out involuntarily. Good thing the Listening Room was soundproof.

Lara, still shaking, got up and, leaving her iPad behind her, stepped beyond the glass doors and began to navigate the perimeter of the Arkhiv. It took four complete trips around the vast building this time before Lara could compose herself enough to head back to the Listening Room, four trips before she could settle down enough to do any work.

Pushing on the thick glass door, she was startled to see a man, enormously big and muscled with closely cropped hair, seated now before the middle of the three Dictaphone machines. He had his huge head in his left hand, poring over some papers at the edge of the communal worktable, looming over the tablet computer that held her notes. The man was practically staring down into the bag of wax cylinders Lara had left on the floor. He was beefier than any academic Lara had ever seen.

She made a little noise so he would look up, and she smiled a greeting. After a moment he arranged his face into a corresponding smile and shifted his work so Lara would have room to sit down. She retook her seat and, placing the iPad in her lap, hurriedly put the headphones on, isolating herself as best she could from the one who had invaded her space.

We come to Dictaphone recording number five, Robert old man. Or should I say, "Meacham for the Defence," as the tabloids have it? I realize I've mentioned the quatrains, but have failed to describe all the fun I had in writing them. So, here goes.

While there is no surviving example of a prophecy or anything else in Nostradamus's own hand, there are one or two pages of printer's proofs of his books with handwritten notes in the margins — possibly the seer's — that have come down through the centuries. Anthony was to write out his translation of whatever doggerel I gave him, in a manner consistent with those notes, on the flyleaf of the Bible we'd selected . . . as long as I limited myself to twelve lines in all.

So, what to write? And how to write it? First, a confession: if I absorbed any history whatsoever in all my schooling, it was purely by accident. I found myself poring over books in the public library any child in the sixth form would consider beneath him. In fact, I got the fish eye from one such urchin when he saw me lapping up Wells's *Outline of History.*

Next, I hit upon the idea of reading aloud (no, not in the

library) from the little book young Kennedy gave me. When I believed myself to be 'at speed,' I would babble out some of my own words and phrases, like "the people of the Rhine" and "in the name of St. George," in a similarly singsong manner until I had something suitable, sort of the way I came up with "Mad Dogs and Englishmen."

I determined early on that, if I had only three quatrains to work with, the first would seemingly foretell the rise of Hitler; the second would describe, rather murkily, actual events leading up to the war, so the Germans would know this Nostradamus fellow was 'spot on'; and the third would predict, in a kind of easily-broken code, Hitler's defeat of Stalin.

I threw in the birthplaces of both Il Duce and the Führer, and the exact count of river crossings from Berlin to Moscow, if the man needed a roadmap. My best bit was a quick mention of the German warrior-king Barbarossa, the Holy Roman Emperor who was leading the Third Crusade in the East when he died in 1190 . . . someone I'd never heard of until I read about him the day before.

Then Noël Coward stopped and coughed a loud hacking cough, perfectly captured — like his sneeze — on the wax cylinder. He said, "Nigel, dear lamb, pass me that glass of water, would you like a good fellow?"

Lara took her headphones off and rubbed her ears to get the blood circulating before putting them back on. She could clearly hear the long-dead playwright drinking the long-gone water. Looking around, she noticed her fellow Listening Room occupant had put away the papers he was studying and was, instead, writing with a pencil on a pad in front of him.

He must have sensed she was looking at him because he turned and looked her way. A generic one-day Arkhiv guest pass dangled from a chain that barely made it around his thick neck. Lara smiled hello at the man and tapped her headphones, signifying that she had a lot of work to do and was returning to it.

The man smiled back and held up *his*

work. Lara looked at the pad and was startled to see he'd drawn the beginning of a game of Hangman, just the scaffold.

Noël Coward started clearing his throat on her recording and she turned back to her work, wondering why anyone would travel out to the edge of nowhere just to play a pencil-and-paper game. And why there was no cylinder in his machine.

I've got my little ditty still, scribbled on a sheet of copybook paper, one I carry around in my pocket to this day. Here it is:

From the deepest part of
   dark Europa
A child will be born. Though
   poor, he will
By his speech induce a great
   multitude,
And his renown increase
   among people of the Rhine.

In the name of St. George
Will come the winged one
   from across the water
Warlike at first and then
   subdued
By the rising Danube and the

162

Ligurian Sea.

Eight centuries on, with
    Barbarossa's sword,
This hero will ford twenty
    rivers at decade's dawn.
Into a cage of iron is the
    usurper drawn,
When the child of Germany
    overcomes him.

To sum up, Anthony and I intended
Hitler to believe a mystic four
centuries earlier had foretold
his rise. And that he would
unite the Germans, pick up their
hero's fallen sword, and lead an
army to the gates of Moscow,
where he would imprison the Communist leader, Joseph Stalin.
    Neat trick, if we could pull
it off.

Chapter 24

With a start, Lara realized she'd been so distracted by the strange man sitting next to her that she hadn't taken any notes. Or heard a word Coward had said. She'd have to replay the recording. Risking a look out of the corner of her eye, she was shocked to see the interloper was gone. Now she was really confused.

He'd left his pad behind. Unable to help herself, Lara slid out from under her headphones and walked over to look at it. On the sheet of paper was a completely drawn hanged man now. Under it, written in the spaces where the solution to the game would go, he had entered, "L E V K L I M T."

CHAPTER 25

Lara yanked the cylinder from the machine, dropped it and the iPad in the shopping bag and raced out of the double glass doors and down the Arkhiv corridors to her study carrel. She fumbled with the key and unlocked the door, hurriedly locking it again once she was inside. Still huffing and puffing, she called Lev's number in Alaska on her mobile.

A sleepy voice answered on the seventh ring. In English he said, "Who . . . who is it? It's nearly midnight!"

"Thank God you're there. It's your sister. Someone's threatening you."

He was instantly awake on the other end of the line. Shifting to Russian, he said, "Threatening . . . me? I can't imagine anyone who'd —"

"Listen to me for a minute." She told him of finding the pad the big man had left behind.

"Maybe it was a joke, someone we went to school with in Perm."

"I'd have remembered this guy."

"Okay, I hear the worry in your voice, Larashka. First, nobody's been threatening me. Second, I've got a call in to Craig; we didn't connect today, but I'm sure I'll see him in a few hours. He's a big guy, huge. If I need a bodyguard . . . just let me get a few more hours of shut-eye, okay?"

"Okay. Sorry I woke you up. Take care of yourself, Levishka."

"You too. And don't worry."

CHAPTER 26

She took the bag of recordings from her cubicle and headed back down the corridor to the Listening Room. Lara wanted to sit there and figure it all out — Gerasimov, the woman from the flirt party, the moose of a guy right here in the Listening Room who had it in for Lev, everyone who'd come bursting through the protective shell of her quiet life. But she didn't have enough data. Instead, she'd have to replay the wax cylinder she'd been too distracted to listen to, and take good notes. What else could she do?

No steroidal thugs were playing Hangman when Lara cautiously peered in from the main reading area. Three empty chairs sat in front of three idle Dictaphone machines. This time she took the seat nearest the glass doors, the better to keep tabs on the comings and goings in the main room beyond. A couple of the usual academics were engrossed in their work.

When she'd heard Coward's Fifth up to the point where she'd left off before, she lifted the lever. While the man's words were still fresh in her mind, Lara wanted to decode the writer's poetry.

The first quatrain was easy. *A child born in the heart of Europe who by his speech will lead a great multitude on the Rhine . . .* that could be no one but Adolf himself. Check.

She typed "St. George" in the Google query box. It came back, ". . . adopted as the patron saint of England." Helpful. She did the same with "Ligurian Sea," and found it was the body of water off the northwest coast of Italy where Mussolini was born. She was starting to understand this particular brand of babble: some winged someone from England crossed the water only to be confronted by the sons of Austria — Hitler had been born in Linz, on the Danube — and Italy (the Ligurian Sea).

Who had flown from England to — Chamberlain! Neville Chamberlain had flown across the English Channel to Munich in 1938, only to be "subdued" by Hitler and the Axis into accepting their guarantee of "peace in our time" on a scrap of paper. Double check.

But was the Führer crazy enough to

168

believe a French savant four centuries earlier would be writing his life story and get every detail right? Lara went to Google Maps and counted the rivers a German Army would have to cross eastward from Berlin. The twentieth was the Moskva that ran alongside the Arkhiv, the one she could see right outside her study area, guarding the western approach to the Soviet capital. What comes after double check?

There was another clue: Coward had used the phrase "Meacham for the Defense." Full name, Sir Robert Meacham, apparently. Lara called up a site she'd used before in her research, burkespeerage.com. It came back with "SIR ROBERT MEACHAM, CBE (1938), born Headley, Surrey, 10 March, 1896; died, Inns of Court, London, 9 October, 1944."

Wait a minute. Lara scrolled back through her notes; yes, there it was: Coward's first day of testimony was October 2. Meacham, the man he was doing it all for, died just a week later. Hmmm.

Next problem: if Anthony Blunt turned an ordinary Bible into a vehicle to trick Hitler into attacking the Soviet Union, what happened to it after it did its job? Lara knew practically everything the Soviets had boxed up from the Führerbunker and his "Wolf's

Lair" in East Prussia, overrun by the Red Army in early 1945. She'd have remembered a Bible. The Americans had their own files of what came out of the Adlerhorst at Berchtesgaden. Unlike the Russians, they published what they found. No Bible there either.

Her brain was once again sending her a message, an email from her unconscious mind. Now she remembered where she'd read about a book.

Leaving the Listening Room, she strode across the main gallery's polished wood floor, past the researchers engrossed in their own work, and slid her ID through the card reader that guarded the door to the "stacks" on the far side.

The box for September 1940 was on a higher shelf than Lara was used to, and she had to get one of the round, rolling library footstools and make sure not to kill herself taking it down.

In the strange German system, the last day of the month, the 30th, was the one in front. Lara stuck her hand into the middle of the box and came up with a memorandum from the 17th. Behind it was the very gold she was panning for, a paper summarizing a meeting of the *Oberkommando der Wehrmacht,* the high command of the

German armed forces. Hitler was thanking Heinrich Himmler for a book he had been given a few days earlier.

She *had* remembered reading about a book.

Now Lara went backward in time through the files from the war council on the 16th. The most massive air raid in the history of war, the Luftwaffe's 1,000-plane multi-wave blitz that climaxed the Battle of Britain, was just returning to base after attacking the English capital on the night before. The men in the Adlerhorst were discussing the direct hits on Buckingham Palace and making rude jokes about the Royal Family.

Though the City around St. Paul's Cathedral was in ruins and the East End docks were ablaze, Lara knew their hopes of achieving a dictated peace in 1940 would be thwarted. She thought she knew how God must feel, looking down and listening in on the puny dreams of men, their fates already determind for them.

The day earlier must have been a strange one in Germany. Those closest to Hitler knew the planes bound for London were just taking off, and there was little to do but wait. Around three in the afternoon Johanna Wolf typed up notes from Hitler's working lunch on the terrace above the Obersalz-berg.

One paragraph stood out like a seam of precious metal in a wall of dull rock. "At 13:43, Reichsführer-SS Himmler asked whether everyone was finished eating. He then gave a signal to Stürmbannführer Edlitz, who came forward with a heavy package that was wrapped and tied up with a ribbon. H.H. said, 'For you, mein Führer,' and placed the gift in A.H.'s hands. Then he and Edlitz simultaneously stepped back three paces. The Führer laughed and said, 'What is it, a bomb?'

"Those around the table enjoyed the joke as the wrapping was removed to reveal a heavy book, very old, with a tooled leather cover. A.H. said, 'This Bible will make an excellent doorstop.' Again the others laughed. Himmler came forward and opened the book, indicating the writing on the flyleaf. A.H. studied it for a moment and said, 'I do not understand this language.'

"Edlitz handed a sheet of paper to H.H., who gave it to A.H. 'Here is a translation, mein Führer. You will see the significance.' A.H. placed the translation inside the Bible without looking at it and put it down on the table. 'I thank the Reichsführer-SS for his

172

generosity, as always. I promise to read it when I get a chance.' With that the luncheon adjourned."

Lara leaned back, thinking it through. She had skipped over the incident when she was writing her history over the summer; it had seemed just an inside joke at the time. Clearly, it wasn't the Bible that was important but what was written inside on the flyleaf. A certain prophecy, perhaps, that all this was about? She allowed herself the slightest smile of satisfaction: Lara Klimt, the last of the armchair detectives.

After returning the *yashchik* of wartime papers to its resting place in the stacks, Lara retraced her steps. One of the scholars working in the main room had packed up and left. Fortunately, the Listening Room was still unoccupied. Wherever the truth lay, she had to know the rest of Coward's story.

Replacing the Dictaphone lever on the fifth cylinder, she went back to work.

Now, dear listeners, we're up to a hot summer's day in July 1940, the day Anthony rang me up to say he was ready to dip his quill in our homemade ink and did I want to watch?

I did not want to watch. As it

was I was terrified his hand would slip and all our work would go for naught. Besides, I was trying my best to pull together something I'd dashed off on shipboard, a thing I was calling *Time Remembered,* and it was taking every waking moment. Anthony was good enough to call later in the day to say the writing had gone off without a hiccup.

Then, it took another forty-eight hours for the ink to dry. Two entire days before he would even take the baby beetles out of the box!

In summer of that year, remember, the overriding question for Anthony Blunt and me, as it was for you and all of Britain, was invasion. Was Hitler coming over, and if so, when? The French had given up, we'd left everything in the way of guns on the beach at Dunkirk, and the *Lüftwaffe* were making reconnaissance flights over the Channel.

Everyone knew the Home Guard

marching in Hyde Park and the sandbags piled up in Westminster wouldn't be nearly enough. It was a terribly trying time to be an Englishman, especially one who thought he might have a weapon against the Hun that wouldn't be ready for a month and a half!

Fortunately for my sanity, there were a couple of tasks to keep us busy in the meanwhile. It fell to me, as our project's "casting director," to obtain the services of the man who would actually hide the Bible where the Germans would find it, just as it was Anthony's job to identify the dupe who would be induced to do the finding.

His job first. Anthony had decided a man named Gerhard Bauer would be our appointed target. Bauer was — is — a collector of Renaissance paintings who also runs a tony German art magazine on his wife's money. He befriended Blunt before the war, or maybe it was the other way round. At any rate, Anthony knew

175

him now to be Procurator of the northern department of the *Einsatzstab Reichsleiter Rosenberg,* occupied at that moment with scooping up all the artworks of any value in the overrun territories . . . primarily (but not solely) those left behind by the Jews who been sent to the East.

Posting the letter immediately, even before Winston okayed our plan, was absolutely necessary due to the time required for it to reach Bauer by way of Lisbon, the only remaining conduit for communications with Germany. I have to hand the English translation Anthony made, which I will read into the recorder:

My Dear Gerhard,

Permit me to thank you in this roundabout way (London to Berlin via Portugal is nothing if not roundabout) for your kind mention of my trifle on Poussin in your brilliantly explicated piece in the

Deutsches Kunstblatt of March of this year. I would have thanked you earlier but the postal service here, as you know, have decided to absent themselves from delivering any and all periodicals from Germany, even high-minded ones such as yours. So the March *Kunstblatt* has only just come my way.

Old friend, I know you will be traveling with your military through the Low Countries, overseeing the removal of certain pieces of our mutual European heritage back to Germany for safekeeping, as your publisher's note puts it. Well, there is something a student here was working on before the war in what is now your neck of the woods, and I'm rather hoping you might keep a weather eye out when it is catalogued, so he may find it when hostilities are over.

Young Weidmann discovered the volume in the monastery at Villers-devant-Orval. It's a rather ordinary late-fifteenth or early-sixteenth century Bible of little interest on its own, but with quite an intriguing notation on the flyleaf. He believes the writing may be from the pen of Michel de Nostradamus. If so, it would be the only extant example of the man's own hand, and might fill for him some rather yawning *lacunae* for the year 1562.

Would you be a dear and put a tick mark or whatever you do on your list if and when your people find it? Weidmann made a note of its location when he was there in '38: on the third shelf from the top, next to a quite nice and very early Book of Job.

I lift a glass of sherry to you now, absent friend, in the hope of seeing you in the not too distant future. Until then I remain . . .

Your colleague and friend,
Anthony

Of course, there *is* no Weidmann.

It was Anthony himself who visited Orval in '38 and made a note of that Book of Job, in hopes the Courtauld might snatch it for themselves in the event of war. Our friend Gerhard would know Nostradamus isn't Blunt's line of goods, so we had to invent the studious young man.

I personally saw the letter being put in the diplomatic bag at the Ministry to be forwarded on to Lisbon so it could be placed in the post over there.

Now I had a casting call to conduct, if our little scheme was to succeed.

CHAPTER 27

An incoming video call on her iPad brought Lara back to the present. The digital clock in the upper right corner showed it was nearly 2:15; she'd been listening to Noël Coward for a good part of the day.

It was Lev. She told him to hold and hurried out of the Listening Room with her brother's face bouncing along on her iPad. The Ladies Room was unoccupied and she sat down in the last stall. Lev's image was distorted with worry.

"Levishka, are you all right?

"I, I don't know. I'm totally sleep-deprived, but I have to talk to someone who understands."

His raspy voice was bouncing off the tiles. She lowered the volume. "What's happened?"

"I couldn't get back to sleep after you called, so I watched the last ten minutes of some old movie on TV. I still wasn't sleepy and I started channel surfing. One of the local stations had something typed across the bottom of the screen, a breaking-news thing, you know?"

"Uh huh."

"A few hours ago, a guy jumped off the Knik Arm Bridge. The whole thing's crazy. The jumper . . . it was Craig, the American I work with . . . worked with. He's dead."

"*Bozhe moî!* Your friend killed himself? I'm so sorry."

"Best friend, I guess. But I don't think he really did. When I called the police, told them I was a colleague, all they would tell me was that he left a note in his apartment . . ."

"Then . . . it *was* a suicide."

". . . typed out, to someone named Melissa. Said he couldn't go on without her."

"I see . . . then why do you —"

"Craig was gay! Totally, completely. Still in the closet, but . . . there couldn't *be* a Melissa. And there's something else. He keeps his iPad at the test station, turned on. After the news, I drove out there and downloaded his latest emails and stuff. They aren't password protected."

Lara waited for her brother to continue.

"Apparently, the Americans are all set to announce an oil strike up here, a big one, in

181

the Wildlife Refuge. They were offering Craig a huge raise and a promotion somehow because of it. The crazy thing is, he turned them down. Said he 'wouldn't be a party to it.' "

"Lev, listen to me, this is important."

"You don't have to tell me. That's why I'm gonna . . . early flight . . . to find out."

"Listen, I'm worried that — What?"

". . . getting . . . plane out . . . to Prudhoe. Catch a . . . winks . . . and head out to the strike. Nose around. Find out . . . made Craig so upset."

"Lev, you're breaking up."

"Crap! . . . battery's just about —"

Then he was gone. Lara tried three more times, but she couldn't get him back. He was gone before she could tell him everything that was going on at her end, so she hurriedly put it down in an email and sent it. He'd get it when his phone was back up and running.

Lara gave herself a pep talk. Everybody gets bad news; everybody deals with it. She shouldn't have bothered him with the Hangman thing. Lev was going to be fine. Everything was fine.

She did her best to believe it.

CHAPTER 28

Lev's call started her worrying about him all over again. His friend was dead, and in murky circumstances. What made it especially troubling was the knowledge there was nothing she could do from seven thousand kilometers away.

Then, as she sat there alone in the stall, the one-hour-to-closing bell shrilly rang from the speaker in the ceiling, as it was doing throughout the Arkhiv. Damn, she remembered, the place closed early for staff meetings on Wednesdays.

Lara left the Ladies' Room and headed back along the hall toward the Listening Room. She was being pulled in too many directions. There was the end of Coward's tale still to listen to, with his talk of Germans and art historians. And her brother to fret over. And the bullnecked man, who might still be lurking around.

She couldn't have picked a worse time to have one of her eureka moments.

CHAPTER 29

That business about German art historians and their scientific tests had tripped a wire connected to something she'd read months or years ago. Not in the humidity-controlled wartime files, but right out there on the *postwar* shelves lining the reading area.

Her footsteps again echoed off the Arkhiv's wood floor as she hurried over to the section marked "Nuremberg." Here were stored the official transcripts taken down by Allied stenographers, translated, printed on color-coded onionskin, and distributed to the non-German-speaking judges and prosecutors of the four countries that defeated Germany: light blue for the Americans and British, yellow for the French, light green for the Russians.

Luckily, the box marked "Albert Speer 4" was on a low shelf. Speer was a special case: sentenced to twenty years in Spandau prison, he freely discussed his case with his captors and admitted his complicity in Nazi war crimes. *Yashchiks* 2–5 contained conversations held after the trial was over; in the case of number four, long after — the conversations recorded by hidden microphones.

She had read something in this box when she was researching an earlier book, something that hadn't computed at the time. The green-colored flimsies flew under her fingers until she found the one she wanted.

None of you believe me when I say it, but the Führer had a wonderful sense of humor, even in times of great moment.

I remember being summoned in the middle of the night to his office in the Old Reichschancellory. He hated the place; called it "Bismarck's soap factory." So I had four thousand men working around the clock, building him a new one. The clanging of the ironworkers sent the others, the light sleepers, off to get their earplugs. But not Hitler. He worked right through the din. And then slept the sleep of the just.

I found him looking out the window toward the east. He didn't turn around when he heard me come in. "Speer," he said, "what if you know for certain something is going to happen? You know it for a fact, the way you know the sun will come up tomorrow? And what if, at the same time, you know equally well that it is impossible, that it can never be? What would you do? Would you go crazy?"

"Yes, mein Führer," I answered. "I probably would."

He kept staring out the window. His voice was very low. "You see? A lesser man can't deal with contradiction. Only the great are able to believe two entirely opposed ideas at the same time. It isn't a question of intelligence, but of the will."

"I can see that."

He turned back from the window and fingered the little brass paperweight on the writing desk, the one I'd given him after the rally in '37, engraved with, EIN

VOLK, EIN REICH, EIN FÜHRER. He sighed. "Ah well, someone has to be in charge."

There were two invasion plans on his desk. The latest from the Luftwaffe had the 11th Corps capturing airfields twenty-five to thirty-five miles from the English coast and then landing infantry divisions on them, avoiding the beaches altogether. The other was *Unternehmen Grün,* Field Marshal Bock's Plan Green, a full-scale invasion of Ireland in support of Sea Lion.

But it was a third paper that he picked up now. He read it aloud, some sort of scientific report. Earlier the previous week — oh, this was in September of 1940, didn't I say? — Himmler had given him a book, which he then turned over to the *Kunst-historisches* to authenticate.

It was a Christian Bible, very old, and they were going on about when it was printed and where, with these absurd prob-abilities: seventy percent that it was from the Rhineland and

188

thirty percent from eastern France. Crazy, minute details like that. The kind of ink, the kind of pen that was dipped in the ink. I remember dust samples had been put under an electron microscope. I'd never even *heard* of an electron microscope.

It was the wormhole that I remember. The report described this hole that went from the binding through the flyleaf and several pages of the Book of Genesis, partially obliterating some of the text, both handwritten and printed.

The Führer showed me the last line of the report: "The object thus analyzed is genuine in all respects. Heil Hitler!"

Then he turned on his heel to the massive map of Europe he was always studying. "There are exactly twenty rivers from that very window," he nodded toward the one he'd been staring out of when I came in, "to Moscow. Twenty from the Wuhle to the Alte Oder all the way to the Moskva." He ran his fingers over the map south to Italy. "Right there is Liguria. Duce was born in Liguria, and I myself on the Danube. I will tell you something, Speer, something I've never told anyone. My mother said that, on the morning I was born, a cow on my uncle's farm gave birth to a two-headed calf.

"Then, when I was in the Army, in the trenches on the Somme, men on both sides of me were killed in the same instant and I was spared. Spared by the Almighty, so I might achieve . . ." he waved his hand in the air over the map of conquered Europe ". . . all this. Don't you see? Triumph in the East is *ordained*!"

Of course I didn't see. When he was going on like that I found it best to say nothing and wait for an explanation. But he didn't explain.

Instead, he started in on this character in *Die Walkure*, Hunding, the husband cuckolded by his brother; Hunding and his helmet of ox horns. It was the horns he was thinking of, I suppose, the horns of a dilemma no less painful than those stage props.

"It is impossible." He was leaning with both elbows on the map table. I thought he might actually put his head in his hands. "Here it is already September. Even if I postpone Sea Lion tonight, even if we mobilize tomorrow, we cannot invade the Soviet Union now, not with the Russian winter coming on. And yet, it is preordained."

That's when he handed me a sheet of paper that was lying on the map. I ran my eyes down the page, thinking it must be a battle order. It was poetry, of the strangest kind.

"I don't quite see, mein Führer . . ."

Impatiently, he stabbed at it with his index finger. "There, there, in the third verse. *At decade's dawn.* The prophecy specifies victory now. But we're not ready."

So, it was a prophecy. I read

it again, this time noticing the part about the child of Germany picking up Barbarossa's sword. I had to be honest. "I do not see the problem, mein Führer."

"1940! The dawn of the decade! The year of my destiny, this very year, 1-9-4-0, is all but over!"

Then I understood. "Here, mein Führer, look at my fingers." I spread my hands, palms outward. "If I count them, I go *one, two, three,* and so on, up to ten."

"*Natürlich.*"

I'd learned to remain calm when he was agitated. "A decade has ten years, as I have ten fingers. One, two, three . . . so, the first year of a decade isn't zero. It's one."

"You're saying . . . the decade begins, not in 1940 . . ."

"But in 1941. Exactly. You are, if this message from the past is to be believed, predestined to master the Slavic race *next* year, in 1941."

Hitler sat down a little heavily in his chair, drained by all the excitement. "Very good, Speer. You can go."

I clicked my heels and headed toward the door.

Hitler stopped me. "Speer."

I turned back. "Yes, mein Führer?"

He smiled. "If you were anyone else and had played that game with me, by now you'd have only nine fingers."

You see what I mean? What a sense of humor!

The joke was lost on Lara, but not the story's significance: it was one more piece in the jigsaw proving that Noël Coward's story really happened.

CHAPTER 30

Her stomach rumbled, reminding her she hadn't eaten all day, when her phone rumbled too. Caller ID said "Grigoriy Gerasimov." She'd forgotten to call.

"Glad I caught you, Lara. Look, I'm in the car . . . how about I pick you up for that practice session with the prompter?"

"I'm at the *Osobyi Arkhiv* for another quarter hour. Do you know where it is?"

"I'm on my way."

Gerasimov was waiting for her at closing time not in a Mercedes — the standard choice of the Russian privileged class — but in a restored Alfa Romeo. She got in the little sports car and he drove her out of Moscow past the big War Memorial up there on the hill at Poklonnaya Gora. It wasn't long before the thought came to her that she was living the dream, at least for the moment, of every unmarried woman in the faculty lounge, and not a few of the married ones — being whisked away in a convertible by a tall, dark Prince Charming.

"Are you hungry?" he asked.

"Starving."

"Me too. We'll eat before I take you back home."

They took Vozdvizhenka Street westbound across the river to the Kutuzovsky Prospekt, joining the fleets of buses, trucks, taxis, private cars, and, everywhere, motorcycles heading for the M-1. Storm clouds were gathering overhead, big, dark thunderheads, and Gerasimov was worried that they would have to pull over and put up the top if it started to pour. He was going on about his car, how the Italians were great at bodywork but terrible with electronics. "Take the turn signals. No matter how much I spend, they never seem to work in the rain."

When Lara tried to talk instead about the problems his change in her teaching schedule had caused, of what the superintendant was trying to pull with a vote of the Faculty Senate, he used a break in the traffic to speed up and pass a number of cars, increasing the wind noise and making conversation impossible.

So Lara didn't get to complain that, on a call she'd just made from the Arkhiv, Nazimova had threatened her newest full professor if she made a stink in front of the Department. "Last in, first out," she'd repeated, as if it were a commandment handed down by Moses. Then, to compound matters, Lara had told her in memorable language exactly how she'd felt. So now she'd probably have to write an apology. Ugh.

The traffic jam was a new, post-Soviet phenomenon, the inevitable consequence of Western consumerism coming late to an oil-glutted country. Try as she might to hold on to it, Lara felt her anger starting to seep away in the gathering gloom. Poking along, there was plenty of time to notice the enormous blue banners depicting the smiling world leaders of the G20 countries, two to a flag. Each of the dozens lining the fifty-meter-wide boulevard for more than a mile bore the single word, *Vmeste!*, and its English translation, *Together!*, at the bottom, as if the owners of the world's twenty biggest economies — so often rattling sabers at each other — were in Moscow for a series of nice tête-à-têtes. Now that the motorcade had come and gone, dozens of workers were stacking the pedestrian barricades back on the trucks.

Gerasimov broke his silence by pointing to one of the banners, showing the new

American president and his Russian opposite number. "So, my Russian-American friend, how do you feel about your two peoples getting together?"

She thought about it. "Talking is better than shooting, I suppose." She looked at him in the rearview mirror. "And you?"

"Wasn't it an American who said, 'My country, right or wrong'? I'm with him."

Gerasimov steered the car toward the exit that led out of town toward St. Petersburg and points west. The surprise of it made Lara blurt out, "Where is this prompter of yours, Grisha? Poland?"

He smiled. "I have a media room upstairs at the dacha."

"Wait a minute. *Your* dacha?"

"We do remotes from there sometimes." He looked over at her. "Don't worry, everything's on the up and up. My son will be joining us."

But she *was* worried; she barely knew this guy. What was she getting herself into? Leaving the Arkhiv, she'd called her roommate to say she'd be late getting back from practicing for her telecast and Katrina, predictably, had said, "With your man . . . of mystery?"

Still, Lara had never seen a dacha. Not a nice one, anyway. Oh, they'd tried. A long time ago, under Brezhnev, her father piled the family into the Zhiguli and drove the twenty miles from Moscow to Uspenskoye. The woods, when they could see them, were dark and beautiful, with little clearings that would have been perfect for the picnic lunch they'd brought. But a NO STOPPING line was painted on the edge of the road, all the villages had TRANSIT ONLY markers and, just to be sure, a ten-foot-high green fence set back from the road ran for miles in both directions with NO ENTRY signs on every side street. The workers, who theoretically owned everything in the Soviet state, were as unwanted as capitalist spies.

When she looked up, Gerasimov was pulling off the main road and heading the Alfa across a little wooden bridge and up a lane dotted with the comfortable cottages of which every Russian dreamed. He was saying, "Can you believe it, ours was once Nikolai Bulganin's place. The official retreat of the Soviet premier and just one bathroom! As the Americans say, it needed an extreme makeover."

Lara thought back to the picnic. By the time they'd driven past the forbidden district, the children were hungry and complaining, and Father pulled over in the yard behind a closed gas station. They ate their pirogis on the rough wooden table where the workers had lunch. Some picnic.

The worst of it was, her parents had acted as if it was what they had intended all along. Two beaten-down victims of the Soviet state, grateful for the crumbs they were thrown. No wonder she'd jumped at the chance to go to university in the States.

His place, as they approached it, was originally one of those Grimm's fairy tale cottages in the Russian style, with eaves that came down practically to the ground. Put up in the 1920s or '30s, it had recently doubled in size, and there were all manner of satellite dishes on the roof. "You can use the room to the right at the top of the stairs to freshen up, the one with its own bathroom. Then come back down and make yourself comfortable. When I return, we'll begin."

"You're going?"

"I have to get a few things. I promised you food, remember? I won't be long; why not listen to some music here 'til I get back? We have iTunes."

Lara must have dozed off for a while in the overstuffed chair that sat in front of the unlit fireplace, because she awoke with a start, nearly pulling the headphones off her head.

Someone else was in the house, she could feel it. She called out Gerasimov's name. No answer. She could hear water running. Was it the rain? She looked out the window. Nothing yet.

Lara crossed the hall and opened a door that led to the vast, updated kitchen. A young man of not more than twenty-five, with longer hair than was stylish, was washing something in the utility sink. He was shirtless, with blue and black tattoos covering his well-muscled body. Just as Lara saw that whatever was in the sink was making the water turn red, the young man looked around.

He smiled. "I'm the son . . . Nikki. Like what you see?"

Lara blushed and turned away from the door. The young man continued his washing and added a little whistling for good measure.

CHAPTER 31

Uspenskoye

Lara would eventually discover the no-longer-bloody shirt outside on a line, the stains still visible on the cuffs and under the buttons. But that would be later. Right now, she was sitting with her legs drawn up under her on the cushioned built-in piece that ran the length of the big front window, her brain in disarray, watching the first drops come down outside while going through the motions of working on a chess problem. Trying not to run into Nikki again before his father came back.

The little folding wooden chessboard her father had hewn for her, with the tiny holes in each space for the pieces to fit in, was the one good thing to have come out of Perm. She was staring at a discovered check Tal had sprung on Smyslov in their championship match. Should he have seen it coming? A dirty American pickup truck was parked where the little Alfa had been. The rain was starting to clean it off. She knew her mind was wandering and she let it.

When, at the Radisson, Lara had said all the best historians were in the camps, she'd meant it. She still thought of her father and his colleagues as prisoners behind the Urals. Perm was a true Soviet city, with rutted streets, numbered "dormitory" blocks and architecture so ugly it must have been a deliberate choice. A closed city which opened periodically to swallow "deviationists" like Lara's parents and the other faculty members in the years right before Stalin died, when the terror was building once more. And then, miraculously, Perm spit them out again in the "thaw" under Khrushchev.

Lara's mother died there. Not in body, but in spirit. Once they were returned to Moscow, there was no work for which they were trained, not for a pardoned *kosmopolit,* a cosmopolitan (okay, Jew), and his Muslim wife. So the man who understood the history of the West better than most Britons and Americans plastered crumbling ceilings and fixed leaky pipes and began his own long descent into uselessness.

She took the picture out of her handbag and studied it, as she had a thousand times.

Two young, fresh-faced university graduates on their wedding day: the son of the Old Bolshevik, a brilliant career ahead of him, and his just-as-brilliant bride, the scholarship student from Tajikistan, two thousand miles and who knows how many centuries away to the East. Decades too late, they tried to make their world more normal, more "Russian," by making a family when they were almost old enough to be grandparents. So Lara — named for the heroine of the Pasternak novel, naturally — and her brother Lev had been Brezhnev babies, the youngest children by far of all her parents' Moscow friends.

The tattoos made it all come flooding back. The inky, unearned prison insignia she'd seen on Nikki's back and chest meant he was in Nashi, the marauding band of young nationalists Lev called "our own Hitler Youth." While the father professed democratic ideals. And here she was, under the same roof. Crazy.

In the quiet of the country, the sudden ringing of her mobile phone made a terrible racket. "Yes?"

"Larashka, are you all right?"

"Oh, it's you, Viktor. Of course I'm —"

"I called the house. Katrina said your classes have been cancelled."

"Postponed. It's a . . . a short sabbatical. I'm doing research outside the city."

"Your voice sounds strange. Can I come see you? I can get a two-day pass, more if I want."

"Viktor, I can't talk right now. Let me call you back."

"You're at some man's place? At his dacha?"

"It's not like that. Look, I'll call you back."

"Larissa Mendelova, as long as I'm still your —"

Flipping the phone closed ended the noise.

Lara prided herself on the ability to compartmentalize, to put her personal life in a mental cubicle as she plowed on in her work. Now was just such a time. A wayward husband, hiding behind his Army uniform as he broke his marriage vows in one former Soviet Socialist Republic after another . . . no, she wouldn't let herself think of that now. She had work to do. Azerbaijan, Chechnya, Georgia, everywhere he went . . . no, she wasn't going to get into it. That's what divorce lawyers were for. After she got the back rent, she would wring Katrina's neck.

Lara looked up and was startled to find Grigoriy Gerasimov standing there, a slightly rained-on paper bag of groceries in his hands.

"Who was that?"

"My husband, though I don't see —"

"You seemed upset, that's all."

"Viktor and I, we have . . . issues."

"You mean the divorce."

She was startled. "You know about that?"

"Separation decrees are public documents. And I'm . . . the public." When he saw her expression darken, he quickly added, "If talking to him bothers you so much, why do it?"

"Can I help it if the phone rings?"

"You can keep it turned off. Or . . ." he said quickly, seeing her brow start to furrow again, ". . . you can give each of your callers a different ringtone. Then you'll know right away which to answer and which to let go to voicemail. May I show you?"

Putting down the groceries, he took her phone and punched in some buttons. "Let's say I'm calling you from *my* mobile. What ringtone should *I* get?" The phone's screen displayed a list of possibilities, most of them from current pop songs.

Through gritted teeth, Lara said, "It should be something subtle. Maybe cannon shots from the '1812 Overture.' "

Unfazed, Gerasimov clicked onto the

"Classical" list. "Tchaikovsky. Good Russian choice."

He scrolled down a little more, clicked on a listing and entered his phone number before handing her mobile back. Then he took his own phone out of his pocket and called hers. It rang with the first nine notes of the "Hunters' Theme" from *Peter and the Wolf.*

Lara answered it, and spoke into the phone to the man standing next to her. "I thought you'd give yourself the Wolf's theme."

He said, "Me? I'm one of the good guys," and, smiling, closed his phone.

Under duress, Viktor acquired the old Red Army Hymn for his future incoming calls. But Gerasimov wasn't satisfied until she had assigned individual ringtones to her ten most recent callers. Her friend Vera was assigned *Swan Lake* and Pavel, who'd called again, got something called "Pavel's Song" from the Pop list.

Gerasimov was taking things from the grocery bag: a container of Georgian chicken *satsivi* and a box of toothpicks, the better to pluck the cold chunks of white meat from the walnut sauce; little lingonberry cakes; a half bottle of wine. Outside, afternoon had turned to dusk.

He sat down opposite her. "I gather you've met Nikolai."

Lara pulled herself together. "We weren't formally introduced but, yes."

"Nikki . . . Nikki's a good kid."

He was staring at her. Lara had a small dark spot on her cheekbone a couple of centimeters under her left eye. When she thought about it at all, she usually told herself it was a beauty mark. Now it felt like a flaw, a weak place. A way in.

Gerasimov spread a bit of the Vologodskoye maslo he'd brought on a thin slice of coriander-studded rye bread. He handed it to her. Not cheese but a nutty-flavored butter, it was sumptuously creamy, a true Russian indulgence. He poured them both some wine and held up his glass.

"To the interesting Dr. Klimt. Welcome." He took a sip and said, "There's something I don't understand about you, Lara."

She took a sip from her glass. "Oh, what's that?"

"You spent a dozen years, almost your whole adult life, living and teaching in America. Why come back?"

Yes . . . why had she? "It was strange at first, to be a Russian in America at the end of the 1980s. The Iron Curtain was torn, but it was still up . . . the Berlin Wall . . .

everything — and to be free to think what you wanted, to say what you wanted, it was all so *seductive.*

"Everybody there is part American and part something else: In New York you're Italian- or Irish- or African-American. My parents were so different from each other, one a Muslim, the other a Jew . . . I guess I've always *been* a hyphenate, so I fit right in."

Even as she was speaking, the answer came to her, surprising her with its simplicity. "When the Soviet Union was gone, the Wall down, the Curtain opened, I was free to be *all* of something, just another Russian in Russia. So I came back." She took a bite of the buttered bread and then looked back at Gerasimov. "And, well, I like it."

He was sipping his wine and looking at her, the lines around his eyes crinkled in an odd expression. Interest? Skepticism? She couldn't tell. All he said was, "Shall we get to work? Take your wine. The media room is upstairs."

As they walked up the flight of stairs, the rain beat a tattoo on the roof just over their heads. But inside the padded door at the top of the landing, it was just a whisper. He answered her unspoken question. "Sound-proofing . . . it actually works."

Gerasimov's "media room" would have made an American anchorman jealous. There were huge flat-screen TVs, laptop and desktop computers, scanners, the works. Gerasimov picked up a remote and suddenly the TVs were playing a dozen different broadcasts at once: A Ukrainian soap opera, a pitchwoman selling earrings, a newscast showing the Russian president walking alongside his American counterpart up the fifty-eight steps of the Red Staircase where, four centuries earlier, Ivan the Terrible killed the messenger who brought him bad news.

A variety show was playing on the bottom monitor, with Alla Pugachova, the most popular singer in Russian history, crooning her biggest hit, "Dreams of Love." As Lara watched, the picture froze with Pugachova's mouth open grotesquely wide.

"Grisha, look! You have a problem on that network!"

He smiled indulgently. "That one's offline. It's the pre-build for Friday's Conception Night telecast. She'll be the second act to go on live, so they slugged in what they had of her in the archives and extended it another forty-five seconds to make the schedule work."

He clicked all the screens off with his

remote. "As the director, I get to approve the various stages of a production in progress. Now, over here, please."

He was standing in front of a pull-down, three-meter-wide screen of light blue material in the corner. Lara joined him, and saw they were facing a small television camera whose red light was on.

He said, "Look to your right."

She did and saw herself on a TV monitor as her host stepped out of the picture. She ran her hand over her hair to tuck it behind her ears.

"Now look back at the camera. I'm going to type in something for you to read."

Instead of doing as she was told, Lara looked to her left, where the man was now hunched over a keyboard, his fingers flying, faster even than Lara could do it.

"Don't look at me, look at the lens."

She did, and saw the words in Russian appear in a small window built into the camera. She said, "Good day, I'm Dr. Larissa Mendelova Klimt, and it's my honor . . ." She turned back to Gerasimov, who was watching her on the monitor, and asked, "How's that?"

He paused. "Well, we've established that you can read. Now, let's see if you can manage an entire sentence. Ready?"

She faced the camera. "Ready." She could hear Gerasimov clicking away on the keyboard. "Good day, I'm Dr. Larissa Mendelova Klimt, and it's my honor to be very beaut—"

She stopped and turned toward the man at the keyboard.

He smiled and moved toward her. "Was there a typo? The word should read, 'beautiful.' Let me see if I got it right." Now he was next to her, pointing to the words on the camera's screen. " *'Dobryĭden, ya Larissa Mendelova Klimt, i eto menya bolshaya chest byt ochen krasivyi.'* Yes, it's perfectly correct. The word you stumbled over is *'krasivyi'* . . . it means lovely, beautiful, gorgeous, with intriguing almond-shaped eyes. Repeat after me: ". . . very beautiful."

"Do you always soften up your translator this way?"

"You mean Boris, the guy with the flu? If he had your legs, maybe." He grinned. "Okay, back to work. This time, I'll type in a sample question. After you say it out loud, look over at the monitor as if the president is sitting there, and translate the words into English. Wait for his answer, and then turn back to the camera and translate it back for your viewers."

211

They practiced with the TelePrompTer for another hour until Gerasimov was satisfied. "You're not just a teacher, you're an apt pupil."

"Thank you, Grigoriy Aleksandrovich."

"Grisha, remember?"

"Thank you, Grisha."

"Now, let's see how good you are at modeling."

She spent another forty minutes trying on different outfits from her suitcase for the camera, changing in the little upstairs bathroom each time, as he murmured variations of *krasivyi*. They settled on a cream-colored blouse and jacket.

Then Gerasimov looked at his watch. "Is it seven already? Please stay for dinner. With Nikki here, Cook is making a little more than usual. It would be an honor to have you join us. Then I'll run you back into town."

Lara said, "Your wife . . . will she be joining us too?"

He didn't look at her when he quietly uttered a single syllable.

"Nyet."

CHAPTER 32

Moscow

The president's "body man," or closest personal aide, sat opposite him in the suite's sitting room. "Body woman" would have been more like it: Sarah Rouke was a curvaceous blonde in her early thirties, unattached and much in demand by Washington party-givers. But today she was all business, unzipping a slim leather attaché and handing over several files to the chief executive.

"This is your address to the G20. You won't have a TelePrompTer, so you'll have to go old school and read it from the lectern."

Her boss smiled and took the papers. "Got it."

"Afterward, we've put aside half an hour for the photo ops with the other leaders."

"Standing or sitting? I'm a foot taller than some of them."

"Sitting. There'll be armchairs."

"Good."

"And please, Mr. President, remember: no texting during the business sessions."

The president briefly thought back to his gaffe at the Tomb of the Unknown Soldier. "Right."

Rouke took another set of papers from her attaché. "And here's the latest copy of your oil agreement. The other side asked for a few minor changes; they're highlighted in yellow."

Her boss cocked one eyebrow above the frame of his reading glasses. "Changes?"

Rouke leaned forward and ran her fingernail under a highlighted area. "Who's responsible for paying the tanker crews if they're delayed in our waters; stuff like that."

The president sighed. "Lawyers."

Rouke gave him one more file. "We've put together a few toasts for after the dinner tonight. They're in phonetic Russian, with the English underneath, so you'll know what you're saying."

The leader of the free world took off his glasses and wiped them on a little cloth he took from his pocket. As he did, he looked intently at the younger woman. "Don't let my wife have more than two drinks. You know what she's like when . . ."

Sarah Rouke stood up. "I'm on it, sir."

The president got up as well. "Don't let me have more than two either. You know what I'm like."

The two shared the briefest of laughs.

CHAPTER 33

Deadhorse, Alaska

The bright green bus was warming up its engine as "Len" Klimt got on. The No Smoking sign over the driver's head was already lit up and Lev knew he was going to need a Winston the moment he got off. To think about something else, he watched the Arctic Caribou Inn fall away behind the tour bus as it got going in the morning light.

Comfortably seated near the rear, he turned his attention back to the Google Earth app on his recharged iPhone. The inn was the jumping-off point for the daily Wildlife Refuge trips run by Tatqaani Tours, an Inupiat word meaning "way up" or "way out north." To prove it, the tip of the red Google arrow indicating the motel's location touched the green-shaded land area on the phone's screen, while most of the arrow's shaft hung out over the blue Beaufort Sea.

Seen from space on Google Earth, northern Alaska had sprouted major new construction just inside the nineteen-million-acre Refuge in what was called t he 1002 Area, undeveloped land opened to commercial interests by the president's recent executive order. Lev had to see it for himself; had to find out why Craig's emails said he "wouldn't be a party" to whatever was going on in there.

His phone's app showed him pumps, drilling sheds, holding tanks and sections of conduit on the screen — all the stuff you needed to get vast quantities of oil out of the ground. It was the place Lev needed to get to.

The Holland America and Princess lines were finished cruising for the season and the Caribou Inn, the closest public place of any size, had transformed itself back into a remote-site camp for oilfield workers. As an accommodation to the workforce, the first roundtrip of the day set off early, dropping roustabouts at the various wellheads and collecting them again in the late afternoon.

Lev was on the second run, the one for family members going shopping in Prudhoe, leftover tourists doing the North Slope on their own, and a handful of naturalists and wildlife photographers staying in the area who didn't want to get up at the crack of dawn. Still sleep-deprived after the plane ride up, Lev felt his eyes closing, involuntarily. No sense calling Lara yet on his recharged phone, not when he had nothing new to tell her.

Across the aisle, two men with their coats on their laps were speaking quietly, their words drowned out by the accelerating bus. Lev's hand rested protectively on his backpack beside him on the seat; if anyone tried to take it while he was dozing, he'd know. Not that there was anything valuable in it — just his old metal hardhat and the camera case he'd purchased in Anchorage. And, he remembered, smiling, as his lids dropped some more . . . his pack of Winstons.

When the bus shifted into cruising gear, Lev heard one of the guys across the way ask the other, *"Kak dolgo vy budete nasosnoĭneft?"*

"How long will you be pumping the oil?" Nothing particularly nefarious these days about Russian being spoken on an American bus, Lev mused, almost asleep. Up here in oil country, Alaska was a melting pot of English, Inupiat, and Russian speech. But, *"pumping the oil?"* It was the very reason he was up here. So he turned on his phone to capture their words.

The second man, also in Russian, asked, "What did you say?"

"Kak dolgo vy budete nasosnoĭneft?"

"Oh. Once they give the word, a week at the most. Depends where you are in the line."

The first man spoke again. "And how far back is your tanker?"

"We're thirtieth, fortieth, something like that."

Thirty or forty oil tankers in a line? Lev opened his eyes. Sure enough, a procession of nondescript oil tankers flying American flags lay at anchor for miles just off the shore. Lev switched his phone to Video and began to film them as the green bus headed east along the bumpy road that ran beside Mikkelsen Bay.

The man by the window suddenly pointed out to sea. "There, you can just barely see it, the one with the orange insignia: *The Atlantic Pioneer.* If you look carefully, you can see where we painted over it."

The driver announced an upcoming stop, and the two men got up to go. Lev didn't know what to make of it.

CHAPTER 34

Uspenskoye

Dinner was awkward. For one thing, Lara was overdressed. Underdressed actually, in her skimpy black sheath and its too-thin straps and scoop neckline. She was usually pleased with what her body brought to the scoop, but now she kicked herself for not wearing Vera's outfit with the cap sleeves.

The rain outside was intensifying, increasing Lara's discomfort at being bottled up with these strangers. She sat across from the two of them, the older and newer models. Grigoriy with his remarkably handsome features and the beginnings of grey in his dark, glossy hair *could* have been a model. Next to him the young man, so similar in height and weight, was all neck and torso and forearms, twisting the bread in his large hands until he tore off the heel, crumbs flying everywhere except the bread plate. Openly competing with his father for

Lara's attention. Lara, a still slightly married woman.

Was she showing too much skin? She looked down and saw gooseflesh. She could plead that it was chilly and go get her thin blue shawl. But it wasn't chilly. It was uncomfortably warm.

The younger Gerasimov's mood had darkened. He began peppering Lara with questions. Who were her friends, where did she live and with whom, why did she teach what she taught, why had she gone to America to teach under the enemy, Reagan? Instead of a meal it was a job interview. Nikki asked what her father had done to get thrown into Perm.

"Nothing."

"Nothing?"

This boy across from her was too young to understand. So she said, "They had a joke in the camps. When a new arrival showed up fresh from the Moscow trials, he was asked at the gate what his sentence was."

" 'Ten years for doing absolutely nothing,' he'd say."

" 'You're lucky,' they'd tell him. 'For absolutely nothing, it's usually 15 years.' "

The father laughed. The son just went on making waves in his soup with his spoon.

"No one does nothing. He must have written or spoken against the authorities."

"No, he was one of the loyal ones. Even afterward. He simply knew too much about the West."

Nikki looked up from ladling his *okroshka*. "You see? It's what they say . . . a little knowledge is a dangerous thing."

Grigoriy put a manicured hand on his son's arm. "Nikki, Larissa Mendelova is our guest. Stop interrogating. And besides, we already know everything about her. It's all in her file, or we wouldn't be breaking bread together." With his free hand he started picking up the breadcrumbs and dropping them on Nikki's plate. "Use the other spoon, the soup spoon."

The younger man, annoyed, moved his arm from under his father's grip, picked up his unused utensil and wordlessly began slurping up his broth.

But Lara wasn't about to let it drop. "You know, Nikolai, I happen to agree with you. A little knowledge *is* a dangerous thing. So if my dossier says I spend half my life thumbing through yellowed documents or listening on the Arkhiv's Dictaphones to a lot of dead guys, it's because the only antidote to a little knowledge is a lot of knowledge."

The boy's eyes briefly registered some-thing at the word "Dictaphone." Then it was gone.

She turned to his father. "This file on me. What's in it?"

Her question caught Gerasimov with *his* spoon almost to his lips. He went ahead and put it in his mouth, looking straight at her as the liquid went down. Then he said, "Your file? Public stuff. Birth date, school-ing —"

"Who I live with or don't live with?"

He went right on. "— the chess titles you won as a girl, your work record, marriage, separation decree . . ."

Nikki eyed her again, and shared a veiled look with his father.

She had her dander up. "What I think or don't think?"

Gerasimov was still picking up micro-scopic breadcrumbs and dropping them, one by one, beside his soup bowl. "All I'm interested in is that you *do* think. And you do that very well, judging by the degrees you earned."

Nikki said, "Let's go back to those tourna-ments you won. What's the *real* reason you stopped playing?"

She'd been thinking about it ever since the father had asked the same question at lunch. "If you must know, I think it was the injustice of chess."

The young man gave out an unbelieving snort. "What could be *more* just? Equal pieces, level playing field, a fight to the death, just the two of you."

She knew she'd never convince him but she tried, anyway. "Exactly. Chess is warfare without the blood. Everything about it gives the stronger, more cunning player the means to grind down the lesser one, turning the screws until there's no place to run, no place to hide.

"Oh sure, there are once-in-a-lifetime accidents, like Kasparov thinking about something else, maybe his dinner, and overlooking what I was doing with my knight that time. And don't get me wrong, I love the intellectual challenge, the problem-solving. But as a system, in and of itself, chess is simply a way for the powerful to prey on the weak."

Nikki smiled. "I call that justice."

"And I call it tyranny. So, though I didn't fully understand it at the time, I stopped playing competitive chess because I wasn't willing to live under those rules."

For a long moment, the rain hitting the roof was the only sound in the room. Lara needed to change the subject. "Nikki, what do *you* do for a living? Or are you still in school?"

The younger man didn't make eye contact. "No, I've had enough of studying. It's time for a little *doing.*"

For some reason, Gerasimov was staring daggers at his son.

Lara kept on. "What kind of doing?"

"All I know is," he answered, still not making eye contact, "this place needs a complete housecleaning, top to bottom."

Lara decided to add fuel to the fire. "It seems to me you're doing all right. Your father's got a nice job with the Government; you have this place, Bulganin's place . . ."

Lara knew she'd made a mistake the instant Nikki turned back to her. There was fire in his eyes. "We have a dacha, but we don't have a country. Whatever happened to Russia for the Russians? When did we ever have a chance to rule ourselves?

"You teach History, but how much history do you actually *know*? You think your rivers and lakes make history? Or iron and coal under the ground? *People* make history. For three hundred years we were a wholly owned subsidiary of Ivan the Terrible's family. He marries some Circassian woman and we get the Romanovs for centuries.

"Then the Tsars are overthrown by the Jews. Oh, excuse me, the Communists: Marx, Engels, Lenin, Trotsky — true believers, not in Russia, but in something they call the workers' paradise. When they pulled us out of the first Great War, suddenly the Americans and the British were our friends. But only so we'd go back to fighting the Germans, which never happened."

Lara tried to get a word in edgewise. "But after the war —"

Nikki's laugh was bitter. "After came the civil war, the Reds against the Whites. American, British, French troops started fighting one half of Russia in the name of the other. Churchill dropped chemical weapons from planes; I'll bet you didn't know that. Fifty thousand bombs!

"Then, when *their* Russians were losing and falling back, the West abandoned them to their fate and went home in 1920, back to their nice warm beds in London and New York. While the firing squads went to work over here."

He leaned across the table until he was inches from Lara's face. "Instead of a national anthem, you know what we got? When the Reds were done, we got "The Internationale," thanks to the riffraff they brought into *our* revolution: Finns . . .

Poles . . . Georgians . . . Armenians . . . Tajiks —

"That's enough, Nikki! Apologize to Dr. Klimt this minute!" Gerasimov's raised voice startled them both.

Lara murmured, "No, it's okay. I asked, he answered." She returned to the boy. "You're right. My father was a Jew, my mother Tajik. And they were both Bolsheviks. But *I'm* one hundred percent Russian."

Nikki was back to playing with his soup. He didn't look at Lara when he spoke. "You say 'I'm one hundred percent Russian' with an American accent. You just live here. You aren't *of* here."

At that moment, Cook came in and whispered something in Gerasimov's ear. He turned to Lara. "I was afraid of this. The creek at the bottom of our hill has risen over the bridge. You'll have to stay over with us tonight. *Prostitye,* Larissa Mendelova, I'm terribly sorry. I'll drive you back in the morning."

CHAPTER 35

Arctic National Wildlife Refuge

Lev picked up his phone to call Lara in Moscow. No bars. He must be out of cell phone range. Looking out the windows on both sides of the bus, there were no cell towers to be seen. Strange . . . communications were the first priority at any new drilling site.

Lev had the pack of Winstons out and the lighter ready even before signaling the driver he'd be getting off at the first "1002 Area" gate. From what he understood, the tourists, naturalists and photographers usually stayed on the bus till it came to the second gate, the one closer to the uplands where the wildlife stayed when they weren't migrating. The drilling company people, the early risers from the first trip, would use this one.

Standing by the side of the road, he drew the smoke down into his lungs as the bus started up again. When it pulled away, he shoved the cigarettes into his pocket, reaching down for a handful of dirt to rub on the hard, shiny leather of the new camera case. Then he stood there and smoked the entire cigarette before crossing the road and going up to the small "Information" kiosk just ahead.

The information obtained at the wooden shed ran in only one direction: from the visitors to the sentry. Lev knew the state worker was stationed there to ID people entering the Refuge; if any caribou were killed and their antlers taken, they'd know whom to blame.

The guy behind the counter was flipping through an old *People* magazine. Only when he handed the clerk his Len Klimt driver's license did the man finally look up from his reading. He said, smiling, "Do Not Enter means do not enter. Okay?"

Sure enough, there was a picket line of DO NOT ENTER/ACTIVE DRILLING AREA signs that ringed a rise in the ground three hundred yards ahead; they ran toward the nearby coastline. The land open to the public lay due south, across the flat grasses of the Marsh Creek anticline that lay on this side of the Sadlerochit Mountains, twenty miles away.

Lev nodded to the man that he understood, picked up his license and now-dusty camera case and started off in that direction.

Over his shoulder the man called, "Hey, what magazine you with?"

Lev looked back and said the first thing that came to mind. "*People.*"

The guy seemed surprised. "Really? That's funny."

Lev was on his guard. "How so?"

"People's the one thing we got hardly any of."

CHAPTER 36

When he was well out of sight of the man in the shed, Lev turned sharply left and entered do not enter. Then he bent down and got his test station hardhat out of his backpack and put it on, tightening the strap under his chin. Between the empty case around his neck, the hat, and his test station ID, he thought he could pass as a working photographer, if no one got too close.

Nobody saw him or stopped him. After another half hour he came to the crest of a small hill. A little out of breath, he looked down into a valley, a sort of natural bowl, drained by the Canning River just before it emptied into the Beaufort.

The visual was striking: at least a dozen structures large and small, with all manner of drilling apparatus everywhere, constituted a twenty-first-century boomtown. But the sound was puzzling. In the middle of a workday, it was oddly silent.

Lev used his phone's camera to squeeze off several shots before hurrying down the far side of the hill. No cranes were working, no trucks were moving, nobody was loading or unloading anything.

In another ten minutes, Lev knew why. The buildings weren't buildings at all, just tents painted on top to look like buildings from the air. And from space.

He walked under a "drilling shed" and listened as the wind whistled through the tent flaps. Holding it up in the middle was a telephone pole, plain and simple. The edges of the vast tent were held down, like a circus big top, with stakes.

The oil rigs themselves were either rusty iron surplus parked on unbroken ground, or else wooden constructions painted to look like rigs. He remembered reading about General Patton's mythical First Army, stationed before D-Day in southeast England. This was how they fooled the Luftwaffe.

He hadn't wanted to add the weight of a real camera with a real telephoto lens to his backpack, but now Lev wished he had one in the case around his neck. Instead, he held up his phone and took more shots of everything at ground level, moving slowly in a 180° arc and snapping away.

On the far side, stacked against the hill, were piled dozens of huge four-foot-diameter pipeline segments. Instead of anodized steel, they were merely so much concrete drainage pipe, probably hauled in from some municipal sewer project to play their role as props. Lev made sure to get a couple of close-ups before he clambered up the first pipe. He used them in turn as giant rounded steps to start up the hill opposite the one he'd stood on earlier.

At the top, ready for another cigarette, he knocked one out of the pack and groped for the lighter in his pants pocket. You couldn't smoke on a real drilling site, but that sure wasn't what he was looking at down there. A couple more pictures from this side, then he'd get to some place with cell phone bars and call Lara with the news. Maybe she'd know what to make of it.

The bullet arrived before the flame could reach the tobacco, even before the sharp crack of the firing pin that set off the charge. By the time the noise echoed off the phony derricks and wellheads, Lev's boots had lost their grip and he was tumbling down the chalky hill.

A quarter-mile away, the man from the information booth put down the rifle and spoke into his satellite phone. "Got 'im."

CHAPTER 37

The security guard put down the bulky satellite phone, took the rifle, and worked his way up and around the incline toward the guy he'd shot: always the double tap. One to the chest, then one to the head.

At the top of the ridge there was a lighter and an unsmoked cigarette where it had been dropped, but no victim. Looking down, he could see the trail the guy's boots had made on the way up and, right next to them, where the body had tumbled down the dusty slope toward the big pipes. Couldn't see it from here; must have bounced off and rolled under an outcropping.

The guard worked his way down, making sure to wipe out the evidence of the dead guy's boot prints as he went.

At the bottom he looked around for the corpse, but couldn't find it; maybe it took a freakish bounce off the concrete ducting.

He stood where he could see all the openings of the huge pipes. With the morning sun coming from behind the hill, the interiors were in shadow.

Then he spotted a dark brown or black something wedged between two of the pipes. He picked it up. The thick, stiff leather camera case had a bullet hole torn into one side, and it rattled. Popping open the case, he found the spent round from his .22.

Okay, the shot didn't kill him, but the forty-foot fall must have. Or at least, injured him bad. Must have crawled into one of the pipes to die.

Leave him there, or go looking? The guard briefly considered firing a round into each of the darkened pipes, just to be sure, but he didn't have his extra ammo with him. Sighing, he stuck his head in the closest one.

CHAPTER 38

Lev was in pain, but the fear was overwhelming it for the moment. His ankle must be broken; his fingers were starting to swell. The crazy thing was, it was the hardhat, crushed in several places and digging into his skull — the thing that saved his life in the fall — that hurt the worst.

The shooter was out there, and he saw it was the guy who checked him in at the gate. No time for the why of it. Lev watched him raise the rifle and aim it at the opening of the bottom pipe closest to the slope of the hill, next to the one he'd crawled into. The tubes were stacked like so many cells in a beehive; if his idea was to shoot into every one in turn, Lev was a goner. Crawling back deeper wouldn't save him from the bullet. So Lev inched up closer to the opening, worked the hardhat off his head, and waited.

Instead of shooting, the man walked up to the first dark opening and put his head in, the gun barrel resting on its concrete bottom, prepared to fire. Then he raised himself up and did the same with the pipe that rested above it on the hill. He bellowed, "C'mon out, Klimt. I got the gun and you don't!"

Then he shifted to his left and peered into the one next to it, the one that lay halfway on Lev's. One of his legs was visible just inches from Lev's face.

The man was yelling, "Hey, what kind of Commie name is Lev?" his voice echoing down the pipes, when a metal hardhat swung out and rammed itself into the side of the guy's exposed knee. The satisfying snapping of his anterior cruciate ligament also echoed down the pipes, as did the clatter of the dropped rifle into the pipe above.

The man, yowling in shock and pain, fell to his left as his leg was taken away from him. It put his face right in line with Lev's hiding place, and the wide-eyed surprise was evident just as Lev brought the hardhat down on it with as much force as he could muster. By the third blow, the look, and the face, were pretty much history.

For the longest time Lev just lay there, eyeing the gruesome mess he'd made of the man's face. His ankle was throbbing. The ring finger and pinkie on his left hand were broken too, or at least dislocated. Even so, he couldn't help falling into a deep black pit.

CHAPTER 39

Uspenskoye

Lying in bed in the guest room, Lara found sleep impossible. Too many images were flashing through her mind, like a slide show whizzing by at a hundred miles an hour. Father and Mother chopping wood in the camp; Lev, her brother, in his Young Pioneers uniform, explaining some experiment at a school science fair that used two spinning cans to generate electricity; which morphed into a spinning Dictaphone cylinder.

Gerasimov made an appearance, leaning toward her and uttering over and over the word *"krasivyi"*; which became an old movie poster for *Love Story* she'd seen in the lobby of a revival movie house on the Upper West Side; which magically turned into Lara and Viktor the way they'd been in the beginning — but, again and again, the leering face of the cocky young man saying, "You just live here. You aren't *of* here." And then, "a little knowledge is a dangerous thing."

Enough! It was exhausting, the rods and cones behind her eyes firing off in crazy bursts. Then some part of an idea came to her, something for later when her mind was functioning normally. Reaching for her phone on the bedside table, Lara turned it on and pressed the Memo button. She spoke as quietly as she could, not wishing to wake up the others in the dacha. "Who'd want to show the world proof that America and Britain got Hitler to attack us? And who in present-day Russia would do whatever they could to stop it?"

Before turning it off again, she saw all the messages from faculty members. There must be a dozen! She clicked on the Superintendant's. "An outpouring of support for our colleague, Larissa Mendelova Klimt, convinces me the waiver should be granted so she may appear on television."

Finally, some good news. Lara turned off her phone and closed her eyes, hopeful of getting at least a few hours of sleep before facing the new day.

CHAPTER 40

Arctic National Wildlife Refuge

The sun had circled the hills and was lighting up the inside of the big concrete duct when Lev opened his eyes again. He roused himself enough to sit up, sideways, with his back against the curve so he wouldn't have to face the body.

Luckily, his brain was still working. He knew he was supposed to be sitting in the middle of the biggest oil strike on the North American continent, at least since the East Texas gusher of 1930, and it was all a fraud. He knew Craig had been killed because of it, and that he'd nearly gone the same way. Someone was desperate to keep the fiction going, but who? And why?

It couldn't be the dead guard lying on the ground over there, he was only the trigger man. How high up did it go?

Lev's cell phone had no bars, so he couldn't tell anyone what he'd found, or call for help. He made himself get up and out of the concrete pipe.

He walked around the guy's booted feet, coming up behind him so he wouldn't have to look at the pulpy features, and went through his pockets. Nothing. No ID, no phone. Lev tried to think. The guy must have gotten his orders somehow.

He'd have to make it out of here and over the encircling hills to the security shed on a damaged ankle. He looked at the sun and then at his watch. Five o'clock. An hour till the bus came back on its return loop.

Lev picked up the camera case with the bullet in it where it had been dropped in the dust. Time to get going.

CHAPTER 41

It took Lev three quarters of an hour to hobble back to the gate and the road beyond it. Once there, he inventoried the information booth. There was the visitors' log, a satellite phone hanging on a nail, the *People* magazine the dead man had been riffling through, extra ammunition for the rifle, and a half-eaten sandwich with a thermos of coffee. That was all. Maybe there was something more in the guy's dusty Jeep Cherokee, parked in a little turnaround.

On the floor of the Jeep he found a day-old *USA Today,* and a Styrofoam cup in the cupholder. Guy liked his coffee. He opened the glove box. Just a couple of maps. No car keys. Lev had gone through the dead man's pockets, looking for them. When he hadn't found them, he assumed they were here. Now he realized they must have fallen out when Lev hit him. Damn, they were probably back there under the guy; he'd been too squeamish to roll the body over.

Lev limped back to the kiosk and scanned the list of visitors admitted through Gate One of the Refuge. Two people in a Land Rover yesterday, photographers. They'd both checked back out by nightfall. His own name was still the only one down for today. Funny, the guy had written down "Lev Klimt," even though the driver's license he'd handed over said "Len."

While he searched the little shed, no car came by on the road, no one passed by on foot. Lev's own foot was throbbing, swelling so much he'd had to take off his boot. Thank God the bus back to civilization would be along any minute; he'd get medical attention back at Prudhoe.

He turned his attention to the bulky satellite phone with the extra-long antenna. He took it down and worked the buttons, looking for the list of Incoming Calls. There: one from an Anchorage number that morning; nothing since. He switched to the outgoing calls. That same number had been dialed a little later, around the time Lev was shot.

He hit redial.

"State House, Carl Hendricks."

Lev didn't speak.

After a moment, the man said, "Ray, that

244

you?" Another pause, then, "I didn't want to send the copter, it could be seen going in. So the guys are driving up . . . should be there any minute. Make sure you don't leave any of Klimt's stuff behind. Ray? You got that?"

Lev pushed the phone's End button. More bad guys on their way? There was no place to hide; plus, if it came to it, he couldn't outrun anybody on a broken ankle.

And then, salvation. He saw the bright green Tatqaani Tours bus coming up from the south. Hailing it, he showed the driver his ticket and painfully hoisted himself up the three steps. Taking the first open seat, Lev leaned back and let his backpack drop down next to the window. He had a couple of pieces of evidence in there, the camera case with the bullet in it and the guy's satellite phone. The real proof, though, was in his pocket: all the pictures on his cell.

The satellite phone! He could use it to call Lara. It was five in the morning in Moscow, so he'd leave her a message. He undid the backpack. Before he could get to it, he saw a black Land Rover speed past the bus in the direction of the gate and turn in — the guys coming to retrieve a dead body.

There was a body, all right. Good thing it wasn't his.

Chapter 42

Uspenskoye Thursday

When Lara came down to breakfast, she looked out the window and saw the foliage outside was still dripping from the rain overnight. The shirt Nikki had been washing was pinned to a clothesline, as wet as before, brick red stains clearly visible even at a distance. The Alfa Romeo was gone again, but Nikki was out there, adding to the water table by hosing down his pickup truck.

Breakfast for one was set out in the big kitchen. She was going to ask Cook about it when her mobile rang with *Peter and the Wolf.* It was Grisha.

"Good morning, Larissa Mendelova, I hope you've found the food. My boss, too, has a dacha out here, and he roped me into an early-morning budget meeting. Nikki left me a note, told me he wanted to drive you back in, make amends or something, so I thought I'd let him, if it's all right with you."

His boss? Didn't the State Director of Broadcasting report directly to the Kremlin? Lara was about to say something, but he beat her to it. "Look, I'm terribly sorry about last night. These kids, they think they know everything . . . you and I were that way once, weren't we? I don't mean the bad manners, no, I'm sure you were never — I just mean, well, it's a generational thing these days, isn't it?"

Three beeps from her mobile told her she had another call coming in. Gerasimov's half-baked apology hung in the air. Looking down, she saw the caller was Viktor. Listen to him hem and haw over signing the divorce papers? Not today.

Natalya the Cook had filled her cup with tea. Lara gave her a silent nod of thanks as she held the phone to her ear, ignoring the incoming call.

"What I said just now . . . I didn't mean to imply that you and Nikki are in different generations . . . nothing like that . . ." Gerasimov paused. "I seem to be apologizing for my apology."

"No apology is necessary." Lara lifted her teacup so she wouldn't have to say anything more.

"Cook will make you whatever you want.

When you're back in town, call me on this number and we'll go over the arrangements for tomorrow."

Nikki walked into the kitchen, his trousers wet at the cuffs. Ignoring the fact that she was on a call, he said, "Just let me change and we'll go." She took a second sip of the tea and said, "Okay," to both father and son.

Cook picked up a tray of *ponchiki,* sweet Russian doughnuts covered in powdered sugar, and silently offered them to Lara, still holding the phone.

"May I have one for later?"

"Have two."

The woman wiped her hands on her apron and picked up two of the sweet rolls, wrapping them in paper towels. Lara dropped them both in her purse; she was a morning person, not a breakfast person.

In a dry change of clothes, Nikki stowed her wheeled suitcase in the truck bed, started the engine, and steered the big Dodge Ram pickup down the hill. As they passed over it, Lara could see the stream was still high, just inches below the rough boards of the little wooden bridge.

Out of nowhere, Nikki said, "My father likes you."

"I like him too."

He took his eyes off the road for a moment to meet her gaze. "You shouldn't. He's not the nice guy he appears."

"And you are?"

He turned back to his driving. "No, but I don't pretend to be."

Another silence, and then he said, "About last night . . . well . . . I could see Father was taken with you so, naturally, I had to do what I could to drive you away."

She looked across at him. "And so this morning you're driving me away?"

He smiled, briefly. "I shouldn't have involved you in a family fight. *Prostitye,* Larissa Mendelova."

"*Spasibo,* Nikolai Grigorevich."

Nothing was said for the next five kilometers as Lara gazed out at the traffic in her side-view mirror. If objects are closer than they appear — the printed warning on the truck's mirror said as much — traffic must be right on top of them, especially the silver-and-red motorcycle flashing in and out of her line of sight in a mirror that was the size of her iPad's screen. Which reminded her — she hadn't checked her email since yesterday. She'd do it first chance.

"My place is on *Lubyanskiy proyezd.* It's a one-way street, so you have to —"

He smiled. "I know my way around."

CHAPTER 43

Moscow

Lara's apartment, three blocks from the Kitay-gorod metro stop, was on the fifth floor of a building that had been put up in the '50s to house minor party officials. In other words, the lift worked.

She prayed her tenant/roommate had gone to work today, hawking her lipsticks and eyeliners at the counter in TsUM, and that she hadn't left her stuff all over the bathroom the way she usually did, because Lara was looking forward to a nice long soak in the tub.

"Katrina! Trina, you here?"

The silence was wonderful. Lara made a quick visual survey of the place. A dishtowel was draped over the kitchen doorknob, the fern was dying from a lack of water, and the goldfish, Mr. Russky, was frantically splashing in his bowl close to the unopened jar of fish food. Next to it, her grandfather's prized Prussian helmet, booty from the First World War, was covered in dust. If Lara wasn't around to do it . . . Katrina couldn't cook, she couldn't sew, and she wouldn't clean. Or rather, she performed what Viktor called "Chechen battlefield housekeeping." She'd make some poor schnook the perfect post-Soviet wife.

Lara quickly fed the grateful Mr. Russky and looked around. A few pieces of mail — bills, apparently — had been left on the little half-moon table in the foyer. Her backup handbag was lying on its side next to the mail. She hadn't left it like that, had she? She strode into the bedroom, shrugging off her jacket and dropping it on the bed.

There was a brown wallet, a set of keys and some pocket change on the bedside table. Opening the wallet, she saw a laminated ID card for a Major Vassily Bondarenko. Under the name it read, "Commanding Officer, Sakhalin Island Garrison," but the clear, sharp picture grinning back at her was definitely that of her husband, Viktor.

Behind her she heard the bathroom door start to open. She turned and saw, walking into the bedroom and wearing only a bath towel, Russian Intelligence Officer and Hero of the War in Chechnya Viktor Nikolayevich

Maltsev.

He was drying his hair, not that it looked wet, with one of the hand towels and saying, "You've never seen that before, have you, Larashka?"

"What is it? Who's Bondarenko?"

"Nobody."

Lara sighed. "Is there anything about you that isn't a mystery?"

"My love for you." The man grinned, just like his picture. Thanks to the Army's free dentistry, his capped teeth were his best feature.

She sighed a bigger sigh. "What are you doing here, Viktor?"

"Is that any way to welcome your hero, home from the field of battle?"

"The battle of the sexes, you mean." She hated playing the bitchy wife, but he gave her no choice.

"Okay, I'll rephrase: Is this any way to welcome your husband, home from the wars?"

"Ex-husband, Viktor. Ex-husband."

He was rubbing his hair vigorously, so his words were somewhat muffled by the towel. "Not until I sign the papers. Till then, I'm all yours."

Lara had never noticed that thinning spot of his, right on top. How long had it been since she ran her fingers through his hair? "You were never all mine. That's why we're getting the divorce."

He dropped the crumpled hand towel. "*You're* getting the divorce. I like things just the way they are."

"I'll bet you do." She let herself drop down and sit on the edge of the bed. "Viktor, why are you here?"

He parked himself in the chair across from her. "I told you I had some leave coming, so I came. Thought I'd surprise you and let myself in. Then, when you didn't show up, I called your mobile a few times. But all I got was your recording. Let's see, what did I do next? Went through your old handbag, but it was empty. Listened to the calls on your landline's machine, and then . . ."

"You listened to *my* calls?"

"Yeah. Maybe one of them was from that Gerasimov guy you're seeing, and I could —"

"What? Call him back and threaten him?"

Viktor flashed that smile again. "I don't threaten to do stuff; I *do* stuff. No, I just wanted to ask him where you were. But then I heard a couple of messages from Pavel. Are you two having an —"

"Me and Pavel?" She wanted to laugh and cry, both. "No, we're not . . . having . . .

anything."

"He sure sounds jealous of you and that Grisha guy. Anyway, since I knew I had no way to get in touch with you, I guess I . . . dozed off."

She stood up again and walked around the bed, away from him. "I don't like you listening to my private calls. In fact, I hate it."

He shrugged. "Hey, I'm the head of Electronic Intelligence, that's what we do. Besides, this guy you're working for, Gerasimov, seems like one bad dude."

Lara picked up the crumpled hand towel from where he'd dropped it on the floor. She'd have to get a fresh one from the linen closet in the other bedroom. She started to move toward the bathroom hamper when Viktor took the towel from her hand and began smoothing it out. "It's just a little damp. Don't go tidying up on my account."

He put the towel on the towel bar. Immediately, Lara took it off the bar and dropped it in the hamper, saying, "I'm not drying myself with that. It's been on the floor."

She moved toward the door to Katrina's room and Viktor stopped her, grabbing her wrist. "Can't we try again, Larashka? Forget the towels, come to bed with me, I miss you." He was actually pulling her toward their bed.

Lara let herself think it over. For the life of her, she couldn't remember what she'd ever seen in him. She broke free of his grip. "I'm over missing you, Viktor. I want you to go."

With the officiousness of a chambermaid at the Ukraina, Lara pushed open the door to the far bedroom and strode over to the linen closet. She looked around. Her roommate never made her bed. She'd left all the bedding in a vast lump down the middle of the mattress. Better get out a set of sheets and pillowcases while she was at it.

Looking a little closer, Lara saw there was a bit of color amid the tousled sheets on the bed. A bit of khaki color. Lara gave a little tug, and she was holding Viktor's Army-issue boxer shorts.

"I was sleepy from the flight here, so I took a nap till you got home." He walked over and took the boxers, putting them on with the bath towel still around his waist.

Lara said, "Sleepy? Is that what you call it?" She was looking at a square inch of exposed female flesh where the boxers had been. Taking hold of the duvet cover, Lara pulled it and the tangle of sheets off the bed. There was Katrina, wearing nothing but a smile.

Not again. Not in her own flat.

Trina tried to pull the sheet up around herself, but it was caught under her. Her embarrassed giggle didn't go with the mood in the room. "Larashka, I won't insult your intelligence by saying it's not what you think."

Lara turned to leave the room and came back with Viktor's wallet. When she threw it at him, she missed his ear by a couple of centimeters. Damn. She said, "Viktor . . . Vassily . . . whatever your name is . . . you and Katrina have five minutes to clear out. That's what I think."

Retreating to the kitchen, she fixed herself tea with shaky hands. Just as the teapot whistled on the stove, she heard the apartment door slam behind the two of them. She sat down with her tea and cried.

.

CHAPTER 44

With the shock wearing off and the tear from her one working duct drying on her cheek, Lara knew, if she wanted those divorce papers signed, she was going to have to make up with Viktor. But not right now. Right now, she desperately needed a long hot soak.

At least the bathroom was reasonably presentable. She dropped the stopper in the drain and turned on the taps. Grabbing the mat from the towel bar, she spread it on the floor. On a shelf above the soap dish was her collection of American bath salts from the '40s, each a different floral scent in a colorful paper packet, like seeds. She reached for Lily-of-the-Valley.

Some cold warrior from Washington or New York must have brought them in to trade for — what? A drink? A meal? Information? Who gives away the location of a missile base for a bunch of bubble bath?

Black market collectible or not, Lara ripped open the packet and let the powder run out under the faucet.

Almost immediately, the strong, and strongly artificial, fragrance filled the air. While the tub was filling, Lara went and got her mobile. Letting her clothes fall to the tile floor, she carefully placed the phone on the wide flat edge of the tub. It was reckless, she knew; one false move on her part and it was checkmate, electronics. But she needed to be connected to the outside world.

As soon as she put it down, the phone rang. It was her brother. "Larashka!"

"Lev?"

"You were right! Someone did try to kill me, but I got him instead."

"Lev, what? How? Are you all right!? Where are you?"

"I'm fine, but you should see the other guy. I left him in the wildlife area where they've started drilling. Or rather, not drilling."

"Lev, slow down, I don't understand."

"I'm up near Prudhoe, calling you on a satellite phone. They're supposed to be drilling for oil, only they're not. That warning you got . . . it was for real. The guard here tried to kill me, almost did too. Look, I don't know how much more juice this baby still has, and I have to call around for an emergency room."

"I thought you said you were okay."

"I am, mostly. I'll get back to you first chance I get."

She put down the phone, not at all reassured by the call. The worst part of it was, there was nothing she could do.

CHAPTER 45

Milky-white bubbles threatened to flow over the top of the tub. The scent of chemical blossoms was now overwhelming. She turned off the water, shivers from Lev's close call still running up and down her spine, and lowered herself in. Keeping her hands out of the water, Lara summoned up the messages on her phone.

Pavel's calls were lined up in voicemail like planes at Sheremetyevo waiting to take off. He'd phoned her when she and Gerasimov were driving out to the dacha, and was going on about their next lunch not being so swanky.

His second message was different. "Larashka, I'm worried about what I got you into. I know you're up there at Gerasimov's place, with him and his kid. He's a bad guy, that Nikki.

"There's something else. Someone I know here at the Broadcast Center, someone who does, did, the weather — look, it's complicated. This isn't about me, it's bigger than that. I'll explain everything when I see you. Just this once, call me back."

Pavel's third voicemail was an angry outburst. "Did I embarrass you at the restaurant? Is that what this is? Are my hopes and dreams so pathetic that . . . Anyway, I told you this isn't about me: I'm sending you a text. If your parents' pain and suffering mean anything to you . . ."

Now she was alarmed. What did her mother and father have to do with anything? Pavel's fourth message, in its entirety, read: *itms://ax.itunes.apple.ru/WebObjects/MZStore .woa/wa/ViewVidPodcast?id= 120315179&ign -mscache= 1.*

She got up out of the water, wiped her wet hands on a towel, and picked up the phone. Carrying it across the bedroom and dripping on the carpet, she put it down and got her iPad from her bag. The she laboriously typed the entire text message from her relic of a phone into the iPad's Google search box. Almost immediately, the iTunes icon in the dock at the bottom of the screen activated itself and started bouncing up and down. Could Pavel possibly have wanted her to hear a song?

Lara carried the little computer into the

bathroom, setting it down where the phone had been. Slipping back into the still warm bath and touching the Play arrow — the advantage of having Wi-Fi all over the flat — Lara was startled to see a woman's face fill the entire screen. Stranger still, wasn't that Tatiana Ivanova, the woman from the flirt party?

"The following vodcast has been prepared for those members of the regional committees of the United Russia Party who have already indicated your support. If you are not a committee member, turn this video off and delete this file now. Unauthorized individuals will suffer the prescribed consequences."

The picture went to black and the word *Background* briefly came on before dissolving off again to reveal Tatiana, if that was her real name, standing in front of a map of the world.

"The European oil and natural gas 'monopoly' we currently enjoy drives our national economy. At the same time, unlike the West or the other large 'emerging' economies — those of China, India, Korea, etc. — we produce virtually no consumer goods that foreigners (i.e., Americans) wish to buy."

As she moved in front of the large map,

the camera followed her over to China. "Without export-quality flat-screen televisions, mobile phones, or cheap shirts and shoes, Russia's balance of trade and our economic well-being depend overwhelmingly upon this energy dominance."

The tall, confident woman now walked slowly east across the Pacific Ocean and the United States, stopping at the eastern seaboard. "And, because global energy markets are traded in dollars, events here on Wall Street and in Washington have enormous consequences in Moscow." The camera pushed in slightly on her. She held up a dollar bill and started to ball it up in her fist. "When the American dollar weakens, the way it did in the middle of the last decade, the price of oil goes up. From $55 a barrel back in 2006, it reached nearly $150 in 2008, tripling the value of Russia's vast oil reserves."

Like the TV weatherperson she was, Tatiana Ivanova gestured back at the American Midwest as if she were discussing a cold front. "Then, thanks to the American home mortgage debacle that raced across the country, it took only five months for the price of oil to plummet to under $35. Hedge fund traders who had 'parked' their dollars in energy raised cash by selling off their leveraged positions. That selloff weakened our central bank's ability to secure international credit lines.

"Thirty months later, the 'Arab Spring' uprisings of 2011 and the continuing conflicts in Libya, Egypt, and Syria increased instability in the region and enabled oil to recoup some of its losses." She paused and looked straight into the camera. "In hindsight, though, it is evident that no national economic planning can proceed when a country's assets are constantly in flux."

Lara was confused. What could this possibly have to do with anything? Her frustration with these Russians who don't or won't explain themselves made her want to scream.

Tatiana Ivanova started walking again, this time across the Atlantic and into Europe. "With energy so volatile, the Americans and their friends are making aggressive efforts to conserve and to find new/alternative energy sources. Consider: if every automobile on the world's roads had one of today's new induction engines, fuel consumption would come down by thirty-eight percent."

She pointed back the way she'd come. "On the other hand, the enormous quantity of new natural gas produced by fracking and wastewater disposal has led to more than

2,100 earthquakes in the midwestern state of Oklahoma alone. American environmentalists are fighting hard to end the practice. Still, the math is working against us here in Russia."

By this time, Lara's bath was lukewarm. She paused the — what had Tatiana called it? . . . the *vodcast* — so she could pull out the stopper and let some of the water drain away. The plug came out with a wet plop. After thirty seconds, when the water level had gone down far enough, she put the stopper back in and turned on the hot tap. She dried her hands on the towel hanging down from the bar, all the while wondering if Pavel had written down the wrong URL.

Deciding to suspend her disbelief, she turned off the faucet and, reaching over, un-paused the image. Almost immediately, a new title came on the screen: "The Current Geoclimatic Situation and the Opening it Presents."

Tatiana was back. "While the Americans (Al Gore in his movie, etc.) bemoan global warming or deny it, our best scientists predict that current worldwide warming trends will continue and even accelerate." The camera pulled back to show that she was now in front of a blow-up of Russia's northern frontier. "The receding polar ice has already — and will continue to — open sea lanes into and across the Arctic that have not been navigable for ten thousand years, giving us access to untapped energy resources under the Barents, Kara, Laptev, East Siberian, and Chukchi Seas, along with the ability to ship the oil and gas we recover to any existing pipeline."

What was that signature phrase of hers, from the forecasts she used to do on Channel One? Ah yes: "Let's set the map in motion." Tatiana was setting the Arctic in motion so it spun 360° around the Pole, showing the various countries bordering the Arctic Circle. She was saying, "Naturally, the same warming trend exists for the Canadians, the Americans in Alaska, the Danes in Greenland, and the other Scandanavians. They too will have freer access to their own previously ice-locked energy resources when they awaken to the possibilities. In all, we estimate as much as forty-five percent of the world's undiscovered oil and gas reserves lie under the polar ice, making the Arctic 'the next Saudi Arabia.' The nation that controls that oil will dominate the world's economy through the rest of the twenty-first century.

"Under existing law, The International Seabed Authority of the United Nations permits drilling for oil only within each nation's coastal waters, *unless it can be shown that a submerged geological feature extends past the '320-kilometer line.'*

"It is our scientists' belief that the Lomonosov Ridge" — she now used some kind of light pen to draw a large shape on the blue Arctic area — "extending from our waters into the Arctic Circle all the way to the North Pole, is precisely such a geological feature. If the ISA concurred, all natural resources (oil, gas, manganese nodules) lying under the ice between Russia and the Pole would be ours to exploit, denying the same resources to our Western competitors and guaranteeing our economic (and political) future.

"Sadly, despite the scientific and legal merits of our case, the Americans, the British, and their Canadian partners have opposed any Russian effort to claim the Arctic Ocean for ourselves." Her smile was rather cunning for a weatherperson. "We hesitate to use the term *Cold War* when discussing the Arctic, but when the next appeal is heard a year from now, the West can ask the International Seabed Authority to deny our application yet again. *And they have the votes to do it.*"

This time, when the title "Political Implications" came on, they didn't bother freezing the frame. The presenter was looking in the camera lens and saying, "Fortunately for us, the Americans now have a president who doesn't concede that global warming exists. Even better, he wishes to appear to the American people as the hero who, by unleashing 'free market forces,' single-handedly guarantees America's energy independence from foreign oil. Including *our* oil. His first act as president was to open a tract of wilderness in Alaska to commercial drilling. Eight months later, the oil — if it's there — is still in the ground."

She smiled. "I said it was fortunate for us that America has such a president. Even more fortunately, our own leader understands the challenge — and the opportunity — this new attitude presents.

"So, through back channels, he has made the US president the following offer in exchange for a reversal of their Seabed vote: With the help of our associates at Lukoil, we will covertly furnish the Americans, at no cost, with enough of our surplus petroleum to support the idea that they have found the largest oil field in history under their own Alaskan permafrost. We will paint a fleet of our oil tankers in American colors and dispatch it to Prudhoe Bay, ready to start pumping the oil into their pipeline. We will promise to continue to secretly ship the crude oil across Arctic waters to the Americans, gratis, through his four-year term in office, his reelection campaign and his second term . . . after which we will turn the faucet off."

The camera moved in as she lowered her voice. "And there's this dividend: once their oil 'discovery' lowers world prices for fossil fuels, there will be less incentive for Americans to conserve energy; and it will be harder for alternative sources of energy — wind, biofuels, geothermal — trying to compete. That in turn will increase the US reliance on burning their own oil and coal, providing jobs for the president's blue-collar base but befouling the air over American cities, where his opponents live. So our offer will effectively reinforce the partisan divide that already exists in the United States while it forecloses their ability to become truly energy-independent for decades, if not the entire century.

"In effect, we would be buying the American's reelection . . . so that we may control the supply the moment he's gone and dictate economic terms long into the future."

Lara pressed the Pause button once more.

Well, the woman sure wasn't working for Garry Kasparov, that much was certain. As Lara understood it, the Russians were proposing a classic sacrifice of material. Give up enough oil now — a knight or bishop's worth — to reap a King's ransom later: in other words, win the whole energy game.

She unfroze the screen. Tatiana's brow furrowed. "Ah, you say, what if the American President takes our free oil and then, a year from now, reneges on the deal at the UN? Not to worry: we are in the process of acquiring an 'insurance policy.' Should we obtain it — and we are confident we will — its release to the media would turn our people permanently against America and the West . . . as well as the pro-democracy types here at home, whom the Americans are so eager to back."

There was a new background to the video, a still shot of one of the opposition rallies in Red Square complete with all manner of signs and banners denouncing the Russian strongman. "Why are we going to such lengths to explain all this? Because, the minute the Americans announce their Alaskan 'discovery,' the law of supply and demand will drive down the price of oil on world markets and depress the Russian economy with it. This is the unavoidable cost of playing the long game — appear to lose now in order to win much more later. And, due to the confidential nature of our leader's plan, it means our internal enemies will be emboldened to try to bring down the government without our being able to respond publicly. You must not allow this to happen."

The image behind her changed once again, this time to the classic photograph of the president of the Russian Federation on horseback, shirtless and smiling.

"When and if it becomes necessary to ensure public order by imposing martial law, your supporting votes in the Presidium — in the face of what may prove to be strong, if uninformed opposition — will be crucial to bringing Russia back to the forefront of nations.

"Your consent to the entire plan we've just outlined is implicit in viewing this vodcast. Now, delete this file."

Lara lay there in a rapidly cooling tub, wreathed in white Lily-of-the-Valley bubbles as the video's implications sank in: The US and Russian leaders were planning to con the rest of the world into thinking they'd found new oil in Alaska? One of them was ready to sell his country's future to stay in power while the other was planning to ensure his continuance in office by using the state oil company Lukoil . . . while the Lukoil Professor of Geohistory stood idly by?

She rose so abruptly it set off a small tidal wave of soapy water that would have engulfed her iPad if she hadn't hurriedly snatched it up with slippery fingers and set it down almost as quickly in the sink.

She kept repeating the same four words to herself: "Over my dead body."

CHAPTER 46

Lara, her still-wet hair wrapped in a towel, sat down at the desk in her bedroom and tried to get past her anger so she could think. A fairly unsavory stranger hands her a half-dozen Dictaphone recordings and tells her there are clues in there that will lead her to a valuable book. Then a woman comes up to her and says she'll pay double for it.

The same woman, obviously working for the party in power, describes an under-the-table deal with the Americans, whose head of state is in town at this very moment — the man Lara will be sitting beside in twenty-four hours.

And the "insurance policy" that would turn the Russian people against the U.S. if their leader reneged on his end of the bargain? Might it not concern a hoax hidden in a four-hundred-year-old book? A hoax perpetrated on Hitler . . . that had the effect of devastating Russia instead of Britain and, possibly, America?

Then and there, Lara determined to do everything in her power to find the Bible, and put it in the right hands. Once she figured out whose hands those were.

This was a job for Larissa Mendelova Klimt, the online Sherlock Holmes. Picking up her iPad, she began by searching the German government's wartime archive with the keywords "prophecy" and "Nostradamus," and got exactly what she expected: nothing.

Lara tried again, using "Hitler + Bible." A half-dozen links all led to the same wrong thing, a crazy sort of replacement Bible the Nazis distributed during the war. "Honor thy Führer and master" was Commandment Number One. Not at all what Lara was after.

The archives of the various Allied powers came up blank, as well as more general searches on Google and Bing. By now it was late afternoon, her stomach was rumbling from a lack of food, and going through all the crackpot postings about Nostradamus on the Internet could take the rest of the day.

She leaned back in her chair and let her mind go blank. Himmler gives Hitler a heavy, leather-bound Bible swept up during the war by the Nazi art thieves. The Führer, occultist that he is, believes something written in it four centuries earlier is all about him, and that it foresees his coming triumph in the East. Does he toss it aside when he's read it? Or send it to some warehouse to be stacked with a thousand other tomes?

No. He keeps it nearby, possibly to open it and reassure himself of the prophecy whenever times get tough, like after Stalingrad. She looked over at the goldfish, Mr. Russky, swimming in his bowl, and asked him, "So why didn't the official sites, when they catalogued everything else they captured at war's end, have any record of it?"

Whatever the goldfish had to say was lost in her eureka moment: grandfather's German helmet on the other side of the fishbowl! The official archives weren't the whole story; private soldiers the world over picked up stuff and took it home.

Quickly she scrolled through the major military memorabilia sites. There were thousands of listings on germanmilitaria.ru, ww2collectibles.com, and the others, including hundreds of books. Some of them were Bibles carried in the war by various soldiers, but nothing remotely like what she was looking for. An hour of that and she was almost ready to quit again.

But Lara had one or two more tricks up her sleeve, Russian search engines that sometimes got stuff the others overlooked. Lara typed in her query on Yandex.ru, hit Return, and scanned the results. Nada. She did the same with Rambler.ru.

Halfway down the page came her first real hit. It was a link to eBay.de, the German-language auction site. When she clicked on http://cgi.ebay.de/ HitlerBibel, the slow-loading connection showed just the web-site's header at first. In German it said, "Great Deals on Hitler's Bible on eBay!"

The fully loaded page was better, exciting, but still a disappointment. It read, "Hitler's Personal Bible, item #Z280377684250. This listing has ended."

How do you see something that was bid on years ago? Viktor, a whiz at all things electronic, once showed her how to navigate the site when she'd gone on eBay to buy Mr. Russky his bowl. It was coming back to her. Clicking her mouse on the button labeled Advanced Search, she typed in the item number and scrolled down to Completed Listings.

Ta-da! The original 2006 listing page for Hitler's Bible appeared on the computer, with the description of a book posted by someone with the screen name WattsUp from Fort Myers in the U.S.

There were seven thumbnail photos across the bottom. Lara clicked on each one in turn, filling the screen. The first was of the cover, an old leather binding embossed in gold, taken straight on. The next was snapped from the side, showing how thick the book was. There were a couple of the centuries-old typeset pages, with crabbed handwriting in the margins that Lara recognized as Hitler's own, ending in the initials "A.H." A fifth picture showed a page penned in a kind of French poetry, and then another, this one typed on a separate sheet in German.

She moused over to the final image, a black-and-white snapshot of an American soldier in a Jeep with the Bavarian Alps looming far above, before going back to the German translation.

There they were, the same three stanzas of doggerel Coward had described, ending with, *"Into a cage of iron is the usurper drawn/ When the child of Germany overcomes him."*

Tseluyu! She scrolled back up to read the seller's description.

"My grandfather, Delmer Watts, was a corporal in the 506th Parachute Infantry. In the last week of World War II, his unit was looking for German Army holdouts in the village of Berchtesgaden when he banged on a door with his rifle and it fell off its hinges. Inside, he found a 400-foot-long tunnel of polished stone with an elevator going up inside Kehlstein Mountain to the 'Adlerhorst,' Hitler's 'Eagle's Nest.'

"The Airborne had fought their way up the face of the mountain the week before and they'd already taken the ceremonial swords and such. All that was left were a few things protected from the bombing and overlooked in a maintenance shaft behind the elevator. This Bible came home with Granddaddy. Now that he's gone, it can go home with you."

Excitedly, Lara dropped back down to the pictures and clicked on the one showing the original quatrains. She leaned in closer to the screen and peered at the image of the French writing. Was that a wormhole obliterating a couple of the letters? *Da!!*

Okay, now for the jackpot question: What happened to it?

The Bidding History button told her there had been eighteen bidders. The winner, at 1,902 euros, was a buyer called adler01, with the number 34 and a yellow star after it in parentheses.

Lara got up, took from her handbag one

of the *ponchiki* Cook had given her, and wolfed it down with the last sip of her lukewarm tea. Pacing around the room again, she stopped in front of the goldfish and asked, "What do you think, Mr. Russky? Is it someone named Adler? Or, *adler* being German for eagle, is 'eagle01' their screen name?"

The fish pondered the question and then swam away. Lara sighed. "You're right, there's no way to tell. Let's get some feedback."

She remembered Viktor's explanation. "Every time someone buys or sells something on eBay, the other party can leave feedback afterward for everyone to see. 'The seller sent me the thing I bought and it wasn't a fake.' Or, 'The buyer's check didn't bounce.' It's how the site builds trust in the whole cyber system of unseen buyers and sellers."

The screen now said, "View all feedback for adler01." What followed was a series of comments in German scrolling up the screen, like blurbs for a movie in a newspaper ad. "Great buyer, paid on time!" "Couldn't ask for more!" "Quick payer!" The most recent posting was a month ago.

Lara clicked the Leave Feedback button. Instead of a statement, she typed in a few questions for the unknown buyer. "Who are you? Where in the world do you live? Do you still have the Bible? Would you be willing to sell it?"

It had been years since the auction ended. Adler might not be checking out his feedback anymore. Still, that number and the yellow star after his name meant he'd done at least 34 transactions on the site. And if other eBay members were still posting blurbs about him as recently as a month ago . . .

"Nothing ventured, nothing gained," she told herself, clicking the Feedback button and posting her questions online. Then she gathered up her things for one more trip out to the Arkhiv and Noël Coward's big finale.

Four kilometers away, eyes fixed on another computer monitor widened as the keystrokes appeared on the screen. One of the watchers said, "She's asking some guy if he still has the book. Better tell the boss."

The second man said, "Before I do, hack into the German server and get me a current address for that adler01." He rubbed his massive neck and allowed himself a rare smile. "I told you this program would work."

CHAPTER 47

Obersalzberg, Germany

Ulrike Preisz felt things were finally looking up. After all the Sturm und Drang of going hat in hand with Horst to the Tourist Office, then to the blowhards on the local Council, then the Preservation people in München and back to Tourism in an endless tail-chasing of meetings and payoffs — only to have the European recession knock everyone for a loop — the place was finally nudging into the black.

It was absurd that politics should decide whether a restaurant succeeds or not, but of course the Kehlsteinhaus was no ordinary restaurant, sitting as it did on the very top of the mountain, with a fifty-mile, 360° view of Bavaria and nearby Austria. Ulrike and her husband, who'd taken over after the previous concessionaires' default, had made a few simple requests of their landlord, the Berchtesgaden Tourist Office: money for new tables and chairs, an automated window-washing system, a computer at the dining room workstation for entering the orders and one in the kitchen for receiving them, and, best of all, a website — so she and Horst wouldn't have to be on the phone all day booking tables and rooms in their *gasthaus* at the foot of the mountain.

The Tourist Office, packed with left-wing holdovers from the previous government, had dragged its feet on the improvements. The place had once been the Adlerhorst, Adolf Hitler's favorite wartime retreat, and the Socialists didn't want to appear to be subsidizing "Hitler's place," even after all these years.

But when the Merkel government's appointees finally gained a majority, the reconstituted Tourist Office had ponied up the money, with enough left over for Ulrike to redo the little alcove in the reception area into a proper gift shop, with wallpaper and new lighting, so she could get the books and postcards out of the dining room and bring her few pieces of Hitlerana out of mothballs.

It wasn't just the view that made people (especially foreigners) tramp through the tunnel to the elevator and come all the way up here. It was the history, Hitler's history, for better or worse. Worse, of course.

The dinner plate, the knife and fork he'd possibly used, the well-worn blotter and the gold fountain pen set had looked a little skimpy, sitting there on the table. They'd needed something to pull them all together.

Ulrike frowned, interrupting her reverie to pick up a napkin and clean an obvious fingerprint from one of the glasses Klaus had set out on Table 21. Klaus would have to go.

When Ulrike was growing up, Germany wouldn't have acknowledged there had ever been a Hitler, much less build a national Holocaust museum in the middle of the capital. Then came the great reversal, the acknowledgement of their country's shameful past. And with it, ironically, along with the dialogue on Hitler, genocide, and national guilt, came a market for the Nazis' possessions, thanks to German eBay.

She moved over to the computer by the door and clicked away from the Reservations page for the bookmarked site. Under the subhead *"Sammeln und Seltenes"* on eBay.de were 219 "rare and collectible" items. It was pretty much the same jumble sale as there had been the day she'd made her find: books about Hitler, some signed by the authors; wartime letters, with Hitler's picture on the stamps; a plate someone was claiming had come from the old *Reichs-kanzlei* in Berlin. What was she supposed to do with two mismatched plates? Now, if she had a service for eight, or even six, they could promote a special dinner "on Hitler's own china," providing the Tourist Office let them. Wouldn't that be amazing?

When she'd found it, under the heading "Hitler's Personal Bible," the thumbnail photo had been dark and hard to make out. Clicking on the listing, she'd found better pictures of a large, leather-bound book, the cover, and a few inner pages. One of the snapshots showed the flyleaf, inked with some old handwriting she couldn't make out. And the whole book was in Latin. Did Adolf Hitler know Latin? Somehow she didn't think so.

But the sheet of poetry stuck in the book — something about Barbarossa's sword — was in German and looked real enough. So did the "A.H." at the bottom of a couple of comments in its margins. The convincer, though, had been the block of text from the seller in Fort Myers in the USA. It read, "This Bible was 'liberated' by a U.S. Army officer in May, 1945, from the Adlerhorst, Hitler's wartime headquarters in the Bavarian mountains."

The Adlerhorst! Think of it . . . something

that old Adolf would have handled right in this room! By the time Ulrike had found the listing, people had already run the price up to 1350 euros.

She remembered going to the bidding page and wondering how many eyes all over the world were fixed on that auction just then, one with a picture of GIs in a Jeep staring up at the very place where Ulrike was sitting now?

Horst was out shopping, so she'd taken the chance without him and typed in a bid of 1501, with a maximum up to 1999. If someone in America was willing to pay more than $2500 dollars, they could have it. There were six bids in the final ten seconds of the auction before eBay's computer flashed her the "Congratulations! You Won!" message. Her winning bid turned out to be 1902 euros, almost the entire rainy day fund.

Now, by turning her head to the left, Ulrike could see her prize, set out with the other things on the table in the alcove just as you got off the elevator. Truth be told, it was the focal point of the place. When she looked back at the screen, she noticed the You Have Feedback link was highlighted, and she clicked on it. Someone in Russia was asking about the Bible. She smiled as she typed in her reply.

Yes, the Hitler angle had made all the difference.

CHAPTER 48

Moscow

This is the last of my six
cylinders and, fortunately for
you and your typists, Robert,
the finish line is in sight.

Lara looked at her watch; it was nearly six.
Her mind was all over the place. Concentrate on what Coward's saying, dammit.

By the middle of August, 1940,
the Battle of Britain had moved
inexorably — as you know — from
a few German strikes at our
Channel convoys to wholesale
bombing of our ports and airfields to "dogfights" (forgive the
vulgarism) in full view of the
population.
    In September, five weeks after

Anthony had let loose the hounds . . . all right, insects . . . I was telephoning him every day, some days more than once, to try to hurry things along.

The very afternoon that Blunt informed me the "simulacrum" was finished, I was told by Churchill's people I had ten minutes on the morrow, whilst they were setting up for a Cabinet meeting, to hand over my supposed "anniversary present" for Winston and Clemmie (though the actual event was weeks off). As I had already cast the remaining actor in our little farce, we were ready to beard the lion in his den.

I remember we were standing in an antechamber just off the vestibule in Downing Street, a little room with a table and four chairs, when the Prime Minister spotted me. A year earlier he was appointed Honorary Air Commodore for the County of Surrey auxiliary Air Force, and so was entitled to wear the

RAF uniform. Now, at five foot seven inches, the blue-grey cloth seemed to swaddle the Great Man in all directions.

He started right in. "Noël, are you here to entertain the Downing Street Brigade? How delightful." Then he spotted Blunt standing there, holding the Bible wrapped in brown paper with string round it. Shifting gears, he said, "Who's your friend, and is that something for me?"

I introduced Anthony, who wordlessly placed the parcel on the table in front of Winston with something of a thud. While his secretary stood against the wall, Churchill took the chair near the window and started working on the string. Acutely conscious, at six feet tall, of looming over the Prime Minister, I took the chair across from him. The secretary pursed his lips and glared at me; apparently one does not sit in the Buddha's presence. To compound matters, Blunt also took a seat because I had.

As the Bible emerged from the wrapping, I found myself trying to re-create the Kennedy boy's pitch to me that night in New York, being careful not to say the actual word "Kennedy," lest the mention of the American ambassador's name spoil everything. I don't know how much sense I was making, so I switched over to describing the manner in which we would plant the article where the Germans would be sure to find it.

"Sir, with your permission, an associate will take that parcel with him by boat over to Flanders under cover of darkness and, in the guise of someone they trust, present himself to the German checkpoint at Antwerp before making his way to a certain monastery we know their army of looters will visit, and leave it there in plain sight."

The PM looked up at Anthony, dubiously, and then over at me. "Is *he* your 'associate'?"

I had to laugh. "Not quite.

It's your godson, Ian."

Surprised, Churchill left off what he was doing to look me in the eye. "Why on earth would the Germans trust Ian Fleming? I'm not sure *I* trust him."

"Because, sir, I intend to have him show up in Antwerp as Sir Oswald Mosley."

"You say Ian will be behind enemy lines, dressed up as the leader of the British Union of Fascists?" He seemed troubled. "I don't know . . ."

"He's already agreed to do it, sir."

Churchill still appeared troubled. "Of his courage I have no doubt, but . . . there's a problem: Don't the Boche know Mosley's safely tucked up in Holloway Prison?"

"That's why I need you to release his wife, Diana, from the women's gaol. When Ian shows up with her, they'll have to believe he's Mosley and that he's been exchanged for British prisoners."

Churchill was still considering the thing when an aide ducked his head in the room and said, "We're ready for you, sir."

The leader of the armed forces of the British Empire and Commonwealth rose from his seat, so we stood as well. I thought he was going to leave without approving our plan, but he returned his attention to the Bible, now exposed to the air.

Anthony produced a pair of white cotton gloves from his jacket pocket and, still without a word, handed them to the PM. He was eyeing the French inscription Anthony had done. Pointing to the last quatrain, he said "There shouldn't be an 'e' at the end of *sabre au claire.* C'est un mot masculin, non?"

Oh my God, a spelling mistake! I was glaring my best glare at Anthony when the PM allowed himself a chuckle. "Well, I suppose they hadn't dictionaries back then. Possibly this Nostradamus you speak of couldn't spell any better in his language than we can in ours."

Ice broken. Winston was about to poke his little finger into the *punctatum*'s freshly chewed hole into the ink when Blunt uttered his only two words of the interview. His "No, don't!" was probably a little louder than absolutely necessary.

With a baleful look at the man, the Prime Minister picked up his "gift" and dropped it back into Anthony's grateful hands. Churchill's aide came back again. All he said was, "Sir" as he pointed to the watch on his wrist.

Winston looked me square in the eye. "Do it." He shook my hand as he walked through the door to the meeting. "Just don't let him get caught. Ian's the only godson I've got."

CHAPTER 49

Before I conclude my "testimony"
as to events of the late summer
of 1940, it occurs to me I've
neglected the most important
duty of a character witness —
for that is certainly what I am:
to attest to the nature of the
man standing in the dock.

Either I'm the worst possible
such witness or the best: I just
don't like Anthony Blunt. I
don't know anyone who does. So,
when I defend Anthony, it's
certainly not out of friend-
ship . . . he *has* no friends.
The man's insufferable, a prig
and a snob (and I should know).
I'm quite certain if we passed
in the street this afternoon, he
would keep on going without the
least sign of recognition.

But what I *do* know is, when our lads were up against it after Dunkirk, when we were all up against it, it was Anthony who saved our bacon. When the Croupier called, *"Les jeux sont fait,"* Anthony rolled up his sleeves and placed all his chips on the spin of the wheel. Even though he was a Soviet spy and we were sending all those tanks and planes against the workers' paradise.

You see, Anthony and his handlers believed that, with proper advance warning, Stalin and his generals would be ready for Hitler. That his five-million-man army would lie in wait for the Austrian paperhanger and deliver the knockout blow once he crossed the border. But Uncle Joe didn't believe them. He doesn't believe anyone . . . especially the people who work for him.

"Love of country" sounds dashed peculiar when one speaks of an admitted spy. So I'll just say this: four years ago, he and I and the others who helped us accomplished something no battalion or even division could have done. My proof? That the jackboot has not yet trod this earth, this realm, this England.

Now, with apologies to Mr. Shakespeare, I end my tale with a bit about how we planted the Bible where the Hun would find it. And here I wish to make a request: do not allow anyone but yourself to listen to what I'm about to read into the record; dismiss the typists for the afternoon. A woman's reputation, such as it is, is at stake, and I would not want this part read out in open court or gossiped about in the Ladies' Room.

Ian Fleming, Peter's brother and the "fill-in" at table for Marlene's party that evening in 1939, is, as you know, serving in Naval Intelligence with the rank of Commander. He heads up a little group called 30 Assault Unit, a band of what they're calling "commandos" these days. When I was writing *In Which We*

Serve, I thought I might use Ian's bit of stealth as one of the officers' flashbacks whilst the men from the torpedoed ship were in the water, so I prevailed upon him to set down in detail those first few days of September 1940. Here is what he sent me:

"Noël, for several weeks after I agreed to pass as Oswald Mosley, I began cultivating a moustache like his. Now, the day before departure, I darkened my hair with dye, brilliantined it, and brushed it straight back instead of giving it my usual part. We had the passport chaps take a few snaps and do their usual magic with stamps and visas and lo! — I was now Sir Oswald, fresh out of Holloway.

"At least I was a fair enough approximation of the man — about the same height and weight — that I might hope to pass under the eyes of some functionary at the Wehrmacht checkpoint. Especially if I should have Lady Mosley with me in the flesh.

"What did they call her in the

papers when the bastard was courting her? 'Diana, Goddess of the Chase.' But a black-and-white photo fails her . . . the blond hair, the small, rosebud mouth, and those eyes, the colour of perfect star sapphires.

"Of course she refused to do it at first. I mean, the woman is every bit the Fascist her husband is; married in the home of Joseph Goebbels, weren't they? With Hitler in the wedding party! But she *had* to be my *laissez-passer* through the German lines so, as you suggested, I told her we'd hang Mosley if she didn't go along. Winston would have done it too.

"Anyway, once we *did* get through German security at Antwerp, it took us three days to make our way down to the Ardennes, doubling back every so often to make sure we weren't followed and staying each night in some out-of-the-way *auberge*. I insisted Diana keep up the pretense of my being Mosley, acting affectionate during the day and sharing rooms with only one bed at night.

"Speaking man to man, she adjusted quite well to the part. She was trapped and she knew it. Another thing we both knew: Diana was no debutante. She'd left her first husband in the lurch to take up with Mosley. And she'd spent the last two months in prison. Sorry, Noël, if I'm being rather indelicate, but you asked how it really was, didn't you?

"I was thinking, afterward, standing there in the clearing amid the towering birches and pines with the monastery behind me and the moon overhead, a man could make a very nice life for himself in wartime, provided he wasn't actually killed. There was, first and foremost, the adrenaline rush of the operation itself, the release that a few minutes or hours brought after long, boring days and weeks of planning and rehearsal. Almost as good as sex.

"Speaking of which, I'd brought a perfume sprayer with me, filled with Blunt's age-old dust and dust mites, that I'd sprayed all over the place — the books, the shelves, but mainly on myself. I began to have this fit of sneezing standing there in the clearing, loud enough to wake the old boys just up the road. Diana was very good about using her hands to work the dust off my monkish robe. And then under my robe, where I don't think there *was* any dust.

"It was quite dark under the trees, and I have this mental picture of her, later, shaking two cigs out of her box of Benson & Hedges. She lit the match and, when we put our heads together for the flame, it came back to me again how amazingly beautiful she is.

"Exhaling, she blew out the match, casting us both back into darkness, and we stood there smoking in the night, the glowing tip of Diana's cigarette barely coming up to my chest.

Now that the job was over, I was thinking of the name you once called me. "Shamateur," remember? I can't shoot straight or operate a wireless set but I get to run my own operations behind enemy lines because I'm the PM's fair-haired boy.

"You were right too: You don't get to pluck the wife of 'Britain's most dangerous man' out of gaol so you can travel incognito with her on his passport unless Winston Churchill gives you the high sign.

"In my own defense, this whole business — Dietrich to the American to you to Blunt to Winston to me — none of it would have been worth a farthing if I hadn't been the perfect one to take the ball, the winger who cut back inside when they weren't expecting it and went in, untouched, for the try.

"So I'm asking you now, Noël, to think of me not as a 'shamateur' but as a true English amateur, a lover of the game. I believe I've earned it."

There you have it, Robert old man. As I watch your man Nigel prepare to put this final cylinder in the valise and lock the whole business onto his wrist for the long journey home, I'm at a loss over what to make of it — several magical California evenings wasted, so I might help you defend a man who would cut me dead in the street.

Ah well, what do they say? "Bedfellows make strange politics." Or is it the other way round?

CHAPTER 50

It had been a long day and it was only going to get longer. The G20 session had gone well, everyone said so. Now he just had time to take a quick shave and get ready for the state dinner. The protocol officer had carefully instructed him to toast the Russians every time they toasted him, tit for tat. Did that go for the French, too?

The call came in on his wife's Samsung Galaxy. No surprise; he'd thrown his own phone against the wall and the backup governmental one with the scrambled lines was next door with his chief of staff. He walked over to where she was reading the *Wall Street Journal* and took the call.

"Carl! What's up?"

He listened for about thirty seconds before saying, "Carl, two things. One, it's your problem. Two, you're fired."

When he handed the phone back, she gave him the one raised eyebrow thing. He said,

"Anger management in action: If I threw yours too, how would I tweet?"

CHAPTER 51

An hour later, on the other side of Red Square from her flat, Lara was standing before the lemon-yellow façade of the Moscow Botvinnik Chess Club, familiarly known as the Central House of Chess. In the 1920s it housed Russia's Supreme Court; now a few aging kibitzers lounged on the raised bench, gazing down and judging the play. Strange, the places you go to have questions answered.

In the '50s, back in Botvinnik's day, the House of Chess would have been packed to the rafters to watch a world champion play. Or tie his shoes, for that matter. Even an ex-champion like Garry Kasparov. Chess then was a Russian obsession.

Lara remembered the Russian Girls semifinal she played here. It wasn't her home club, so she'd been given the side of the table closer to the door. The place was so full of patzers and gawkers, every newcomer who arrived pushed the crowd more tightly up against her back. She distinctly remembered going for a quick mate so she could get away from the guy with greasy, unwashed hair, leaning over her shoulder and whispering dumb moves into her ear.

Today, what with kids playing video games and texting all day, Russian chess is in such a sorry state the current world champion is Norwegian. Imagine. This all-comers match tonight against the retired fifteen-time champ was, sadly, just one more proof of the game's decay. Twenty-two players were arrayed in a circle, and the only people pressing up against the challengers' backs were one or two of the younger girlfriends.

Kasparov was in the middle of the circle, still going on about Russia's need for closer economic ties with the U.S. to his captive audience of uncaring pawn pushers. Lara congratulated herself on missing most of his speech. When The Other Russia's motley group of parties had been unable to agree on a Presidential candidate, it had rendered them irrelevant on the political landscape, Kasparov the most irrelevant of them all. But that didn't keep him from bloviating.

Lara's hundred-ruble entrance fee entitled her to stash her stuff in a cubbie and take down a shopworn set from the shelf by the door, under the *"net mobilnykh"* reminder. She dutifully turned off her mobile and passed by the jumble of clocks on a table; these games wouldn't be timed.

Kasparov finished his talk to a smattering of applause. Waiting for the matches to start, Lara fingered a rook where one of the little turrets on top had broken off the castle. In public, in private, Russia was decline and fall everywhere you looked.

Garry was older than she remembered, of course, with gray mixed into his thick black hair. To make it just that much harder on himself, he was playing Black on every board, so he would be dealing with twenty-two opening moves from twenty-two eager beavers. Even so, when the bell rang, he took no more than five seconds to size up a board and push a piece ahead before taking three steps to his right and repeating the process. The twenty-two of them were like twenty-two roses and he was the only bee, going flower to flower.

She needed to do something unorthodox to get his attention, so Lara moved her knight forward. He was across from her now. Without looking up he moved his queen's pawn up one space. Then he was gone to deal with the pimply boy on her left.

If you simply tried to defend against a great player, you'd be sliced to ribbons. *L'audace, l'audace, toujours l'audace.* Lara wanted to open up the center before she lost the advantage of playing White, and brought her own pawn out. The situation called for a flanking maneuver, a discovered check, anything to make him think a little about this game, this opponent.

By his eighth circuit of the boards, he'd already mated over half the players. With fewer competitors, he was coming around faster, leaving her barely enough time to plot a move. Here he was again. He looked at the Botvinnik Fork she was lining up and said, eyes still on the board, "Haven't we played before? I remember your hands."

"Yes, we played when my hands and I were a lot younger."

He stopped and looked up. "You beat me that time, didn't you? With the same fork." Without waiting for her to answer, he interposed his bishop.

Five more players on the next go-round conceded defeat, either toppling over their king or reaching out for a handshake. Kasparov was practically running around the circle now that there were just the four of them left.

Lara had seen his bishop coming. She

abandoned the fork and, instead, took the exposed pawn, the one the bishop had been defending, en passant. This nicely opened up the long defile for her own bishop.

She looked around the circle. One of the players on the far side was up and walking away from his board in defeat. Sore loser. The other guy on that side looked for several minutes at his position and finally stuck out his hand.

And then there were two: the history prof and the kid with the pimples who couldn't be more than fifteen, sitting next to her. The other players and onlookers were now congregating behind them five deep. One was even standing a little too close. Just like old times! She looked over at the kid's board. He had a nice modified Caro-Kann going. Would he castle now and bring his rook into play?

She hadn't noticed Kasparov standing in front of her board, studying it. He startled her by saying, "I like your inventiveness," before moving his queen out, threatening a number of nasty possibilities.

She put her hand on her queen's bishop. Moving it she said, "There's something I want to ask you."

His face took on a quizzical expression. In the old Soviet days, when there were no rock stars, starry-eyed nymphets propositioned chess champions all the time. Now there was no Soviet, and she was no nymphet. He looked down and moved his other bishop forward, offering to exchange pieces. It was a simplifying move for both of them. Without speaking, he sidled over to the boy.

The teenager *had* castled. The great Garry Kasparov took his time before moving his king away from the square threatened by his opponent's newly emboldened rook. Then he stepped back to Lara.

She waited for him to refocus on the board before taking his bishop. She too desired a simplifying move. He smiled a little and said, "So ask."

She could feel the other forty people in the room press forward in anticipation. What did this woman with the Asian eyes want from the celebrity? To have her picture taken with him? Something more? Her question was not what they expected. "What would you pay to get your hands on the Bible?"

Kasparov raised a bushy eyebrow before taking her bishop. Then, without replying, he moved to his right, where the whiz kid had him in a pickle, having developed a nice three-pawns-to-two thing on the left-hand side. Lara looked back to her own board.

She could retake his piece with her queen, the way he wanted her to. But she could look down the road and see only bad things if she did. Or she could do the spectacularly flamboyant thing and sacrifice her queen right now, giving him an enormous edge in material but denying him the tempo he needed for his attack. It might just be her winning line.

He was back. After a silent minute that they both spent studying the position in front of them, he said, still looking down, "This Bible you speak of. If I have to bid for it, Larissa Mendelova, then you're not your father's daughter."

Lara sat there and studied the man's face. Nothing in the room was moving — not the pieces, not the players, not even the onlookers. But tumblers were turning in her mind, over and over, back and forth. And then a mental something dropped into place, one tiny cog in a much larger mechanism, and Lara knew what she had to do.

She reached out her hand and took Kasparov's chess piece with her queen, the move he wanted her to make. It would be over soon. Let the kid be the last man standing. Or sitting. She had things to do.

CHAPTER 52

Obersalzberg

Ulrike Preisz had a sixth sense about people and desserts. Which customers would order straight off the menu and which ones had to be coaxed with the rolling trolley brimming with the *Sacher tortes* and *apfel kugels* and all the pastries *mit schlag.*

The two businessmen at Table 23, closest to the entrance, would need the cart. Not the musclebound fellow whose clothes were straining at every seam; he looked like he carried a fork and napkin around with him in a jacket pocket. No, the other one, tall and bony; he'd just have coffee if Ulrike didn't bestir herself soon into a little tableside selling. No wonder the previous leaseholders hadn't made a go of it. You couldn't just sit up here and let the scenery do all the work. Always be selling.

The proprietor scanned the room. Nineteen tables occupied on a Thursday! You

313

couldn't tell her Hitler didn't sell. The heavy one was still going at it, working the last of the veal off the bone. The one with him, Mr. Johnson, appetite long gone, was looking at his watch. Better get the trolley from Inge.

Chernuchin knew the hostess had been looking at him. At them. Was she suspicious? Out of the corner of his eye he watched her tap a young waitress on the shoulder and take the rolling dessert wagon from her. He looked at his watch and thought, two more minutes. What did it matter if she *was* suspicious? What could she do?

If the next 120 seconds went as scheduled, they'd write this one up in a training manual some day; a book, even. That is, if the KGB ever started up again as an aboveground organization. Step One: Drop malware, literally, into a motherboard to locate a desired object. Step Two: Snatch that heavy object while it was on display in a public place, when the only escape route is a single elevator leading to a long tunnel inside a mountain. Added Difficulties: do it speaking another language in another country, with less than half a day to organize, execute, and escape. Ha! It would take the CIA two weeks, minimum.

He looked at the dessert menu, but his

mind wasn't on all the heavy pastry. In fact, he was full up to here. His stomach was definitely upset from all the flying and the time zones. They'd hardly unpacked after London before being shoved back onto the flight to Munich. No time to plan, just adapt something you've done before and slide down the pole into your boots like firemen.

Still, he had to admit there was real satisfaction when a plan came together, even one as straightforward as Find the Tins, Grab the Tins, Follow Where the Tins (and the Professor) Ultimately Led.

He looked over at Suslov, the bottomless pit. Two old farts they were, one tall and one wide. He chuckled to himself: what if the positions were reversed and they were the ones down there in the valley, while Alexei and his flamethrower was up here in the Kehlsteinhaus dining room . . . Alexei, whose thing for pretty girls was exceeded only by his love of guns and high explosives? By now, fifty innocent people would be fried to a crisp. No, better the sane ones are up here. He chuckled again.

Without looking up from the worried-over veal bone, Suslov said, "Care to share the joke?"

"I was just thinking of the kid. Like a bull

in a china shop."

Suslov gave him one of his looks. "There are no china shops anymore. Everything's online."

"It's an expression."

The woman who had seated them now glided over to the table with a cart full of fattening German sweets. She said, "How was everything?"

They made the appropriate noises, so she went on. "And for dessert? What may I get for you gentlemen?"

Chernuchin, trapped, was about to order the strudel, not that he'd have to eat it, when Suslov said, "I'll have the cookies."

The woman was puzzled. "Cookies? We don't —"

Suslov said, "It was the cookies that brought us here. Isn't that right, Mr. Black?"

Chernuchin gave him a withering look, a flamethrower look, and said to the frowning woman, "My colleague will have the apple strudel, as will I," even as the last five seconds were ticking off his watch.

Boom!

The detonation of the first old truck going off in the valley far below reverberated all the way up the mountain. Had bright boy used too much kerosene?

Another crash, louder, as the second, big-

316

ger truck exploded, sending metal fragments thirty feet into the air.

The third one, a farmer's hay wagon, seemed muffled in comparison with the first two, though the wooden bed of the wagon did a spectacular cartwheel, sailing off in one piece even as the next two trucks were going off.

Boom! Boom!

Each new explosion rattled the dishes and the glasses on the tables and over the bar. By now everyone — the diners, the wait-staff, even the host who doubled as bar-tender (was he adler01?) — had jumped up from the tables and had their faces plastered against the panoramic windows, looking at the precisely spaced fires in the farmers' fields down on the floor of the valley.

Boom! By the sixth explosion, halfway through Alexei's handiwork, Chernuchin and Suslov were already in the entrance alcove on the opposite side of the restaurant from the windows, with the elevator doors open. The kid had sent the cab up to the restaurant level when he'd disarmed the elevator's call button down below.

The big cowhide-covered book was now in the sack, the one Chernuchin had kept hidden under his jacket during the meal.

The doors closed and they were on the way down.

"What was that crap about cookies?"

Suslov let the heavy sack lean against a corner of the elevator. "Just having some fun. You remember fun, don't you?" Suslov straightened the lapels on his jacket and shot his cuffs, the way he always did. "Computer cookies, get it? The ones on the eBay site that remember your name and password, the ones that led us right to adler01. If you were the least bit tech-savvy, you'd be laughing your ass off."

Chernuchin didn't think so. Jeopardizing a job never struck him as humorous. "And *you're* Mr. Black. I'm Mr. Johnson."

"Yeah right, the Russian Mr. Johnson. To be honest, I was thinking of calling you Mr. Pink. Spice things up with a little Quentin Tarantino."

Chernuchin was doing a slow burn, matching the maddeningly slow pace of the elevator down the inside of the mountain. Of course, the slowness was the beauty of the thing. It would be just as slow going back up, so no one would be following them for at least ten minutes. Certainly not the cops, who were at that moment still rushing to the scene with the volunteers of the *Feuerwehr* to help put out a burning neck-

318

lace of a dozen car fires. Would the police be on to them fast enough to stop a tour bus that had been parked at the base of the mountain along with a half-dozen others, a bus with three drivers going out for a beer while their tourists were having dessert? Hardly.

He looked over at Suslov, with his bullet head and his impossibly large neck distorting his shirt collar. "If anyone is Mr. Pink, it's you."

CHAPTER 53

Prudhoe, Alaska

Discharged bright and early from America's northernmost medical facility, Lev Klimt hobbled outside in his walking boot and lit up his first cigarette of the day. A confirmed night owl, he needed the hit to get himself going. And then he remembered Craig and why he'd come up here. The pictures! He took out his recharged phone and was scrolling down to Lara's name when the dark green Land Rover pulled up to the curb.

Uh oh.

He barely had time to attach the material and hit Send before the first guy to reach him took away the phone.

CHAPTER 54

Moscow

All those mental tumblers tumbling, but still the vault door wouldn't budge. If Tatiana the Weather Girl wasn't working for Kasparov, she must be playing the Black pieces for The Powers That Be. But then, who was the red-headed kid, Alexei — the one with the tattoos and the muddy shoes who'd given her the recordings — playing for? Kasparov? He obviously knew about the Bible.

Lara sat down on the broad granite steps of the House of Chess and pulled out her trusty iPad. She'd let her brain stew over that one while she quickly caught up on her mail.

The most recent message was from Lev, except there was no message at all, just a bunch of attachments. Pictures of an oil field, and others of an abandoned carnival somewhere, all empty tents and stuff. She'd have to call her brother later and find out what the story was.

The next thing down was a three-hour-old reply from adler01, who turned out to be a German restaurateur named Ulrike Preisz. The news was decidedly mixed: Yes, we still have Hitler's Bible here at the Kellsteinhaus in Bavaria, but no, we have no thought of selling, as it's "an integral part of our presentation." Sure enough, when Lara Googled "Kellsteinhaus," the first thing visitors saw on the restaurant's virtual tour was the Bible in its place of honor in the foyer.

With a sigh, Lara headed for the Metro. There was still the little matter of a conspiracy to control the world's energy, and therefore the world.

Half an hour later, Lara was walking up the steps from the Kitay-gorod stop. At Moscow's latitude the sun, having dropped below the horizon, still managed to illuminate the late summer sky above her head with two hours to go to midnight. So, a block from home, Lara was easily able to see the extra-long, late '90s Russian Army cargo van, the insignia inexpertly painted over and the rear doors wide open: Viktor's.

And there was Viktor coming out of their building, several jackets on hangers in one hand and their living room floor lamp in the other. Their floor lamp. His and hers.

Gerasimov, Kasparov, an antique Bible, and all the carefully worked-out plans tumbling around in her brain were replaced by the latest image, of Katrina, leaving the building with her own rolling suitcase, the one she'd originally shown up with, and handing it to Viktor, who put it in the truck. So that's how it was.

There was no light or crosswalk, so Lara had to wait for a break in the four lanes of traffic. Viktor and his new girlfriend — Lara's behind-in-the-rent tenant — were back in the building by the time she made it across.

Lara looked inside the open rear doors. They worked fast. Her floor lamp and the carved wooden wall clock . . . the one she'd haggled over that time at the Izmailovo flea market . . . were already stowed in the old van's cargo area. He was taking everything. She closed the truck's doors, hurried around to the driver's side and looked in. Damn, no keys. Okay, she'd wait.

It wasn't that comfortable leaning with her back against the rear doors, blocking them. The handles met in the middle of her spine. She tried just standing in front of the doors, but after five minutes that was uncomfortable too. To make matters worse, it was starting to rain.

Then Viktor and Katrina appeared again, carrying his old Army footlocker between them. He was facing the street and saw her first. In his surprise he dropped his end of the trunk. "Lara, what do you think you're doing? Stopping us?"

Katrina let go of her end, and the footlocker dropped with a thump.

Lara didn't budge. "What do you think *you're* doing . . . with my stuff?"

"Our stuff."

"Okay, our stuff. Not yours. Ours."

Katrina wasn't saying anything. She just stood there with her mouth hanging open.

Viktor marched up to Lara. Was he going to hit her? She flinched, but he was reaching around her, trying to open the truck doors. Lara pressed back against his hands, pinning them.

Viktor said, "I'm taking half of *our* stuff and all of *my* stuff to Trina's new place; she found a studio right near the store. I thought you'd be happy we were going." With that he walked deliberately back to Katrina and picked up his end of the trunk, motioning for her to do the same.

They came toward her and stepped down into the street. At a signal from him, they dropped the trunk an inch from the toes of her shoes. Now Lara was pinned.

Gerasimov's Alfa Romeo chose that moment to pull up behind Katrina, boxing everyone into a two-meter space between the vehicles. He approached the group on the run. "Is there a problem, Lara?"

It was Katrina who spoke first. "Who the hell are you, gorgeous?"

Gerasimov acted as if he didn't hear. "You must be Viktor Maltsev, the about-to-be-ex-husband."

Army officer Viktor Maltsev stepped up to go chest to chest with the taller broadcast executive. It was no contest; Viktor's chest won. "So this is the *druga*," he sneered, dragging out the first syllable of *boy* friend.

Still backed against the van, Lara asked, "Grigoriy, what *are* you doing here?"

"I've been calling you about tomorrow. When you didn't pick up, I thought something might be wrong. So here I am."

"I was in the Metro."

Ignoring the intruder, Viktor turned back to his wife. "Lara, step out of the way."

"Why should I?"

"Because I'm doing what you asked me to. I'm taking my woman and going."

That last bit was too much. "*Your* woman? You're still married to me."

Viktor reached for something in his jacket pocket. "No, I'm not. Here, I signed it." He threw the divorce decree at her.

Lara sat down heavily on the footlocker, the breath knocked out of her a little.

Viktor sneered. "Oh wait, here they come, the one-eyed tears."

"Stop it, both of you!" It was Katrina, who was in the process of dropping down onto the trunk alongside Lara. "I want to be with Viktor, Lara, and you don't. And unless I miss my guess," she nodded toward Gerasimov, "you want to be with Ivanhoe here. Can't we do this like adults instead of fighting in the street?"

She was right, of course. But fighting in the street felt a lot better.

CHAPTER 55

The floor lamp was back in its place next to the couch. The clock was back on the nail in the wall. Viktor was packing the last of the things from his side of the dresser in an Army duffel bag and giving the stink eye to Gerasimov, who was booting up the iPad borrowed from Lara.

Katrina had tuned out. Instead, she was watching the week's last contestant on *Fabrika Zvezd,* Russia's *Star Factory* — a talent show that was a lot like the American show, *The Voice* — when she interrupted the staring contest to ask Gerasimov, "As the Director of Broadcasting, do you approve everything before it goes on the air? Do you already know who'll win tonight's *Factory*?"

Grateful to stretch his legs, Gerasimov got up and walked toward the kitchen. "I only see the work we produce ourselves, not the other stuff." He took the carafe of coffee Katrina had just burned and started filling the four cups set out on a tray. "*Fabrika*'s a live show; it's this Conception Day thing that takes all the work ahead of time."

Now that he was on his feet, Lara could look over and see what he was working on: her iPad screen showed the log-in box for the Conception Day extravaganza set to air tomorrow night.

At the dacha he'd told her how teams of video artists, music directors and sound mixers labored for much of the summer to supply the recorded content for the three-hour show. And that, as each segment was finished, it was posted online at a password-protected site so the various bigwigs could sign off or suggest changes wherever they happened to be around the city or country. Gerasimov, as the boss, had the final okay. "It's one of the reasons they gave me such a nice media room," he'd said.

Having handed out the coffees, Gerasimov sat down again at the iPad, inputting his ID and password on the keyboard. Viktor commented, "*Romantika* and then *Deti.* Very good."

Gerasimov frowned. "You're not supposed to see the show's password."

Viktor ignored him. " 'Romance' followed by 'Babies'. Someone at your place has a sense of humor."

All Gerasimov said was, "Thank you."

For years, the world's biggest light show has been the one mounted by Russian leaders every May 9 on Victory Day, marking the end of the Great Patriotic War in 1945. Swathing the four palaces and an equal number of cathedrals that make up the northeast façade of the Kremlin in a dazzling display of colored floodlights and projected images to the music of the great Russian composers, the show — paid for and coordinated by the government through Gosteleradio, which broadcasts it live to every viewing device in the country — is usually the most-watched TV event of any year.

With the growing popularity of Conception Day and the state's interest in promoting population growth, a second annual son et lumière event was inaugurated. Lacking the military parades, Air Force flyovers and other trappings of Victory Day, the organizers determined that this new production would be even larger and more spectacular, inviting celebrities to intone selected texts and dignitaries from around the world to join the celebration, including — this year — America's new president and other world leaders. And maybe, just maybe, it would give the protesters in the streets something else to do.

Ballet legend Mikhail Baryshnikov would be leading off the evening, reading his favorite poem about — what else? — a pair of dancing lovers. Gerasimov pressed Play on the computer and Baryshnikov's still picture came up. The Broadcast Director fast-forwarded through the five minutes of airtime the ballet star would get.

Next there was the now-completed montage of scenes from the career of torch singer Alla Pugachova, including the image Lara saw at the dacha. She'd sold as many records, all love songs, as the Beatles ever did, though not many recently. The images from her life and career would accompany her singing "Dreams of Love" and "Million Roses."

Viktor glanced at Gerasimov. "Pugachova? I thought she was dead."

Gerasimov shrugged. "It wouldn't be Conception Day without her."

Next came the section a team of young artists had been struggling to get done, a series of psychedelic images set to Stravinsky's *Firebird Suite* that would play as fireworks filled the night sky over Moscow. Gerasimov murmured to himself, "Better. Much better this way."

Lara, sitting apart from the others, was

letting her coffee get cold. She was worried about a dozen things at once. Was Lev all right? What about those photos he'd sent? And what about the kid with the red hair and muddy shoes? And Tatiana Ivanova, the weather lady on the video? And Viktor and her divorce . . . how did she feel about that, now that she finally was free? And back to Lev, was he all right?

"Oh, look at this! It's the thing you're doing tomorrow morning!" On TV, *Fabrika Zvezd* was over and Channel One had moved on to the news. Katrina swiveled the little television on the counter so the others could see it.

They were showing stock footage of schoolchildren in class, with the now-familiar image of the smiling US president juxtaposed next to them in a split screen. Trina dialed up the sound. The anchorwoman was saying, ". . . an online press conference, in effect, for five million students, after which the American leader will meet with ours."

"That reminds me," Gerasimov said, "I'll have to pick you up early."

The anchorwoman had moved on. "In a fitting touch, we're told the Americans' visit has been extended a few hours so the president can attend the Conception Night light show tomorrow evening at the Kremlin along with other leaders of the G20. Fitting, because he's also the father of five. In other news . . ."

The image was now a string of evenly placed fires glowing in the night as firemen played their hoses over them. "In Berchtesgaden, Germany, a string of car and truck fires apparently was started to distract authorities from the theft of memorabilia from Adolf Hitler's wartime headquarters. An old book with Hitler's initials in it was stolen from the restaurant that now sits on the site. The book, a Bible, is valued at 2000 euros."

Lara stared at the screen. "*Bozhe moi!* Oh my God! That's the thing I was looking for all week — Hitler's Bible!"

"What are you saying?" Viktor got up. "That you were trying to find something . . . a Bible . . . that just got stolen?"

"Yes, exactly. I just can't believe the coincidence."

"Was it valuable? I mean, to a private collector? More valuable than they say?"

The screen was showing a gilded plate and a pen-and-pencil set on a table with an empty space between them. Then the scene cut to a view looking from the valley below back up to the restaurant. It was eerily similar to the one she'd seen on the eBay page.

"Not the book itself. What's written inside. Someone offered me two million rubles to find the thing."

"Really? Wow!" Touching the iPad lying on the table, Viktor asked, "This computer of yours . . . have you been sending emails from it?"

"A couple. And feedback to a guy on eBay."

Without asking Gerasimov's permission, Viktor closed out the Conception Night file. Then he began typing on the iPad's virtual keyboard like a madman.

Lara said, "Do you know what you're doing, Viktor?" She didn't mean it as a put-down, but that's how it came out.

He didn't look up. "You said you don't believe in coincidence. Neither do I."

He kept entering things on the keyboard, pulling down various windows and opening files on the operating system even as he replied to her question. "I'm an intelligence officer, a pretty good one, actually. In the twenty-first century, nobody passes little pieces of paper around with codes written on them, or gives up state secrets in bed." Viktor looked up briefly at the two women, one his ex-wife and one his new lover, and added, "Of course, we still try."

He entered another something, continuing his thought. "These days we run electronic intelligence sweeps, hunt for cyberterrorists, that sort of thing." He stopped and peered at the screen. "Okay, there's your problem."

The three others looked at him, uncomprehendingly. Gerasimov asked, "Do you mean it's okay, or that there's a problem?"

Instead of answering, her ex swiveled to face Lara. "You have a key-logger."

Katrina said, "Is that bad?"

"Well, if you want the bad guys to know everything you've entered on this computer since you've had it, it's perfectly fine."

Katrina sat down in the chair next to Viktor. "But how can they? It's a portable; there aren't any wires."

"Okay, my little noodlehead, since you asked . . . right this minute, there are at least five ways a software programmer can hack into this computer from another one. There's Blue Pill, though that's mainly for Windows, not Mac. It sort of runs *underneath* the operating system, taking it over. There's also hooking, there's polling, there's —"

"Viktor, please," Lara said. "In simple Russian."

"All right. But if I tell you, I want the floor lamp." He smiled. "Just kidding. Somebody installed malware in your machine, maybe in a spam email you opened and then trashed. It left behind a cookie, a sort of footprint of a file that left behind a kernel-based rootkit. Very hard to detect, the kernel-based ones. It grabs any information typed on the keyboard as it goes to the operating system, transmitting it . . ." he paused to look at Katrina, ". . . *wirelessly,* maybe to a predetermined email address or a website, but more probably, if they used the ethernet, they can directly access the logs stored right on this machine. Have you left your iPad alone at any time?"

Lara tried to think. "I took a ten-minute walk around the Arkhiv, no more; came back to find this enormous guy in the Listening Room."

Viktor beamed, inappropriately, in triumph. "Well, that's when he dropped in the spyware. Probably used a flash drive. Thirty seconds and you're done."

"So everything Lara typed —" Gerasimov didn't finish his thought.

Lara did. "The eBay search, the feedback, the vodcast, my notes in the Arkhiv . . ."

Viktor said, "It's worse than that. Even though I think I disarmed all the spyware, whoever planted it knows what I just did, all the entries I just made looking for their 'trojan horse' before I destroyed it. If they're any good — by that I mean, if they're really bad and mean you harm — they're on their way here right now."

The sound of four people not breathing filled the room.

"Get just the stuff you absolutely have to take. Grigoriy Aleksandrovich, is there somewhere you can take Lara for the evening? Trina's flat is awfully small."

"My place in town. I'll drive her in my car."

"Then let's get going."

Two minutes later, the van and the Alfa Romeo had made it only a hundred meters up the road to a little park, where Lara was busy being sick in the bushes. The rain was coming down a little more and Gerasimov was with her. Katrina was in the van, sitting next to Viktor, inspecting her nails and thinking, if she made it out of this in one piece, how much she needed a manicure.

Lara was coming back, wiping the last of the regurgitated *ponchiki* from her mouth with Gerasimov's handkerchief and feeling rotten. Rolling the van's passenger window down, Viktor leaned past Katrina and said, "Hurry up, Lara, or you'll run right into the bad guys." Then he gunned his motor and pulled away from the curb, yelling, *"Udachi!"* out the window.

In the circumstances, they'd need all the "Good luck" they could get.

CHAPTER 56

"Keep your friends close and your enemies closer." Sun Tzu would approve of the way Lara was jammed right next to Grigoriy Gerasimov in the little Italian sports car. Her hair was damp from the rain when she'd been ill, the moisture working its way down the back of her neck as he pulled away.

"I'll make you some hot tea when we get to my flat."

"This flat of yours, it's in town?"

He grinned. "In the Arbat, where else?"

The new-money quarter of Moscow was all glitzy casinos and high-rises. "Okay, but just for tea."

Craning around to get some tissues from her purse behind and under her seat so she could dry her wet neck, Lara glimpsed a red-and-silver motorcycle pulling into traffic behind them.

Her thoughts, though, were on the man

sitting beside her. Once and for all . . . friend or foe? She'd share a piece of information and see how he reacted. So she told him of the death of Lev's American friend, Craig.

All Gerasimov evinced was surprise. "My God! And your brother, he's all right?"

"I wish I knew for sure."

"You'll feel better when you've had a little something to eat."

"Eat? I don't think so."

Right then her phone rang in her handbag. She groped for it, but only succeeded in pushing her purse further under the seat mechanism. Then it stopped, and Lara realized it was the ringtone she'd given Pavel. She'd call him back, finally, once they got to Gerasimov's place.

They were heading west, tooling along Novy Arbat, the huge five-lane boulevard, with the rain increasing. The wipers were laboring to keep the windshield clear, but the neon signs and the headlights of cars zooming in and out of the side streets produced a blinding white haze.

"This isn't good," he mumbled.

She looked over at the man peering through the occluded windscreen and tried to tune in on his thoughts. Was he Mr. Right or Dr. Evil? If he was involved, somehow, in any of this, there was no sign of it in his handsome face.

For no reason, Lara pressed the button on the little glove box in front of her.

"Don't do that," Gerasimov said, sharply.

Too late. Lara was staring at the gun nestled inside. "Is it loaded?"

"Naturally. That's the only way it works."

"Why . . . why a gun?"

He sighed a big sigh. "If you have to know, I took it away from Nikki. He said a friend gave it to him to hold. A 'friend.' " Lara looked over at him and, briefly, he looked back.

"With friends like his, you don't need enemies. Lara, please, close it up again."

When she leaned forward to do as he asked, her eye caught a glimpse of red in her side mirror. A moment later, there it was again in the rain-slickened traffic behind them.

"I think we're being followed."

They were coming up to the Garden Ring road; beyond it was the flat. Gerasimov, instantly tense, peered at the driver's side mirror. "The truck?"

Lara looked in her mirror again. "Behind it. A silver-and-red motorcycle."

"I see him, with the black helmet on the Ural Volk. Well, there's one way to find out."

Instead of continuing ahead, Gerasimov made a last-second turn onto the ramp that led up to the Garden Ring. So did the cyclist.

Surprisingly, she felt Gerasimov relax. Speaking into his mirror, he said, "It's not enough you tapped her computer. So now you're *stalking* her? Us?"

He gunned the engine. In less than a minute on the elevated highway, they were approaching the exit for Barrikadnaya, named for bitter street-fighting in the 1905 revolt. Gerasimov took it without slowing down.

Lara peered into the mirror outside her window, looking to see whether they were still being followed. They were. "Now that I think of it, I saw him when Nikki was driving me in."

They moved in and out of traffic, the motorcycle in their wake. Halfway to the Third Ring Road, Gerasimov eased off the gas pedal, closing the distance back to the motorcycle behind them. "Roll down your window."

"But, it's raining."

"Just for a moment. My turn signals aren't working. Point to that exit coming up. Let's have it out right now. They wouldn't dare try something out in the open."

341

Against her better judgment, Lara rolled the window down just enough to be able to stick out her arm and point. The Alfa's three-piece seatbelt was constricting, so it meant unbuckling it and raising herself as she leaned out. She was halfway through the maneuver when Gerasimov violently swerved left and yelled, "Duck! Get back in, he's got a gun!"

Her body was thrown against the partly open window, bruising her under the arm. Craning her neck to her right with the rain coming in, she saw the guy on the motorcycle holding what looked like a big, black cannon.

Gerasimov floored the sports car, jamming Lara back against the seat. Over the suddenly deafening engine whine and the road noise from the wind and the wet tires, Gerasimov yelled, "Ha, feel it?! That's the turbo!" He had a strange grin on his face. He was *enjoying* this.

She was being crunched by the g-forces kicking in as she struggled to get the seatbelt back on. The tach pushed past 7500 revs and the speedometer needle flirted with 150 kph. The motorcycle, now two lanes to the right, fell back.

With the window back up, all she could do was hang on to the door handle with her right hand and the edge of her seat with her left. She couldn't tell which was worse, the gun or the fear of dying in a crash.

It was the gun. When a slight opening appeared in the traffic, the man on the motorbike raised his hand to fire. A lorry with a load of lumber was to their left, leaving them nowhere to go. As Lara watched, a hole the size of a beer can bloomed in the canvas that was covering the wooden boards. He'd shot just over the top of them.

Gerasimov refused to give him a second chance, spinning the wheel hard right and sending them careering on a diagonal through three lanes of traffic the way a bishop might cut through a cluster of pieces to end up all the way on the king's rook file. If a bishop could hydroplane at 150 kilometers an hour.

They were already under the Third Ring. Lara felt her stomach trying to climb out her throat. It was getting harder to see through the windshield. Apparently Alfa engineers don't care that much about defrosting either. "Wipe it for me," Gerasimov yelled. "With your sleeve."

The way the glass was curved, she'd have to use her right arm. It hurt her to lift it but Lara managed to do it. The corridor of vision she revealed showed the southbound exit for the expressway coming up. We're going too fast, she thought, and closed her eyes.

For the next twenty seconds, the centrifugal force of the turn kept her injured arm pinned to the door. A moaning sound seemed to be coming from the tires, and then she realized it was coming from her.

Gerasimov reached out to touch her good arm and Lara opened her eyes again. They were hurtling south along the Third Ring, the motorcycle still twenty meters behind them.

"Keep your hands on the wheel, damn it!"

He looked at her in the rearview mirror. "Okay, hold on. Let's see if he can stay upright in this rain." He gunned the car till the needle passed the 9,000-rpm line and then drove onto the roughly paved shoulder, passing a slow-moving van and a camper ahead of it.

Gerasimov was weaving in and out of the two right lanes of traffic. Every now and then, looking behind them in the mirror, Lara could see a smudge of red in the gloom, keeping up. She turned around and tried to see through the plastic back window of the convertible's top. Impossible.

Now the motorcycle was on the shoulder too, shuddering over the broken tarmac directly behind them. At least it would take both hands on the handlebars to stay upright. The turn for *Shmitovskiy proyezd* was almost on them. Gerasimov shifted left a lane as if to go on, and then pulled another hard right at speed, fishtailing them onto the ramp, barely. The little Italian car fought to regain its grip. The back end gave a second little waggle and they were through.

Looking back, Lara could see the cyclist had gone for Grisha's head fake left. Now he had all he could do to duplicate their move. They were hurrying away from him. With the side windows starting to fog up, she couldn't tell if the guy had made the turn or spun out.

Gerasimov was taking no chances. The car was now heading away from town and the flat, and he took the bridge over the Moskva River at full speed. He was still doing 130 when they turned off onto one of the promenades that sliced a short way through the Moscow Hills. There wasn't another vehicle to be seen. Or heard.

Finally Grisha let up on the gas and they watched the unrelenting rain as they made their way south along the tree-lined allée. At the end, crossing busy Minskaya at the light, he puttered over to Park Pobedy on the other side, the two of them so drenched in their own sweat they might as well have been driving with the top down. Lara was starting to feel the chill. She put a hand up to her cheek. Her hair was matted against her face.

Gerasimov said, "Your arm took a hell of a whack back there. You okay?"

She wanted to say something like, "I'll live." Instead, now that they were safe, the terror came welling up. "You'd better pull over, now."

Good thing she had almost nothing left in her stomach from the time before. She got back in the car, soaked to the bone. Gerasimov had found a clean rag in the Alfa's trunk and was trying to dry her off with it. But it was so threadbare, all she could feel was his hand running over her neck and down her arms and through her hair.

They drove slowly on. Up here, above the city on Victory Hill, they were coming to the spot where Napoleon waited in vain in 1812 for someone to deliver the keys to the defeated city of Moscow. Now there was a Victory Arch on Poklannoya Gora, the hill's formal name, one dedicated to his defeat and the defeat of every other would-be conqueror.

The road to the Arch was blocked off due to the just-completed renovation work on the huge War Museum that lay ahead. Instead of the dark, drafty place where Lara discovered her love of history, they could see lights were ablaze in the remade entrance hall of its fancy successor, three hundred meters away across the vast pedestrian plaza. But there was no place to stop and get out of the rain — the workers had taken down the acres of scaffolding and dumped them on the plaza and here in the car park.

Lara really had to get her feet on solid ground. She pointed across the road to the neighboring building, the ugly box that was the Holocaust Synagogue. Gerasimov nodded and nosed the car into the deserted temple's parking area.

There was an overhang over the short flight of steps in front. Lara's legs were rubbery going up. The bile in her throat tasted bitter. She shook with a long, five-second shiver. Grisha took off his windbreaker and wrapped it around her shoulders. He kept his large hands there, warming her. Despite her misgivings about him, the strange man's hands felt good.

He said, "Do you smoke?"

"No. My brother's a chimney, and I hate the smell on his clothes."

"I think you should start." He pulled a

couple of French Gitanes out of a pack. "It's a good way to warm up, from the inside." When she was slow to accept, he added, "One won't make you an addict."

He lit a cigarette for himself and mimed his intention to light the other. She shrugged and then nodded.

Lara took the cigarette smoke down into her lungs. Almost everyone at the University smoked, which Lara considered a sign of moral weakness. Now she said, with a cough, "It doesn't warm you up."

"I know. I just wanted to take your mind off what happened back there."

They stood smoking in front of the great doors to the holy place, one more Russian palace of the dead. Moscow was a giant mausoleum with people living in it.

Lara asked, "Where did you learn to drive like that?"

"The Army. It's all I did, drive and shoot."

Lara looked up at him. "You were in Afghanistan?"

He laughed. "I was defending these very hills from Afghan attack, eight kilometers over that way. There's a shooting range; my father pulled strings."

He was still holding her. She said, without really intending to, "I'm glad."

He kissed her, adding his cigarette smoke

to hers. It had been so long since a man had kissed her. Even longer since one had meant it. If he was a bad guy, this was so wrong.

She kissed him back and, without making a conscious decision, moved so their bodies touched.

The noise was almost imperceptible, a buzzing like a far-off mosquito, mixed in with the dull throb of the Minskaya traffic on the other side of the trees beyond the car park. But the mosquito didn't go away.

Gerasimov broke off the kiss and looked back toward the war museum. A single light was moving slowly, methodically, among the piles of iron scaffolding. Coming slowly this way.

Lara didn't immediately understand when Grisha said, "I have an idea." He hurried down the synagogue's steps to the Alfa Romeo and opened the door. He got in, flicking on the interior light as well as the radio. Lara couldn't see what he was doing with the car's windows steamed up, but her ears told her he'd turned on a classical station. Then he was out of the car again, taking the steps two at a time. The Alfa's light was still on and the radio was going in the closed car.

"Stay here out of sight, whatever happens.

You understand?" He took what was left of her cigarette and crushed it with his against the rough concrete wall of the building. "And keep quiet."

Lara said, "You left the radio on."

"I meant to." Gerasimov hurried away, leaving her there.

The light on the motorcycle had been going up and down the Poklannoya's narrow paths. Lara saw it hesitate when the radio came on. Almost immediately, the headlight flicked off. In the dark, Lara could hear the machine start up again, coming toward them, an unseen mosquito getting closer in the night.

The sound stopped on the far side of the car park. What was the stalker doing? And where was Grisha?

There was a security floodlight high up on the corner of the synagogue. It picked out the cyclist in dark leathers and full-face Uvex helmet, making his way on foot across the lot, slightly bent over, trying not to be seen from inside the parked car.

The man was now right behind the Alfa, keeping low and creeping around to the passenger side just as the tiny voice of the program's host on the car's radio came on. "Next up on our program of stormy music, Modest Mussorgsky's *Night on Bald Moun-*

350

tain, the original 1867 version performed by . . .”

The figure had stopped at the sound. Now he moved again, all the way around to stand beside the passenger window, Lara’s window. Something in his hand glinted in the strengthening floodlight.

The explosion rocked the parking lot, throwing Lara to her knees twenty meters away. She looked back to see the car window gone and the man with the gun leaning inside.

Before Lara could do or say anything, a second shot rang out. The man wasn’t standing there anymore. He was smeared across the door and slowly, slowly falling to the ground.

From the still-working radio came the sound of kettledrums. Gerasimov was running out of the dark into the circle of light near the building. He bent down and prodded the man on the ground with the gun in his hand, Nikki’s gun, and then with his foot. The figure didn’t move.

By the time Lara reached him, Gerasimov had turned the body face up and was trying to get the helmet off. The strap under the chin was caught somehow. Then it came free.

“Isn’t that . . . ?”

"Yes," said Lara. "It's Pavel. Pavel Samsonov."

CHAPTER 57

Gerasimov handed her the cup. She could taste the brandy or whatever it was in the hot black tea as it coursed through her, defrosting her. Her mind had been frozen too, locked on the horror of what had happened. Now that they were finally out of the rain, she could see the man sitting across from her was going over the same two questions in his mind that she was. Why? And why Pavel?

They had loaded the body into what was left of the Alfa Romeo and discovered there was no room for both of them, so Gerasimov fished around in the dead man's leather pockets and found the motorcycle key. It was hard to start the massive 750cc bike in the rain, but he'd finally fired it up on the third try.

"I don't think you should stay at your place tonight, those guys might still be around," he'd said. His apartment was out, too — no place to park the vehicles without being seen. So they came here, to his office.

On the fourteenth floor of the Gostele-radio offices at Ostankino, eight floors up from where the *Midnight in Moscow* staff was getting ready to put on the last program of the day, the executive level was deserted. Even the babushkas had come and gone. The brass nameplate next to the door of the corner office said, "Grigoriy Aleksandro-vich." He smiled as he ushered her in. "No last names. I think it's friendlier."

There was the standard desk and the standard chairs and lamps and bookcases. The view, though, was incomparable. St. Basil's and the Kremlin were dead ahead in the distance, putting on their light show for the drunks and the insomniacs, which meant practically the entire city. "Through here," he said.

"Here" was the executive washroom, as the little brass plaque on the door put it. Another door on the far side, past the sinks and a shower stall, opened on a sitting room. It too had the amazing view of night-time Moscow. It was furnished with a couch, a coffee table, and a couple of club chairs, one of which enveloped Lara almost entirely when she sank down in it, ex-hausted. You don't appreciate the importance of adrenaline until you use it all up.

"Finish your tea and let's get you out of those wet clothes."

Their little two-vehicle convoy had driven just a few kilometers from the Holocaust Synagogue to the Broadcast Center, but with the passenger-side window blown away, the rain had soaked Pavel's body and, to only a slightly lesser extent, Lara's. (She didn't know which was worse — Pavel's unseeing eyes or his indifference to the rain.) She left him in the car downstairs, next to where Grisha had parked his motorcycle.

He was saying, "I'm going to see about Pavel. I'll be a while."

Lara wasn't listening. "I didn't know he had that motorcycle. Isn't that funny?"

Gerasimov frowned. "Lara, you're still in shock. While I'm gone, why don't you take a shower? You look like you could use it."

Lara did as she was told. The washroom had shower gel, shampoo, conditioner, the works. But most of all there was warm water cascading down her body. For the first time, Lara dared to look at her injured right arm. The black-and-blue mark was already coming up. She couldn't raise that hand high enough to wash her upper back and breasts, so she made do with her left.

There was a little built-in seat in the shower stall and Lara sat down on it, rinsing away the shampoo. She tried to make her brain function, but it wouldn't. After a while, and with the soapy residue long gone, she stayed that way, surrendering to the warmth of the water and giving up thinking altogether.

Wrapped in the white terrycloth robe that had been hanging behind the door, and with a towel wrapped around her hair, she was a caterpillar snug in its cocoon. Who wants to be a butterfly anyway?

Finally, Gerasimov was back, knocking on the door from his office. He had brought her suitcase up from the car. There was a little puddle under it. He said, "I'm afraid your stuff got soaked. When the window was shot out . . ." and then he saw her in the robe and towel. "Mmm, Larissa Mendelova . . . what have you done with Dr. Klimt?"

Back in the sitting room he said, "Look, you're about the same size . . . my wife's things are in that wardrobe over there. She kept them here for when I was . . . working late."

Lara turned toward the armoire in the corner and immediately turned back. "Your wife . . . can you tell me what happened?"

Gerasimov was slumped over the back of one of the club chairs. Lara went over to him. "Grisha, what is it? What's wrong?"

His eyes were wet. "She left me."

Lara reached out with her hand to touch his cheek. When she did, the sleeve of the robe revealed the bruise on her arm.

"Lara, you're really injured! Why didn't you tell me? I'd have found some ice and made you a compress."

He was holding her arm with both of his hands, cradling it. He leaned forward and pushed the cotton sleeve up so he could give the black-and-blue place a tiny kiss. He murmured, "Let me make it better," and, pushing the material a fraction higher each time, kissed her again and again and again, each one a little higher, at first still on the bruise and then kissing the soft flesh of her upper arm. No, no, she didn't know this man, not really; she didn't want this to be happening.

On the seventh or eighth kiss, he hesitated. There was something in his eyes, some sadness. Shocked, she realized she did want this, and lowered her lips to his.

Chapter 58

It was this right now, this weight of the man, his leg, his arm that she had missed as much as anything. The human contact. She was crying, why exactly — for herself, for Pavel — she didn't know, with her one stupid tear duct doing the work of two. The funny thing, she saw now, was that Grisha, on the other side, his stubbled face against hers, still tenderly cradling her injured arm in his sleep, would never know about the tears running down her left cheek.

How could this happen? She was now a fully divorced woman, but Grisha's wife's things were still in the drawers. Come to think of it, why wouldn't he talk about her? Another tear rolled down her cheek. Where could this possibly go?

With the shock starting to wear off, Lara's brain, the brain of a chess player, was trying to turn itself back on. Anatoly Karpov, the champion before Kasparov, once said the only difference between a prodigy and a patzer was how far into the future a player could look. Peering at her mental board, Lara couldn't see much.

Think it through. The book. The recordings. Sometime in 1940, Noël Coward and Anthony Blunt created a hoax involving a book Hitler was meant to read. Acting on what was written in it, the Führer was supposed to turn his armies around and attack the Soviet Union. And he did. And now, anyone who had the book, the Bible, could prove the Allies had deliberately started the Great Patriotic War.

Gerasimov moved in his sleep, his leg rubbing along hers, sending little electric shocks northward that short-circuited her thinking.

No, return to the board. Someone gets Gerasimov, through Pavel, to reach out to Professor Larissa Mendelova Klimt to do a TV show. At the same time, a young tough, a stranger, asks her to listen to some seventy-year-old musings of a dead English playwright. Almost immediately, Pavel starts following Lara and Grisha around on a silver-and-red motorcycle, eventually trying to kill them.

Wait, that's wrong. She could see him

aiming that gun of his at the Alfa's passenger-side window. Her window. Pavel, her childhood friend, had wanted *her* dead. Why? What if —

Grisha muttered something in his sleep, his mouth close to her ear. Chess, go back to chess. Wooden pieces, geometric squares, no place for emotion. She thought of the Karo-Cann opening, the Nimzo-Indian defense. But she kept coming back to one simple move: King takes Queen. Like some schoolgirl, some ingénue, the thought made her toes want to curl. And they would have too, if his feet weren't on top of them, warming them.

And then her mobile rang. Idiot, imbecile, why hadn't she turned the thing off? The racket it was making. She reached out her working, left arm as far as it would go, being careful not to move anything else and waken Grisha. She touched the small, noisy rectangle on the upholstered arm of the pullout bed.

Who would call at, what time was it, 4:25 in the morning? She managed to hold the phone in her palm and turn it open with her thumb. She had to know.

"You have three new messages."

For Christ's sake, it was her own voice-mail! It took almost a minute for her to manage to hold the mobile and scroll down the list with one hand. She finally hit OK and held the phone up to her ear, tightly so the sound wouldn't leak out.

The first one was from the woman at the flirt party, Tatiana Ivanova. "About my proposition, Larissa Mendelova: if you have the Bible, we'll pay you five million rubles for it. You won't get a better deal. Call me back."

The next two were from Pavel, one after the other, the first when she and Gerasimov had been leaving her place after the dustup with Viktor.

"Larashka, get out of his car!" His voice was more urgent now. "I was wrong, wrong, so wrong about them! It's — shit, where are you off to now?!"

In the background, Lara could just barely make out something like a car accelerating. The next thing he said was drowned out by an explosion; it must have been Pavel starting his motorcycle. When the big Ural Volk shifted into gear, Lara could make out his voice again. "His wife worked here, did you know that? Did the weather on the *Weekend News.* I would . . . run errands for her.

"A guy I know, a cameraman, made that tape of her after hours for the Party . . . did you get my text, Lara? Did you see the thing?!"

The rain, the road noise, and the motorcycle shifting gears made it almost impossible to hear complete sentences. "— using me, like they're using you — get what they want. Everyone's dirty, Lara, dirty with a capital D!"

The bike must now be riding on the shoulder. She could hear him say, "I can't hold onto the phone." Was he crying? "I'm so, so sorry I got you into this."

The next call came in minutes later. "Stop and think of your mother and father, Lara, two people with nothing who took in an orphaned boy!"

Pavel was getting louder, his voice distorting on the tiny instrument's playback. Unable to manipulate the volume control with the fingers of her left hand and with her right arm still pinned under the sleeping man, she had to turn away and clamp the phone tighter to her ear to keep the sound to herself.

"Think of their sainted memories! How can you work for the oppressors? Or did you live in America too long and forget what it's like back here? Lara, I love you. Forgive me for what I'm forced to —"

The man lying beside her said something

in his sleep. It was so unexpected she dropped the phone, which clattered down through the pullout's mechanism to the floor.

A moment later, he said it again. "Tati."

For "Tatiana?" Was it possible? Tatiana Ivanova, the weather person?

What had Lara done?

CHAPTER 59

The dream, when it finally came, was the strangest one yet. She was playing chess, but couldn't see whether she was White or Black; there was some kind of veil over the board. Shadows covered her opponent's face. Then the image of the table with a chessboard changed to that table behind the gas station, the one they'd "picknicked" on — there were Father, Mother, Lara, and Lev, the four of them.

She sat bolt upright, fully awake: What if White and Black weren't the only ones playing this game? What if there were three players sitting at the table? Or four?

For some reason she finally felt able to think it through. The figure beside her was breathing regularly now, slowly and deeply. She eased herself from under the covers and rummaged around on the floor for her phone. She had to record another memo to herself, and made her way back through the washroom to Gerasimov's office so she wouldn't be overheard.

She was sitting in one of the desk chairs and actually had her mouth open to begin speaking when the "out of area" call came in. The voice on the other end spoke in English.

"We have your brother."

"What? Who is this?"

"What's important is, we have your brother. A brother you won't have for very long unless you do what we say."

Half an hour later, long after the man somewhere in Alaska had finished telling her what to do, Lara sat alone in the dark, her heart rate finally starting to come down. And then, the way a flash of lightning reveals the midnight landscape in every detail, she saw it all, the way to save Lev, the winning line of attack, complete in her head. And that the way to beat the enemy — make that enemies — was to make them think they'd won. Use their own plan against them.

With that, a peaceful heaviness came over her, and she fell asleep there in the chair.

CHAPTER 60

The muted sound of the "Hunters' Theme" announced itself. "Good morning Lara, this is your wakeup call from the other side of the washroom. Do I snore so much you had to sleep in my office? No one's ever told me that I was that bad. Anyway, I put some of Tatiana's things out for you; your stuff is still wet. Get dressed as quickly as you can and meet me downstairs on the sixth floor, in the studio. We have to get you into Makeup no later than 8:00."

"Da. Is there anything there to eat?"

"A whole spread for the American and his people. Hurry up, okay?"

"Okay."

In the predawn light she moved over to the small pile of women's clothes and underthings, last worn by the wife of the Director (who doubled as the weekend weatherperson on Channel One), with a note on top. "Larissa Mendelova, these should work on camera. — G."

The blouse alone was probably a week's pay. She picked up the underwear and the pantyhose. Wear another woman's lace panties after making love to her husband? A woman whose vodcast aimed to deny democracy to 150 million Russians for the foreseeable future? No, she thought, not Dr. Klimt.

Lara looked over to the window. There was some kind of arrangement she couldn't fathom to close the blinds. She was lucky it was still dark, hating to think what some anonymous engineer looking up from his dials in the old broadcast tower across the way would make of the view: a totally naked Eurasian woman, her black hair sticking out in all directions, with a bruise that was starting to look like something by Chagall on a right arm that was still too painful to lift.

Ten minutes later, a somewhat exotic-looking woman in a flattering jacket-and-skirt set emerged from the executive washroom and, rolling a still damp overnight bag with its "on-camera wardrobe" behind her, walked through the empty offices of Gosteleradio sans underpants.

The voice of the man holding Lev said they'd release him if she did what they said. He'd given her very precise instructions, and she intended to follow them to the letter. With just a little . . . punctuation . . . of her own.

CHAPTER 61

By the time the elevator opened on the sixth-floor studio, Gerasimov was busy dealing with the First Lady and the rest of the American advance party, making small talk in his Intermediate English and describing all the various Russian foods on the craft table.

Lara knew she looked a fright and hurried into the Makeup Room before she was spotted. The cosmetician took one look at her, swore a Georgian oath under his breath, and immediately set about washing her hair. She'd have to call Viktor when she was out of the dryer.

Forty-five minutes later, Lara emerged from Makeup just as the US leader stepped off the elevator with his bodyguards. Though no band was playing "Ruffles and Flourishes," everyone in the room stopped in mid-sentence. The man was tall, taller than Gerasimov, wearing a dark suit and a tie of red dots on blue. His skin was tanned from golfing in the sun at the Florida White House. He had black reading glasses, without a case, tucked in his breast pocket. In short, he seemed altogether presidential.

Tea had been prepared in a large silver samovar. While the president shook hands with the assembled Russians, Lara moved over to it and poured the man a cup by way of introduction.

"I understand we were once neighbors in New York, Dr. Klimt," the leader of the free world said, helping himself to two spoons of sugar. "And now, halfway around the world, we're going to be neighbors again, at least for the next hour. Funny the way life works out."

Lara smiled. "Yes, Mr. President, isn't it?"

The woman who would be directing the town hall — one who regularly directed educational programming — went over the procedures of the broadcast with them, seating them in two identical club chairs before the camera. Then she walked back to the glassed-in booth to confer with the Tele-PrompTer man, a prematurely balding techie of thirty or so, who would type the students' questions for Lara to read on the lens of the special camera.

It was time. The large monitor set up for

the other guests in the booth showed a ten-second countdown followed by *"v efire."* Gerasimov leaned over to the First Lady and whispered, "It means 'on the air.' "

She whispered back, "I know, I was born in Slovenia. They taught us Russian in school."

Gerasimov had forgotten, and just managed to get out, "Sorry," before the recorded Russian and American anthems began the show.

Finally, it was Lara's turn. She welcomed her young viewers tuning in across the nation and introduced the most powerful man in the world sitting next to her. The president gave them all a telegenic smile and settled himself expectantly in his chair, just another pupil ready for his test.

Lara proceeded to invite the students to have their teacher text in questions for the president during the telecast. Thousands had already been received at the Broadcast Center, and they would start with a few of those. Turning to the smiling world leader next to her, Lara was startled to discover the man's eyeglasses — which he had put on, giving his face an intellectual aspect — had no lenses in them.

She asked, "Are you ready, Mr. President?"

He smiled back. "Shoot."

In Russian, Lara told the camera, "Question number one is from Sverdlovsk Primary School Number 6: 'Mr. President, when you arrived here this week, you remarked how much bigger the Kremlin is than your own White House. As someone who constructed buildings for a living before running for office, are you jealous?" Then she turned to her right and repeated it in English for the guest.

The query had deliberately been chosen as an open-ended icebreaker, a softball the president could easily connect with and do with as he pleased. And so he did, happily and at length.

The second question, "Are all American women as beautiful as your wife?" elicited a smile and a simple "Almost, but not quite."

By now the live texts were pouring in. The topics became more serious, covering Iran and the United Nations; governing in a politically divided democracy; how America was dealing with the worldwide immigration problem.

Lara knew it was now or never. To all outward appearances she was merely an interpreter sitting in a Moscow television studio. Inwardly, though, she had become the embodiment of *The Motherland Calls,* the statue commemorating the Battle of Stalingrad: a heroine with a sword, imploring her countrymen to join the fight for freedom.

She turned back to the camera and, more certain of what she was about to do than she had ever been, silently read the sixth question, typed in Russian by the operator in the control room. "The Belgorod Gymnasium asks, "The continuing 'Arab Spring' poses many opportunities and difficulties, especially in Syria and Iraq. How do you assess the chances for permanent change in the region?"

But what Lara said to the president in English was, "From students on Kosa Andrianova, an island in the Chukchi Sea, comes this: "Mr. President, several of our parents work in the merchant marine here, traveling back and forth to trade with Americans in your state of Alaska. They tell us there is great activity in your Wildlife Refuge, and the rumor is that you've discovered an enormous new oil field there. Is that true?"

Lara could see the startled look in the president's eyes as his mouth fell open slightly in surprise. The TelePrompTer man on the other side of the glass, already typing in the next question, scrolled back hurriedly to see what he'd done; the question had been about Arabs, hadn't it?

And then the president smiled. What the hell, he was going right from the studio to close the deal, wasn't he? What better way to put the story out?

Leaning in toward the camera he said, "Yes, our people have struck oil exactly where we said we would. I've been there, walked the ground, talked with the hundreds of scientists and technicians and actually seen the oil gushing out for myself, a billion barrels of new American petroleum. We'll be announcing it later today in America, but I'm glad to be able to provide the students of Russia with a major 'scoop.' "

With that he leaned back, satisfied, as Lara translated her response to more than five million students and teachers — and a host of other viewers — from one end of the country to the other.

CHAPTER 62

The Chinese and Korean plasma TVs were stacked three high and a dozen across in the Electronics Department just inside the dramatic two-story doors that led into the vast TsUM department store from Ulitsa Petrovka. Every TV was tuned to Channel One and each silently displayed an image of the US president breaking the news of the American oil strike that Lara had teased from him an hour earlier, with Lara herself on-screen sitting alongside.

Suddenly, all thirty-six images were replaced by three-dozen more of a blown-up schematic of the Arctic National Wildlife Refuge in Alaska. The station's business reporter stood in front of it, all thirty-six versions of himself ticking off the economic implications for Russia: a drop in the value of their biggest national asset, the possibility of inflation, etc.

Lara took the south escalator up to the

main floor of the giant emporium. The people who held Lev were prepared to exchange him for the six Dictaphone tins that started it all. She'd insisted on a public place for the handover, so here she was.

With her plan of battle finally underway and the bag full of recordings at her feet, and the tiny USB device in her pocket — she tightened her grip on the handrail of the moving stairs. The giant clock high above the shoppers was already striking 12:00; Viktor and Katrina had better be in position.

Unlike an American department store such as Macy's or Chicago's old Marshall Field, TsUM is really a maze of individually leased boutiques, including the cosmetics counter upstairs where Katrina worked. Alexei would think he and his fellow goons could hide unseen amid the shoppers in the stalls and have the upper hand.

But Lara had her goons too. Well, goon: Viktor would station himself across the way in Jewelry. And, too, the store's video cameras, focused 24/7 on all that glitter across the aisle from Cosmetics, would capture everything, if it came to that. Gerasimov, the unknown quantity, was back at the Broadcast Center, wrapping up the "interactive town hall" that had just made international news. So things were on track . . . if Lara was playing White.

She'd been given the Black pieces and, up till now, had desperately tried to figure out where the game was going and what all these strangers were up to. But now that Viktor had discovered that keylogger business, the table was turned. She was White now, wasn't she? She was going to get her brother out of harm's way, and keep herself alive in the process. If she could.

Cresting the main floor, she saw a young man wearing a raincoat with the hood up and looking in the other direction. Two meters away, Katrina stood on the other side of the counter, seemingly helping a customer but keeping an eye peeled. Viktor was where he said he'd be, apparently engrossed in the display of men's watches.

Lara's mobile rang. It was Viktor, whispering from his hunched-over position above the Rolexes. "Larashka, don't look, but whoever it is brought three of them. The enormous guy who might be Mr. Spyware is now ten meters behind you."

A little knowledge is a dangerous thing? Lara was working on a different piece of folk wisdom: knowledge is power. Knowing where the traps were laid meant you could sidestep them.

"Hello, Alexei."

The young man across from her whirled around, the hood of the jacket falling back. He wasn't red-headed.

Nikki replied, "Hello, Dr. Klimt."

CHAPTER 63

"So nice of you to come." He stepped forward and kissed her on both cheeks. "Surprised?"

"What, what are you doing here?"

"Saving my country. What are *you* doing?"

"Freeing my brother. You have him, don't you?"

Nikki smiled. "I believe he's spending the day with American friends of ours."

She involuntarily clenched her fist. "If you've hurt him . . ."

Nikki's smile broadened. "He's perfectly fine . . . except for his ankle. Lev's quite comfortable, really, somewhere in Alaska. Let's call it 'cold storage.' "

Over Nikki's left shoulder, Katrina was staring questioningly at Lara: who the hell is he? Trying to gather her wits, Lara spoke in a calm voice. "My original deal was with the red-headed kid."

"And so it is." Nikki gestured to his right.

Diagonally across the way, looking back at her from within a forest of hanging ladies' handbags, was the kid with the red buzz cut and tattoos. The messenger, he'd called himself. He smiled and gave a slight wave.

Nikki took out an envelope stuffed with high-denomination bills and showed it to her. "A million rubles, I believe he said."

"You're paying me?" Lara appeared stunned. "I don't understand."

The young man smiled again. "You're not supposed to. You rose to the bait, that's all — the old 'loved one in peril' gambit."

The Red Army Hymn announced itself on Lara's mobile. In a hoarse whisper from eight meters away, Viktor said, "What's wrong? You're white as a sheet. Do you need me to —"

In as normal a voice as possible, Lara said, "No, thank you," into the phone and closed it again, getting over the shock. "Tell me something, Nikolai. Why steal the book if you were paying me to find it?"

"But that's it, precisely: *you* found it so *we* could take it." He patted the envelope. "Believe me, you earned this."

He took a step forward until his face was just centimeters from hers. "You're so innocent, I can see why my father came on to you. And you're even more beautiful when

380

those Tajik cheekbones of yours get that pink flush."

She slapped his face, hard, leaving a red welt and bringing Viktor, Katrina, and the red-haired punk to high alert. But Nikki just grinned. He'd been slapped by women before. "Tell me, Larissa, were you always such a bad loser?"

Lara kept her voice calm. "Chess? I wouldn't know; I hardly ever lost."

"You're not playing chess any more. And, as they say on the street, with your brother temporarily detained, we have you by the short hairs."

"Not a classy neighborhood, your street. And who's we? You and your father?"

"Him? Hardly. The other night at dinner, possibly you thought my father was the ventriloquist and I was the dummy. Turns out it was the other way around. No, in our family he's precisely what he seems to be — the innocent bystander."

Lara tried to keep her voice calm at the mention of family. "There's something I have to know: why are you even here? You've got the Bible; why go to all the trouble of kidnapping Lev?"

"Without that English fruitcake on the tapes explaining what it all means, the Bible is just a book with a little bad poetry written inside the cover. We had to have both the book and the recordings. And we finally figured out money wasn't enough motivation for you. So we appealed to something more basic . . . love."

He moved a step toward her, as if to take her shoulder bag with the tins.

Lara backed away. "All right. Payment first."

"You're absolutely right." He reached into the envelope and extracted one of the 50,000-ruble notes. "Business is business."

Holding up the bill, he said, "There. I think the security camera will be able to read the denomination." He put it back in the envelope and placed the thick packet on the glass top of the cosmetics counter.

Trying to look as reluctant as she could, Lara picked up her shoulder bag and put it on the counter as well, holding it open so Nikki could see what was inside. "Six Dictaphone cylinders. Better count them to be sure." She hated to do it, giving the enemy the very material they needed. But her plan, no matter who was playing the other pieces, wouldn't work any other way.

He reached for the bag. "Good girl."

She didn't let go of it. "Lev. First."

Nikki picked up his mobile. He dialed a number and spoke. "We have what we want.

Let him go."

Then he put the thick envelope in her hand. Lara tried to take it, but now *he* wouldn't let go. He said, "I know what you did."

"What I did?"

"You found the key-logger program. Very . . . adroit. I guess I underestimated you."

He let go of the envelope, which Lara put in her purse. She said, "Yes, I guess you did."

He smiled his biggest smile yet. "Well, maybe not entirely. We just established, on that security tape up there, that you sold the recordings to me." He made a small gesture with his hand, which Lara didn't understand. "Now if the question of their — shall we say — English *provenance* ever comes up, it's all on you."

At that moment, Lara realized Alexei was moving across the aisle toward them, still clutching the silver clutch he'd been pretending to examine in Ladies' Bags. A tall, unfriendly-looking man approached as well from the back of the store. If she turned around, she guessed she would see a heavyset, bull-headed guy coming toward them.

Viktor looked up the instant the kid left his position and he too was headed her way.

Katrina, leaving her customer, was at the unwitting Nikolai's elbow, pointing an atomizer of White Shoulders in his general direction, ready to spray it in his eyes.

Nikki started to say, "I'm afraid I'm going to have to —" when a major in the Russian Army came up to Lara. "Larissa Mendelova, remember me? You spoke at the War College. Major Bondarenko."

"Yes Major, I remember. Funny running into you."

As quickly as the three toughs had moved in, they now moved back among the shoppers. Viktor said, "Dr. Klimt, please introduce me to your friend."

The young man looked uncomfortable. He reluctantly held out his hand. "Nikolai Grigorevich Gerasimov. An honor to meet you, Major."

Viktor said, "I'm tight with Lara's husband in the Army. That's how we were able to have her speak about the war. Do you know him? A great, great man, Viktor Maltsev. Smart, tough . . ."

Lara was staring hard at Viktor, but Nikki didn't notice. He said, "No, I haven't had the honor." Then, glancing at his watch, he turned back to Lara. "Oh, look at the time. I must be going."

He picked up the shopping bag with the

384

tins inside. "It was a pleasure, Larissa Mendelova. You've helped me more than you know." Turning to shake hands with Viktor, he said, "A pleasure to have met you, Major . . ."

"Bondarenko."

". . . Major Bondarenko." He moved up the aisle toward the north entrance with a lanky man and a kid with a neck tattoo in his wake.

Viktor and Lara walked in the other direction. An enormous human was coming their way. As they squeezed past him, the man from the Listening Room looked at Lara and nodded almost imperceptibly in recognition before hurrying on.

Lara took out her mobile and called Lev. "Are you okay?"

"Yeah, they took a phone call just now and then walked away. What's going on?"

"Thank God you're okay. Go home. I'll call you when this is all over."

As they hurried down the store's moving stairs, Viktor asked, "What just happened back there?"

"Someone walked into a trap."

"Yours or his?"

"Mine. Now hurry up, we have to get divorced before they close for the weekend."

With everyone gone, Katrina still held the

atomizer out in front of her in attack mode. Then, turning it around, she sprayed the air with White Shoulders, enveloping herself in a romantic, classic floral bouquet rooted in gardenia and jasmine, with a tuberose top note over accents of woods and musk.

CHAPTER 64

Between the Smolenskaya and Park Kultury Metro stops, the Legalization Department on Neopalimovskiy Pereulok is an oasis of leftover Soviet bureaucracy in the arid sameness of modern governmental Moscow. There are four vast halls full of paper files, the clerks still smoke in your face, and they close the place early on Fridays.

When Lara and Viktor handed over their signed divorce decree, the sallow-faced man who took it exhaled a nice cloud of Sobranie Black Russian across the counter. He said, "You know the rules. The decree is posted online for twenty-one days before it's final."

Lara wanted to say, "Know the rules? We've never been divorced before," but she didn't. Instead she asked the man, "How can we see the paperwork on someone else?"

Without looking up, the clerk gestured behind him at the four rooms full of files. "Postwar Births to the left, as well as pre-

2007 baptismal certificates, before the Church reconciled with the Government; then Marriages, Divorces, and, far right, Deaths, as long as they occurred in the federal region."

After explaining for a second time what she wanted, Lara sent Viktor to the left and she took the hall on the right. Like a library, each room was equipped with public computer stations where the human milestones were indexed alphabetically and chronologically. An hour later, they met back in Divorce.

By the time Lara and Viktor were out on the street again, loudspeakers and shop radios were blaring out love songs, the way America's malls play Christmas tunes at holiday time. To put the new exes in the mood for Conception Night.

CHAPTER 65

"Then, Pavel was working for Kasparov?"

Viktor asked the question with his mouth full of egg foo yung.

Lara speared another steamed dumpling. "Your guess is as good as mine. *Someone* wants to keep the Bible from seeing the light of day and ruining everything for our American friends. Pavel just took it a little too far." She bit into the dumpling. "A *lot* too far."

"So, you just gave that guy Nikki what he wanted?" Having posed the question, Katrina daintily dipped a takeaway egg roll into duck sauce, careful not to mess up her newly painted nails before bringing it to her mouth. The afternoon light was starting to fade outside the windows of Katrina's new and very tiny flat, and the Muscovites who wanted to get a place down in front were already making their way to Red Square, five blocks away.

"Yes, everything."

It would be a while before the start of the son et lumière broadcast from the Kremlin, when International Week and Conception Night would come together in one spectacular climax — followed, the organizers hoped, by millions more around the nation. Gerasimov wasn't there; he was overseeing the setup work of his vast broadcast crew from a production truck in the Square.

Viktor rummaged through his Army duffel bag, burrowing under what looked like fifty pairs of unwashed boxers — "well, I didn't exactly have time to do the laundry" — before coming up with a heavy Toshiba portable that had seen better days. One corner was crushed. "My field unit," he shrugged. "Or rather, Vassily Bondarenko's. It will have to do."

He pressed Power and, as the virtual desktop built itself, a message appeared: "For official use/Army of the Commonwealth of Independent States."

Lara glanced over and observed, "That thing's an antique."

"The hardware, maybe. The software's up to date. Anyway, it's all we've got; can't be sure the snoops aren't still watching your iPad."

Katrina was not to be ignored by the ex-couple. "Tell me again how you know this . . . this *trick* . . . will work."

"I don't." Lara let out a bigger sigh than she meant to. "Let's just say I have a hunch, a chess player's read of Nikki, the guy across the table. You should have heard him at dinner; he hates the British and the Americans."

"Why did he steal the Bible now, this week?"

"To plaster the damning evidence of what the West did to us all over the walls of the Kremlin. With the whole country, the world watching. Anyway, it's what I'd do."

"I'm in." Gerasimov's ID and password, *Romance and Babies,* admitted Viktor to the latest version of the prerecorded show. He swiveled his Army laptop around so the women could see the screen as he searched at high speed. When something with a white background flashed by on the screen, Viktor smacked the table with his hand. "Gotcha, boys!"

"What? Really?" Lara searched Viktor's triumphant face.

He paused the streaming video and hit the Back button. This part of the evening was supposed to be the twenty-five-minute light show playing across the Kremlin's façade that coordinated with a fireworks display. Running in reverse, the colors danced crazily on the built-in monitor, the *Firebird Suite* atonally playing backward. After a couple of minutes of running time, though, everything went white, or nearly white. In the middle of the screen was a large leather book, a Bible, open to the flyleaf.

"You were right, Larashka. They uploaded it nine minutes ago, replacing the approved show with this revised one . . . same file name and number," Viktor told her. "Cute. Probably took them all this time to shoot the images in a studio somewhere and then cut them in. Figured no one would be rescreening an entire three-hour show this close to airtime. They're good." Viktor grinned again. "But I'm better."

Lara asked, "How long will it take you?"

"An hour at most," he said. "Let's go over our cues."

CHAPTER 66

Of the nearly half million souls gathered in Red Square as night fell, the handful whose fates were about to intersect had conflicting emotions. The US leader and the Russian president, not far from each other on the temporary metal rostrum just in front of the Kremlin wall, were elated. Hours earlier they shook hands on a deal each believed would guarantee personal, if not national, success for years to come.

Viktor Nikolayevich Maltsev, Katrina Petrovna Chernova, and especially Larissa Mendelova Klimt, in a roped-off section for guests of State Broadcasting and other departments, were as tightly strung as violin strings. *Their* thing tonight had better work. A failure would take place in front of the whole country in real time and on national television.

Meanwhile, the restive Muscovites out there in the cobbled Square were taking the rare opportunity to assemble in numbers without a permit or fear of being jailed as anti-Government demonstrators. There had been warm applause for the G20 leaders as they filed onto the risers, but only whistles greeted their own president. And Lara could count at least a hundred hand-lettered signs starting, "Down With . . ."

It could have been worse. The crowd tonight wasn't concerned with politics, just economics. Surfing their phones and tablet computers or scanning the headlines of hastily purchased evening papers in the meager light of the Square's streetlamps — dimmed to enhance the visibility of the images on the walls — they knew by now the price of a barrel of oil had fallen by 30 percent that afternoon on news that America had all but weaned itself off foreign oil for years to come. And the commentators were saying that, with most US energy traders still asleep in their beds, oil had even farther to fall — threatening to pull Russia's economy down with it. Making more babies was suddenly the furthest thing from any Russian's mind.

As the head of a government department, Gerasimov had to seem unconcerned. He was glad-handing the guests inside the rope, working the crowd before going back to the

TV truck to oversee the production. When he came up to Lara, he leaned in to give her the traditional double kiss of greeting.

"Why couldn't you have told me about your family?" she asked in a low voice amid the general hubbub. "I would have understood."

He pulled back to look at her. "My family?"

"Nikki and Tatiana. Tatiana Ivanova Gerasimova . . . Tati . . . your wife. Your son I can understand. He makes no secret of his feelings. But Tatiana . . . when I saw her Tuesday night, she told me —"

"You saw her? Tuesday night? How is she? Did she . . . mention me?"

Over the man's shoulder, she was watching Viktor, in full Army uniform with major's braid on the visor of his service hat, ducking under the ropes and heading for the production truck. She needed to hold Gerasimov here, not let him return to the truck. "You? I'd only just met you that afternoon and I don't think she knew about it. Besides, what could I have told her . . . then?"

Uh oh, wrong thing to say. He was embarrassed and turning away.

"Why did she leave you, Grisha?"

He turned back, angry now. "Irreconcilable differences, they call it." Lowering his voice he added, "How can there be 'differences' if one person loves the other completely, without reservation?"

"Then, *she* fell out of love with *you.*"

"Over politics, can you believe it? Nikki's politics." He looked around; people in the VIP area were edging closer, trying to hear. "Look, I gotta go, I have a job to do."

Behind him, Viktor was mounting the two metal steps to the truck. He needed more time.

"Over Nikki's politics?"

He was angry again. "Do you have any idea what he does, him and his Nashi friends? They beat up people. Legislators who don't vote to send us back to the Stone Age, to the Tsars, they put in the hospital. Or worse. Two crippled just last week."

"What about Tati's politics?"

"What about them?"

"She told me she was working for Kasparov, told me she was an admirer of mine . . . working for a free press, a more open government. But then I saw the video she made for Putin: it was all a lie."

Gerasimov tried to pull away. "Sorry, I . . . I have to get back to . . . ."

Lara had hold of his lapel so he couldn't leave. She felt all this . . . angst . . . coming up, unbidden. "Where do you stand in all this? It's time for the truth, Grisha. For instance, Tatiana's job on the newscast . . . doing the weather . . . did you get that for her?"

"Why, uh, yes. Are you accusing me of nepotism?"

"No, just of lying. She got *you* the job, didn't she? Her godfather was a Party big-shot back in the day, Mikhail Stoichkov . . . it's amazing what you can find out from a couple of birth certificates, you know. Stoich-kov ran everything in London during the war. Afterward, behind the scenes in the '70s, he ran Moscow."

The head of Gosteleradio started to say something but thought better of it.

A tear rolled down Lara's left cheek, fol-lowed by another. "Everything this week has been a lie. The suicide note of Lev's mur-dered friend Craig. The Americans striking oil in Alaska, that one's a whopper. Oh, and the lie that started it all — the false proph-ecy of Nostradamus you wanted me to find for you."

"Me? Don't be absurd. That was Nikki." A few of the nearby guests, hearing the raised voice, looked at him.

Lara said, "Tell me you're not working for the guy in the Kremlin."

Lowering his voice to an urgent whisper he said, "My wife and son don't get along. Never have. If she says 'up,' he says 'down.' I wasn't a bad husband, just a lousy referee." He stopped and looked at her. "I can see you don't understand."

She grabbed him by the shirt with both hands. "No, *you* don't understand." To her shock, a tear had formed itself in her *right* eye and was rolling down that cheek too. "I felt something for you, Grisha. Dammit, I made *love* to you! I let you . . . *in.*" She was awash in tears now.

He pried her hands, gently this time, from his shirt. "Look, I have to go. The show's starting. I have a job to do."

To his back, as he moved off, Lara whispered, "So do I."

CHAPTER 67

Mikhail Baryshnikov stepped to the microphone. Behind him, the first image of the evening was projected upon the Kremlin walls and music from the Bolshoi Ballet's *Giselle* welled up: archival footage showed his much younger self performing an effortless jeté that took him from the Tsar's Tower all the way to the Arsenal.

"Ugrozy vzryva!"

Seven startled technicians and Pyotr Tamnov, the director in the Channel One truck, swiveled their heads as an Army major strode into their protected area.

"You heard me," the soldier said, "there's a bomb threat. Vacate the premises now."

"But, the broadcast . . ." Tamnov began.

"Just let it run. We received a call threatening the bigwigs out there. Everybody, please . . . I must conduct a sweep. This will take less than ten minutes. Get something to eat, take a bathroom break, whatever.

And give me your keys. No one gets back in till I'm sure it's safe."

As soon as the last man was out the door, Viktor locked it and un-holstered his Yarygin 9mm service pistol. If and when the authorities realized what was happening, they'd be coming through that door. Or at least trying to.

Viktor popped the DVD he and Lara had made thirty minutes earlier into the slot on the console. Finding the exact point in the prerecorded show where the graphics accompanying the fireworks display would begin, he overwrote the entire sequence, Bible and all. Fireworks, indeed.

A knock came from outside. "It's Grigoriy Alexandrovich. Why is this door locked?"

When Viktor didn't answer, the knock came again, louder this time. "Let me in, Pyotr. Now!"

From her vantage point in the crowd, Lara could see Gerasimov on the metal steps, banging on the door to the truck before taking out his phone and using it. Then he hurried off. Meanwhile, Baryshnikov soldiered on, intoning the words of the poet Igor Mikhailusenko as more images from the ballet swept across the walls behind him:

On a quiet night, unearthly,

Over Saturn — first time thus —
Two young beings danced the tango,
Thinking tenderly of us . . .

Two young beings danced the tango,
Danced away outside the Earth,
And to distant cosmos vistas
Rocket ships in peace sailed forth.

Two young beings danced the tango —
Saturn gave that pair a ring,
Cupid aimed straight at their hearts
In that interplanetary Spring!

The young red-haired tough, off to the side in the shadows, saw Gerasimov trying to get in the truck. Something wasn't right; the man was locked out. Nikki's orders were clear: make sure nothing went wrong with the telecast that would expose the Bible to the world.

In the roped-off section, Lara saw him go up to the truck and try the door handle. She turned to Katrina, holding a large takeout container of coffee, and told her, *"Idti."*

Buzz Cut was taking something out of his pocket, a penknife or a pick for the lock. Lara repeated the order, more sharply this time, to her ex-roommate. "Go!"

The woman didn't budge. "Why do *I* have to?"

"Because your *druga,* Viktor, needs you." Lara gave her a gentle but firm shove toward the rope that separated the guests from the working area. "Now, go!"

Finally, Trina moved toward the mobile studio. Just as she was passing the production truck she suddenly tripped, spilling the coffee all over herself.

The guy was still bent over the lock. Damn, had he missed her whole act? Trina was making an enormous fuss now, bemoaning her clumsiness, even as everyone else in Red Square was engrossed in the festivities a hundred meters away.

The kid finally looked down from what he was doing and saw the woman at the foot of the steps, ineffectually dabbing at the huge stain on her dress. Could he help her? Did he have a hankie? She said something to him, and absently gripped the boy's arm to support herself as she dealt with her outfit.

The old Damsel in Distress ploy, not as good as the Lover in Peril, but just as time-honored — would it still work in the twenty-first century? No, Alexei did nothing to help her. But wait, he did nothing to move her hand off his arm either. Then, in her frantic efforts, she managed to spill what was left of the coffee on *him,* too.

Edging the young man down the steps and around the side of the truck, she began dabbing at various places on his trousers, centrally located places mostly, which Alexei didn't seem to mind at all. Finally, Katrina prevailed upon him to move off toward the portable lavatories, so she might get a wet paper towel for them both. Or something. It would buy Viktor a little more time.

Just as Alla Pugachova was following Baryshnikov to the microphone, a woman stepped in front of Lara, blocking her view. It was Tatiana Ivanova, Grisha's meteorologist of a wife.

"Do you still have the book, Larissa Mendelova? If so, you have us over a barrel. I'm authorized to double our previous offer to you: ten million rubles."

"Authorized by whom? Garry Kasparov? You can stop pretending, Tati, I know which side you're on. My friend Pavel sent me your vodcast."

A look of utter sadness flickered across the woman's face. "He was *my* friend, too. In fact, he worked for me."

Pugachova had launched into the sad tale of the artist who sold everything he had to fill the street outside his lover's window with millions of roses, and the crowd was responding, as Russians loved to do. A million hands began clapping rhythmically out there in the Square. There was no way anyone could have a conversation, but Lara tried.

"Worked for you at the Broadcast Center?"

"Worked for me at British Intelligence. I'm a . . . field officer, I guess you'd call it. I wormed my way into making that video so I could . . . so we could . . ."

She looked at her wristwatch. "Look, we're wasting time. The only reason I'm telling you this, blowing my cover, is we're desperate to keep that Bible from falling into the wrong hands . . . my son's hands. Now, how about it?"

It felt like a punch to the gut. Had Lara been wrong about absolutely everything? And everyone? To the rhythmic clapping the crowd now added foot stamping as Pugachova launched into her song of love.

Once upon a time there lived an artist
A house he had and canvases
But he loved an actress,
An actress who desired only flowers . . .

He then sold his house
Sold his paintings, too

404

And with all the money he bought
An entire ocean of flowers!

Lara could see the woman was telling the truth. She pulled Tatiana close and spoke in her ear so she could be heard above the din. "I'm sorry, I didn't know. Nikki has the Bible, the recordings, everything."

The other woman drew back with a look of horror. "Oh my God, have you any idea what you've done?!"

Before Lara could explain, the woman had hurried off into the crowd.

Chapter 68

Inside the production truck, Viktor was almost done with the transfer. The thin aluminum cladding of the metal box only amplified the thumping and stamping from outside. Pugachova was taking them higher, clapping her own hands high over her head, urging the crowd's participation in the chorus of her beloved classic:

Millions and millions and millions
Of scarlet roses
From your window, from your window, from
 your window
You can see
Who's in love, who's in love, who's in love
For real
Will turn his life for you . . . into blossoms
wide as the sea.

Russia's beloved diva had everyone's attention, artfully lowering her singing voice to little more than a whisper for dramatic irony as she reprised the opening verse:

Once upon a time there lived an artist
A house he had and canvases
But he loved an actress,
An actress who desired only flowers . . .

He then sold his house
Sold his paintings, too
And with all the money he bought
An entire ocean of flowers!

It would only be clear afterward, when the feeds from the various cameras in the Square were played back, that the problem began with the gasp from the crowd, reacting to the new sequence of images on the Kremlin walls behind the dignitaries.

As big as a football pitch, the image of the Arctic National Wildlife Refuge had its own kind of industrial beauty, in stark contrast to those of the dancers and roses it replaced: a working oilfield with at least a dozen structures large and small and drilling apparatus everywhere, set in a natural bowl carved out by the Canning River just before it emptied into the deep blue of the Beaufort Sea.

The Russian leader's mistake came in trying to turn around and see what was going on behind him. He lost his balance on the risers and fell several steps to the bottom, just as Pugachova was striding off, blowing kisses to the crowd. His guards at first assumed he was heading down to the microphone, albeit awkwardly, for an impromptu speech. But he'd sprained his ankle in the fall. When he tried to stand up, the ankle wouldn't support him. The second time he fell, he tripped over the exposed microphone cord and killed the mic.

Meanwhile, the scheduled fireworks display was going off in the night sky. But instead of a Stravinsky soundtrack, a woman's narration took over, describing the visual splashed across the Kremlin: "You're looking at the northernmost region of the state of Alaska, the very state in America where one of our honored guests announced his people had struck oil. Those of you with smartphones can go right now to Google Earth, and you can confirm for yourselves that this is what you'll see."

As his bodyguards came to the aid of the hobbled Russian president at the foot of the rostrum, the image behind them changed into one from halfway down the Refuge's hill. Now, even the individual oilrigs were clearly visible. The woman's voice, accustomed to projecting to the far reaches of lecture halls, continued. "This is the very spot where our American guest has walked and spoken with the workers. And seen the oil, oceans of it, that even now — at the start of the working day over there — is pouring up out of the ground."

The American president on the podium didn't know Russian, but when he heard the word *Amerikanski,* he decided to smile.

Now the visual everyone was watching changed again, and what had been oilrigs and production buildings became wooden props and circus tents. Another, louder gasp arose from the crowd. The man the Secret Service called Mogul turned from the scene and, looking down at his injured Russian confederate, shot him his most tight-lipped, anger-unmanaged grin.

Out in the Square, the cameramen were shooting whatever they could: now the giant images on the wall, now the President, now the crowd.

Trina, kneeling in the shadows well beyond the truck, was continuing her vigorous ministrations over the already-dry trousers of Alexei, who seemed lost in the moment. Two other men, though, were in motion; one lanky, one massive, both determined. Lara was perfectly placed to see them leave the anonymity of the crowd and hurry toward the truck.

CHAPTER 69

The laughter started somewhere in the back of Red Square, a little tittering at first. It spread through the crowd with each successive image from Lev's camera of faked canvas buildings and painted wooden props made to look like rigs.

The picture of the lone telephone pole holding up the largest tent — with the words ALASKA POWER AND TELEPHONE COMPANY clearly stenciled in yellow paint across the barrel of the pole — drew a guffaw among those who could read English. The laughing seemed to die down for a bit while the Anglophones translated the words for their Russian-only neighbors, then it burst out again, rebounding off the buildings surrounding the Square, amplifying it.

A line of nondescript oil tankers flying American flags came on next. A man on the video's soundtrack was saying, "There, you can just barely see it, the one with the orange insignia: *The Atlantic Pioneer.* If you look carefully, you can see where they painted over the Russian name."

Another man asked him, *"Kak dolgo vy budete nasosnoĭneft'?"* For some reason, the question of "how long will you be pumping the oil?" set the crowd off again.

The two thugs had reached the door of the mobile production suite with their guns out. The big one, Suslov, peered around the side of the truck, looking for the kid. "Alexei, zip up and get over here!"

The young man pushed Katrina away and joined the others at the entrance to the truck. He took out the knife from his back pocket.

Lara saw everything. In a panic she called Viktor's mobile. "Did you lock the door? Nikki's goons are right outside!"

Too late. In a matter of seconds, there was no longer a door to lock. The crack it made coming off its hinges and crashing to the ground just added to the noise when several fireworks were set off at once. But then the enormous individual who'd accomplished the feat filled the open doorway for a moment before dropping the heavy door on the ground, leaving a rectangle of light where the entrance had been. A second, taller man moved in behind him, and then a shot rang out.

The sound finally caused the TV camera-men to swing their lights away from the rostrum toward the scene, where a third, younger man had something in his hand, something that glinted in the lights.

There were two more shots. Then the whole son et lumière suddenly went dead, and the panicked crowd began racing for the exits. These Russians needed no re-minder of what insurgents from the North Caucasus had done, bombing the airport in 2011 and the Metro a year earlier; or the Chechens' deadly hostage-taking at a Mos-cow theater, and the massacre at the Beslan school, before that.

By this time, the American's Secret Ser-vice people had surrounded him and were trying to hustle him down the temporary viewing stand. Other statesmen were being protected by clumps of their own body-guards, causing a twenty-leader pileup that resembled rush hour on the Outer Ring.

Inside the truck, Suslov had been momen-tarily off-balance when he'd ripped off the door, and his gun had gone clattering under the console. Chernuchin, scrambling in right behind, saw a military man over by the controls. Was that . . . Maltsev, from Intelligence? He delayed before lifting his gun to fire and Suslov, trying to get up, knocked his comrade sideways, making him miss.

Just then, Grigoriy Gerasimov returned with the program's director and a borrowed set of now-useless keys. Before he could stop him, Pyotr Tamnov hurried up from behind and swung his clipboard with all his might, catching the big man above his right ear and knocking him back down to the floor, unconscious. Chernuchin, seeing what happened, whirled and took out the TV director with his second slug.

Viktor had his own gun in his hand by now. Army training had made him an expert shot, but now he hesitated, unwilling to risk hitting Gerasimov. Chernuchin, whirling back around, had no such qualms, and his third bullet was a through-and-through, hitting Viktor in the non-shooting arm. It kept going, shattering the mixer board controlling the light show and putting it, finally, out of action. Then the shooter took one in the gut himself — as the inquest would later show — from the wounded officer working security in the truck, identified as Major Vassily Bondarenko, Commander of the Sakhalin Island barracks, and he fell on his longtime comrade.

Two down, but not the third. Gerasimov

was in the truck, trying to reach the wounded Army major. Before he could, the kid stepped out from behind a panel of machines and calmly stabbed him in the neck, sending him down behind the console. Which gave Viktor a clear shot at the boy, and he didn't miss.

When the security guards reached the scene, they began administering first aid to the dying thugs and the Army major, not knowing good guy from bad. No one saw or heard the head of state broadcasting on the far side of the console as he lay bleeding out from his wound.

It was all over but the shouting. The screams from what was left of the crowd of fleeing people echoed off the bricks and cobblestones of Red Square. Lara desperately tried to get to Viktor and Grisha, but was among those being physically manhandled by a formed-up cordon of security people. The fireworks were still going off in the night sky above the darkened battlements of the Kremlin. So when she was shoved sideways by one of the guards, Lara was able to catch sight behind her of a man slowly, deliberately moving toward the risers from the rear of the Square.

Only now, with no one in charge and everyone jostling to get their own VIPs to the cars that were revving up behind the Square, had the American president made it down from his place of honor on the viewing stand. He'd caught one of his shoes in the corrugated metal planking of the bleachers as he was being frog-marched by his people, twisting his foot, and was now the last foreign leader to be led away, limping in obvious pain.

Had he been shot? The knot of American reporters on the trip had been gathered together below, hemming them in around the now-useless microphone as the First Lady, her press aides, and the Secret Service all tried to get through.

So no one could see what Lara saw: a well-built young man of twenty-five or so, with longish hair, holding a heavy leather book up in front of him.

Nikki!

The young man's eyes were fixed on the politician in the middle of the maelstrom. His lips were moving, muttering something Lara was too far away to hear. As he was the only person actually walking *toward* the viewing stand in front of the Kremlin instead of running away, the T V cameramen who didn't have a good angle on the truck now turned their lights and cameras and mikes on him.

In the T V truck, the monitors with the live feeds were still working. Weakened by the loss of blood and with no one to attend him, Gerasimov looked up and saw who it was on the screen. He tried to rasp out, "Nikki, stop! No!!" but no one could hear him.

Nikki didn't stop. He looked neither left nor right, but kept walking. The directional microphones from the camera positions were picking up his words now. "I don't need a video, I don't need a script! Here's the proof, absolute proof, of the perfidy of the West! Of the so-called democrats, the ones with the blood of twenty-five million on their hands! More!"

And he was still coming on. "Throw out the foreigners! This is our country, made with *our* hands, with our blood. *Nashi!!* Ours!"

And then they saw yet one more gun.

Reporters and security people alike were tripping over each other and the maze of wires at the foot of the viewing stand to get away. Nikki raised his pistol. For a moment, the assassin had a clear shot at his target and, before anyone could stop him, he uttered the words "Russia for the Russians!" and fired, straight at the American's heart.

Miraculously, the bullet bounced off the

slender steel microphone stand. He aimed again. Lara, hurrying toward him but still twenty meters away to his left, knew she had one chance. "Nikki! Over here!"

When he turned to look at her, she stopped and aimed her uncapped laser pen, the one she used on the maps in class, directly into his eyes. With the red dot on its target she pressed the button, blinding him with three hundred megawatts of amplified light.

Afterward the judges, whose eventual verdict was insanity, were able to reconstruct from the din picked up by the microphones Nikki's last words, even as he blindly emptied his gun toward the podium and injured three of the guards. "In the name of God, I defy you and your godless democracy and your Finns and your Armenians and your Tajiks and your Jews!"

Nearly simultaneously, automatic fire from several directions — no one could be certain later which of the bodyguards had fired first — mowed down the would-be assassin, who fell onto the cobblestones in front of millions of horrified TV viewers.

CHAPTER 70

Her mobile rang. It was the "Hunters' Theme" from *Peter and the Wolf*. Grisha! By the time Lara could get to the truck, the wounded man behind the console had dropped his phone. Its clatter brought the medics, but by now there was little they could do.

Gerasimov smiled at Lara and, with a great effort, raised a hand up to touch her face. He seemed surprised to see his hand was covered in blood. "Larashka . . ."

She took his hand in both of hers. "Don't try to talk."

His words were little more than a hoarse whisper. "So much blood. Is Nikki all right?"

Behind her, Lara could hear someone clattering up the stairs of the truck. She bent closer to Grisha. His lips were moving and she tried to catch his words. ". . . if only I was . . . a better referee . . ."

The woman named Tatiana Ivanova Gerasimova tapped Lara on the shoulder. "Let me be with him. He's all I have left."

Lara, reluctantly, turned away. She understood something about loss.

When she joined him outside the truck, Viktor's arm was done up expertly in a sling. She took his good hand and gave it a squeeze. He squeezed her back. There was an ambulance across the Square to take him to the hospital.

Together they walked across Red Square, coming to the place where Nikki's body lay. His hair was fanned out behind him, and medics, no longer in a hurry, were unzipping a black body bag.

The book was lying there on the cobblestones. Lara picked it up. There was a 9mm hole shot completely through it, obliterating any wormhole that had once been there.

They started walking toward the ambulance again.

Viktor turned to Lara. "We still have twenty days left to our marriage. Can we use them to try again, Mrs. Maltsev?"

"I will if you will, Mr. Maltsev."

Then husband and wife walked away together into the night.

AUTHOR'S NOTE

The Bookworm is the second novel I've written that blends fact with fiction. Some people who read this manuscript before publication have wondered which is which. Here's a sampler, starting with the Prologue.

Legend has it that Countess Matilda of Tuscany, who was born exactly 900 years before I was, dropped her gold wedding ring into the waters at the Belgian town of Orval. She prayed for its return and, at once, a trout rose to the surface with the precious ring in its mouth. Matilda exclaimed, "Truly this place is a *Val d'Or!*" and proceeded to establish a monastery in her Valley of Gold. Then the unfeeling French burned it down in June of 1793.

In 1935, Heinrich Himmler founded the *Ahnenerbe,* or Ancestral Heritage Organization, based on the claims of the founder of the Theosophical Movement, 'Madame' Helena Blavatsky. She posited that humans had evolved through various stages, each of which had ended in floods. An elite priesthood had escaped from the lost continent of Atlantis and fled to the Himalayas, and their successors were the Aryans. Others, too, proposed these Aryans, or Nordics, were descended from godlike men and had once lived in the icy north. Go figure.

In 2005, Sergey Ivanovich Morozov, Governor of the Ulyanovsk region 800 kilometers east of Moscow, declared September 12th as Procreation Day and suggested giving couples time off from work to produce the next generation. The first Grand Prize went to Irina and Andrei Kartuzov, whose baby was born the following June on Russia Day. For their troubles (?) they received a UAZ-Patriot, a sport utility vehicle made, not coincidentally, in Ulyanovsk. Other contestants won video cameras, TVs, washing machines, and refrigerators.

What else? Garry Kasparov was one of the prime movers behind a broad coalition of political parties with a single goal: ousting Vladimir Putin from power. The Other Russia chose Kasparov as its candidate for the 2008 presidential election but couldn't get him on the ballot. Seven years later he published *Winter Is Coming: Why Vladimir*

Putin and the Enemies of the Free World Must Be Stopped.

A month before he died, Noël Coward sat for a filmed interview in which he discussed his work as a spy for England during the war, training with his friend Ian Fleming in secret at Bletchley Park. "Celebrity was wonderful cover," he said. "My disguise would be my own reputation as a bit of an idiot . . . a merry playboy."

Nashi, an "anti-oligarchic-capitalist movement," was founded by senior figures in the Russian Presidential administration. By late 2007, it had grown in size to some 120,000 members between the ages of 17 and 25. Western critics have compared its deliberately cultivated resemblance to the Hitler Youth as *Putinjugend*.

On August 2, 2007, a Project Arktika submersible dropped a titanium tube containing the Russian flag on the ocean floor under the North Pole in support of their territorial claims to the Arctic. The International Seabed Authority, established under the United Nation's Law of the Sea, repeatedly has rejected the claims.

And yes, John F. Kennedy's major at Harvard really was International Relations.

Finally, my parents had several floral bath salts in seed packets. When I was seven, I emptied all of them into my bath, and the house smelled of Lily of the Valley for a week.

I made up almost everything else.

ACKNOWLEDGMENTS

First, I want to thank Martin Cruz Smith. I don't know him, but his book *Gorky Park* is so wonderful, and wonderfully imagined, that he made me want to set a novel in Moscow, too.

Thanks also to the people at Pegasus Books. Publisher Claiborne Hancock and his team of (in alphabetical order) Charles Brock, cover designer; Jessica Case, publicity director; Bowen Dunnan, editorial assistant; Maria Fernandez, interior designer/typesetter; and Sabrina Plomitallo-González, art director, took my manuscript and brought it to the life I'd hoped for it.

Thanks as well to my family and friends who read the book, made useful suggestions, or simply suffered through the writing with me. My wife, Ellen Highsmith Silver, is, naturally, foremost among them.

Lastly, thanks to the late literary agent Wendy Weil, who saw enough in this book

to take me on shortly before her untimely
death.

ABOUT THE AUTHOR

Mitch Silver is the author of the critically acclaimed *In Secret Service*. He is an advertising agency creative director who lives in Rye, New York.

The employees of Thorndike Press hope you have enjoyed this Large Print book. All our Thorndike, Wheeler, and Kennebec Large Print titles are designed for easy reading, and all our books are made to last. Other Thorndike Press Large Print books are available at your library, through selected bookstores, or directly from us.

For information about titles, please call:
(800) 223-1244

or visit our website at:
gale.com/thorndike

To share your comments, please write:
Publisher
Thorndike Press
10 Water St., Suite 310
Waterville, ME 04901